Anonymous

Anonymous

A Madison Kelly Mystery

ELIZABETH BRECK

NEW YORK

Copyright © 2020 by Elizabeth Breck

Published in the United States by Crooked Lane Books, an imprint of The Quick Brown Fox & Company LLC.

Crooked Lane Books and its logo are trademarks of The Quick Brown Fox & Company LLC.

Library of Congress Catalog-in-Publication data available upon request.

ISBN (hardcover): 978-1-64385-564-6
ISBN (ebook): 978-1-64385-565-3

Cover design by Nicole Lecht

Printed in the United States.

www.crookedlanebooks.com

Crooked Lane Books
34 West 27th St., 10th Floor
New York, NY 10001

First Edition: November 2020

10 9 8 7 6 5 4 3 2 1

*For my mother and father
and Analise*

Chapter One

It was speared to her front door with a rusty nail she recognized as coming from the banister of the landing on which she stood; she unconsciously leaned her weight forward to avoid resting against the railing. It was a piece of white paper, 8 ½" by 11". The kind you buy in reams from the office supply store for $6.99. Her hair was up in a bun from her run, and the ocean breeze whispered across the roofs of the houses behind her and tickled the back of her neck as if there were someone standing there, on the five-foot square of wood at the top of the stairs, bleached from a hundred years in the sun and serving as the entrance to her apartment. She whipped her head to one side and then back again, expanding her peripheral vision down the stairs to her right and toward the alley to her left. Silence, except for seagulls calling to one another overhead and the sound of waves crashing behind her. The message on the paper was meant for her. More to the point, the person clearly knew where she lived, since it was nailed to her front door. It had only one line, typed with Arial 12-point font:

Stop investigating me or I will hunt you down and kill you. BITCH. No police.

Between the nail and the piece of paper was a strand of long blonde hair, pierced with precision and gently waving in the breeze.

The note and the hair would've been alarming enough, but the main issue, and the one that caused Madison Kelly to stand unmoving on her doorstep for several minutes, was that she had no open cases at the moment. She was investigating no one and nothing. Having closed her first murder case a few months before, she hadn't gone back to insurance fraud investigations. She was at a crossroads. *Stop investigating me.* Huh. The thing was . . . she wasn't.

Chapter Two

~

Madison turned and looked over the railing to the alley below. No unusual cars, and there was no one in sight. She glanced down the stairs into the courtyard garden. Her apartment was built above the garage of a 1929 beach cottage in the Windansea section of La Jolla, California, one block from the beach. A famous surf spot that rose to fame in the 1960s, Windansea still had its small-beach-town charm—despite the gentrification that seemed inevitable when hidden gems became known to the world. Her garden sat quiet and serene, unaware of the march of progress around it. She pivoted again and looked at the ocean over the tops of the houses.

As she stared at a summer storm brewing far out over the ocean, she felt the note burning a hole in her back. The thing about being a private investigator was that she liked to investigate things. Madison had never been able to interpret whether she liked mysteries or she hated them; all she knew was that she was compelled to solve them. So the appearance of a threatening note made her want to drop everything and figure out who had left it. And yet, she'd promised herself she would take time off from investigating to figure out what to do with her life. She had to expand out of the insurance field, or she would go hungry while the big Walmart-type investigations firms took all of her work. Insurance companies wanted quantity over quality these days, and Madison's assignments had been getting fewer and farther between. However, bigger investigations—murders—were very different from insurance investigations.

She enjoyed watching ex-cops stumble and fall when they thought they could retire from the police department and go into PI work with "all of their experience"—which was zero when it came to insurance work. And yet, here she was imagining doing the same thing: moving into a line of work for which she had almost no experience.

Madison turned back to the note. How could she stop investigating someone she wasn't investigating? Since she didn't know what she was doing to make this person think she was investigating them, she couldn't stop. In fact, she might *accidentally* continue, and what would they do next? What came after a threat to kill you?

Actually killing you.

Madison started to get scared, an emotion she wasn't used to. Her fear quickly turned into anger. No, she wouldn't let someone threaten her like this. She reached up to tear the note down but stopped just before she touched it. She saw in a flash what her life would become: constantly looking over her shoulder, checking cars in her rearview mirror, suspicious of everyone, looking out her windows at night to see if someone was watching her; always wondering: was this the note leaver, here to make good on his threat? It didn't matter that she was in the middle of a mini existential crisis. The only way to prevent a life lived in fear was to do exactly what the note was telling her not to do: investigate—but that could also get an escalation of threatening behavior. Damned if she did, damned if she didn't.

She knew that if she turned the note over to the police, she would get a cursory investigation at best. This threat would be a big deal only to her; to the police it would be just one of the many small investigations they had on any given day—if they investigated it at all. The note was terrifying only if it was *your* blonde hair stabbed to your front door. And anyway, the note said no police.

Madison looked down at her sneakers, covered in wet sand from her run on the beach. She kicked them off and pushed them to the side. It was times like these that she wished she still had her father to advise her. He wouldn't tell her what to do—he would ask questions that allowed her to come to her own decision about the best course of action. She didn't have anyone else she trusted to help her. She was on her own. To be or not to be? To fight or to flight? What was the right thing to do?

"There might be fingerprints on that note," Madison said aloud. She went inside to get a pair of gloves.

Chapter Three

Madison went into her apartment, careful not to brush the note on the door as she walked past. She walked gingerly on the hardwood floor, as if she were hiding from someone and trying not to make noise. Even though she wasn't sure what she was going to do about this note, there was no point in contaminating the evidence. She grabbed a pair of surgical gloves from the built-in cabinet along the wall to the left. Her five-foot-eleven frame took her back to the door in five strides. She put the gloves on and then realized she had nothing to store the note in.

Her apartment was a studio, with a floor-to-ceiling bookcase separating the main living area from her bed. She remembered she had a paper bag from Warwick's Bookstore stuffed in the bookcase. It had held a large greeting card, so it would fit the note without bending it. She snatched the bag, returned to the door, and stopped; she should take a photo first. It had taken some skill to pierce her blonde hair just right, not to mention the whim of finding one of her hairs—her strands tended to cling to things—and using it to bring imagery to the threat. It certainly was effective. She went back inside, grabbed her phone, and came back and took several photos.

Setting the phone down, she pulled on the nail; it wouldn't budge. Had the person brought a hammer with them? The use of material from the scene—the nail from the landing, the hair—indicated they hadn't come prepared to place the note on the door, or at least had decided once they got there that those items made a better statement. She put her foot on the bottom of the door to hold it in place and pulled as hard as she could on the nail. She worked out with weights regularly and was no weakling, but this nail was deep in the door. She pulled again, harder. Her pec muscles screamed where they'd been sliced and had healed erratically three years before. She stopped and stared at the nail. She didn't want to use the back of a claw hammer to pry the nail out, because that would leave a mark on the paper. She thought of calling Dave, but he was probably still in the water for a morning surf session. And anyway, she'd rather not rely on a guy to solve her problems for her.

Madison turned and went back into the apartment, bounding to the kitchen. She opened a drawer and grabbed a sterling-silver fork. Returning to the door, she placed the head of the nail between two of the prongs from the fork, careful not to touch the paper, and pried the nail out.

She touched the paper by the edges with her gloved hands and placed it into the Warwick's bag. Setting the bag on the large oak dining table that she used as a desk, she sat down in her office chair with a sigh. She knew what she had to do next, but she didn't want to. She stared at her phone, willing herself to make the first move: a phone call asking for help was a good way to get past awkwardness that had caused months of silence despite a long friendship.

Madison grabbed the phone and dialed before she could change her mind.

"Well, well, well. They always come crying back," he said.

"Hi, Tom."

Thomas Clark, decorated San Diego Police Department homicide detective. Madison hadn't spoken to him in two months. She was suddenly tongue-tied, and the silence went on too long.

"So, how've you been? Busy?" he asked. He was uncomfortable too.

"Can't you see from your spot in the alley?" she said, and regretted it immediately. She'd meant it to sound funny and flippant and like she didn't care anymore—water under the bridge, they'd both moved on, let bygones be bygones—but it came out mean. Well, frankly, maybe she'd meant to be a little mean.

There was steely silence on the other end of the line.

"I'm only kidding, Tom," she said. "I don't care, really."

"What do you need, Madison?"

"I need your help," she said.

Tom laughed. "You need my help? Oh how the mighty have fallen."

Madison started pacing. She didn't really want to get Tom involved, but she didn't see any other way right now. And now she had messed up the phone call. He was highly regarded in the police department, having closed some of the most high-profile cases. He could get things done quickly—and quietly. And no matter what had gone on between them, they'd known each other for ten years and she knew that Tom cared about her and respected her as an investigator. The fact that a couple of months before she'd caught him watching her apartment at night meant their relationship was strained now, sure. But he was still a good cop.

"Someone left a note on my door. A threatening note."

"What sort of threat? What did it say?"

Madison read him the note. "And the thing is, I'm not investigating anybody right now."

"No one?" he asked. "Not some poor guy with a jealous girlfriend?"

"Funny. I don't do domestic investigations and you know it. They're all batshit crazy."

"Okay," he said, and was silent. Madison could tell he was doing the same thing she'd done before she picked up the phone to call him: weighing the pros and cons. Finally he spoke.

"I can have the note processed. Is that what you want?"

It was exactly what she wanted. "Yes, that would be great."

"I can come by at noon on my lunch. Where should I park?"

Madison started to answer but then realized he was joking. He knew all the places around her apartment to park. If he could joke about it, maybe they would be okay after all.

Madison decided to walk to Busy Bee's Bagels; she was starving after jogging on an empty stomach and then all of the excitement. She put on a lightweight hoodie so she would have pockets and put her wallet, keys, and phone in them and walked out her front door.

She put in her headphones and turned on her favorite podcast, *Crawlspace*, to listen to the latest real-life mystery that Tim and Lance were discussing. She liked these kinds of shows and followed several podcasts covering true crime. It kept her faculties sharp. But she had to admit she was obsessed with *Crawlspace*: she often did further research on the mysteries they discussed, especially a San Diego mystery they were currently covering, and she tweeted the hosts constantly. *Too much time on my hands*, Madison thought.

She turned right onto Nautilus, walking away from the ocean. The bagel place was only two blocks away. She stepped over the broken sidewalk where the roots of the huge trees lining Nautilus had busted through. The morning gloom was clearing, and the street was dappled with sunlight coming through the trees.

She knew she would continue to work in investigations; she just didn't know what kind. She had a knack for figuring things out, for getting people to tell her things they had withheld from others, for being lucky when luck was all an investigator had left. It always made her laugh when someone said to her, "You don't look like a PI." She would reply, "Isn't that sort of the point?" She could follow someone for days and never get spotted; she could go undercover in a flash and get information out of someone who would clam up the minute they saw a "cop" type of person. It was rewarding to be good at something. But the freelance insurance investigator was a dying breed. And she didn't know if she could stomach murder investigations.

As she approached La Jolla Boulevard, Tim and Lance started discussing the San Diego mystery that fascinated her. Two young women had disappeared after leaving bars in the

Gaslamp District of San Diego. Tim and Lance used their podcast to bring attention to the case and to discuss theories: Was it a serial killer who had gotten both girls, or was it a coincidence? Their bodies hadn't been found, so were they not dead at all? Madison liked *Crawlspace* because, although the hosts weren't professional investigators, they were thorough and methodical in their approach to true-crime cases.

She paused the podcast and walked into Busy Bee's. She ordered a toasted bagel with sesame seeds and cream cheese. She hadn't even had the one cup of coffee she allowed herself each morning, so she ordered that with cream. She ate and drank her coffee as she walked back home, listening to the podcast. Halfway down Nautilus, the ocean could be seen framed underneath the two huge trees that met over the top of the street. It was like a 3D image of the most beautiful landscape painting you could imagine. The water in the image was so beautiful that a color had been named after it: Pacific blue for the Pacific Ocean. Madison took a deep breath of ocean air and turned into her alley. She paused the podcast again and took her earphones out; she wanted all of her senses working as she got closer to home.

She looked around as she crossed over to her building and walked around to her stairs. No suspicious cars or people.

She walked up the stairs to her apartment and used her key to get in. The note was still there in its bag on the desk. She stared at it like it might move on its own. She threw away the trash from her breakfast and sat in her office chair. Was she going to investigate this? And if so, where to begin?

Suddenly there was a pounding at the door, and she jumped out of her chair; she made it to the door in three large steps and looked through the peephole. Tom thought he was being funny by doing a cop knock.

"You scared the shit out of me," she said as she opened the door.

"Good. Need to keep you on your toes," he said, walking in. "I see the place hasn't gotten any bigger."

Madison stepped out of the way so as not to get run over. "I thought you were coming at lunch."

"I had some time now."

Tom sat in the wingback chair that had belonged to her third-great-grandmother. Madison treasured the chair as a memento of a woman who'd come from Ireland during the potato famine; starving to death, unable to speak English or write her name, she made it six weeks in steerage to a new country and raised a daughter who became a teacher. Madison walked the earth because of the brave women who'd come before her. Seeing Tom in the chair was jarring.

Tom had long legs that he crossed as he sat, but he still managed to look stocky; something about the overbuilding of upper bodies in the gym that cops and criminals tended to favor. His dark hair was slicked back. He loosened his tie slightly and tugged at his crisp white shirt: the uniform of a homicide detective.

"Make yourself at home," she said.

Madison walked over and sat down in the office chair at her desk; she swiveled to face him. There was a moment where they just stared at each other. There had always been electricity; it made the air around them crackle. Early on in their relationship, when they were just a PI and the cop assigned to her case, she'd accidentally touched his hand, and it had felt like her body was set on fire. The fact that it had never gone any further had something to do with timing and everything to do with . . . complications.

"Don't mind if I do," he said.

More silence.

"How's the wife?" she asked.

"Is that how we're going to start?"

"I don't know, Tom," she said. "How should we start? What is the proper way to reacquaint ourselves? I seem to have misplaced my guidebook." Madison got up and went to the kitchen just to have something to do. She got a glass out of the cabinet, filled it with water from the dispenser, and brought it back to Tom.

"How is work? Any good cases?" she asked.

"Work is fine." He took the water with his huge hand. "And the wife and I are working it out. She has forgiven . . . a lot."

Madison looked out the window.

"So anyway, where is this note?" he asked.

Madison handed him the paper bag along with a pair of gloves she'd set out for him. He put the gloves on and then pulled the note out of the bag. He stared at the note.

"Okay. So. You're sure this isn't someone playing a joke on you? What about the surfer?"

Madison picked up his empty glass and took it into the kitchen.

"Dave doesn't have a printer," she said. "And anyway, that's not his style. He wouldn't want to scare me."

That statement hung in the air over them for a minute. She stayed in the kitchen until it had dissipated.

"Okay, I'll take it in and process it," Tom said as he stood. Madison walked into the living room and faced him.

He continued: "You have to promise to let me handle this, though, okay, Maddie? Don't start some investigation of your own."

"Have you *met* me?" She laughed. "I can't promise that."

He stared at her mouth while she laughed. He was about six feet two inches tall; she had to tilt her head back slightly to look at him. Her laugh faded to a smile. He looked at her forehead, then her mouth again, and then into her eyes. "I'll let you know what I find," he said, and turned and walked out.

Chapter Four

Madison watched Tom walk out the door, wondering if she'd just made a huge mistake. Should she be bringing him back into her life so soon? Or at all? Well, it was done now.

She turned on the podcast again as she stared at the copy of the note she'd made before giving it to Tom. The note was just so plain and ordinary that she didn't see how it could be traced to anything. Now that she thought about it, she doubted the person had allowed fingerprints. With all of the crime TV shows, it seemed unlikely anyone would do something nefarious without wearing gloves these days.

But who had so much animosity against her? Madison knew that sticks and stones could break her bones but words would never hurt her, but tell that to someone staring at a threat of death. To Madison, it felt like the words hurt. She looked again at the note, peering at it from different angles. There was nothing unusual about the words used. The *No police* was sort of a cliché, but they also probably meant it. Could she decide that the person was for sure an English speaker, as in English as their first language? Not enough to go on. The sentence was simple enough that even someone who spoke English as a second language could have written it.

It couldn't be someone playing a joke. She didn't know that many people, and the people she did know would have known she wouldn't think this was funny. Plus, it wasn't funny. It had to be exactly what it appeared: someone thought she was investigating them and wanted her to stop.

She suddenly remembered a private investigator that she had royally pissed off one time and he had sworn to get even with her. Could he be behind this note? She'd made friends with his partner at the time, Ted, and so she decided to give him a call. She paused the podcast and dialed Ted's number while looking out the window at her view of the ocean. During the summer it was always cloudy in the mornings at the beach, but by the afternoon the sun came out, as it had now. She looked at a blue ocean and cloudless blue sky that blended together so you couldn't tell where one ended and the other began. It felt timeless.

"Hey, Ted," she said when he answered. "Long time no talk."

"I got a new phone and you're not in it. Who's speaking?"

"Oh, sorry. It's Madison Kelly. You remember, I helped you with surveillance on a truck driver who said he was injured but was playing soccer on the weekends? We ended up tailing him all the way to Nevada?"

There was a pause. And then a huge barrel laugh. "Oh shit, Madison, how ya doin'? Did you ever get the sand out of your ears after crawling through the desert with your video camera?"

Madison laughed in return. "I did finally, yes. Listen. A weird thing happened."

She explained about the note and the fact that she had no current investigations ongoing.

"So I was just wondering if that guy you worked with . . . what was his name? Would he be behind this?"

Madison had replaced the investigator after the company fired him. He was furious and thought Madison had done something to get him fired, and there had been a confrontation. She had done nothing to deserve his wrath except do a good job on the case.

"You're not working right now? Must be nice to live a life of leisure," he said. "But no, I don't think that guy would be after you. His name was John something. I think that was a momentary lapse of judgment on his part. But I could call him and feel it out if you wanted me to?"

"That would be great," Madison said. "Get back to me on this number?"

"Will do."

Ted was a good enough investigator, Madison knew, that she didn't have to tell him not to mention her phone call to the other PI. Ted would bring the conversation around to her name and see how the guy reacted.

It was nice to be able to call Ted. Investigators tended to be loners: sitting in darkened cars, working from home, alone except for witnesses and subjects. On the rare occasion when a "two-man" investigation was called for, it was nice to feel like she had a compatriot.

She turned the podcast back up.

"It seems like we'll never figure out whether this was a coincidence or a serial killer," Tim was saying. "Unless, and no one wants to hope for this, their bodies are found."

Madison went to the dresser in her bedroom and threw on some yoga pants, then got on the floor and started doing three hundred crunches.

As she crunched, she tried to put herself in the place of the girls leaving the Gaslamp when the bars closed: *You've been drinking, maybe you're even drunk. How do you end up missing? What could have happened?* Madison didn't want to be on the PR team for the Gaslamp District: "Come out for a night of fun . . . maybe you'll make it home, maybe you won't!"

And anyway, *Gaslamp* was a bit of a misnomer: while the area was built in the Victorian area, it had never had gas lamps. When Alonzo Horton began development in the 1860s, it was actually called New Town to distinguish it from Old Town, the original Spanish colonial settlement of San Diego, built in the 1700s and still in existence. Horton wanted a more centralized San Diego closer to the water, and he had succeeded: the Gaslamp District was now part of downtown San Diego, mere blocks from city hall and the courthouses—and the water. The area had fallen into a long period of decay but was renewed in the 1980s and became what it was today: a vibrant area of night-life and shopping frequented by locals and tourists alike. During the renewal period the locals had begun calling it the Gaslamp District, and the name stuck. Madison thought the official name was the Gaslamp Quarter, but once locals got a name lodged in their heads, it was hard to change it. You could park near the sixteen-block radius of red-brick buildings and walk from restaurant to bar to shop. Better yet, take a rideshare service, walk around all night, and then get home safely. Well, getting home safely was how it was supposed to work.

The first victim, Samantha Erickson, had last been seen four years before, on security video at Hank's Dive, at 1:30 AM; the camera was positioned over the bar, mostly to watch the cash register and make sure the bartender wasn't stealing money. In the video, which Madison had watched online when she first heard about the case, the bartender could be seen cutting Samantha off because she was so drunk. He even used the universal hand-across-the-throat sign. Samantha stumbled backward, right into the side of another guy, spilling his drink on his shirt. He could be seen exclaiming and yelling at her, and she stumbled out of the frame while he was gesturing wildly at her. She was never seen again. Her VW Jetta was found the next day parked a few blocks away; it was locked and appeared undisturbed.

Madison turned over and began a two-minute plank.

There was no video outside the bar or on the streets nearby. Hank's used to have security video outside, but after a Hank's bouncer assaulted a guy ten years earlier and their own security video helped to convict him—and get the victim a multimillion-dollar settlement from Hank's—their security video "wasn't working" anytime video was sought, which was quite often, considering the number of assaults that occurred at Hank's. The bar specialized in huge drinks, beer guzzlers and shots, and generally consuming as much liquor as possible and still staying upright. The waiters and bar staff all practiced that form of serving entertainment where they were intentionally rude to the customers and everyone was supposed to laugh. Madison had gone in one time and was out within ten minutes. She considered it a frat-boy bar, and she saw a fight start even in the short time she was there. Excess alcohol being served at Hank's meant bar brawls there on a nightly basis.

Two years later Elissa Alvarez didn't make it home after a night at Bourbon Baby in the Gaslamp District. Her friends said she'd gotten into a fight on the phone with her boyfriend and was upset and wanted to go home. She wasn't that drunk; she was more distraught, or else they wouldn't have let her drive. She walked out of the bar to go home and was never seen again. The next day her car was found a few blocks away in a parking lot, undisturbed.

The similarities between the two incidents were striking. Was there someone driving around downtown San Diego at night looking for women walking alone? Madison kept thinking of a rideshare driver preying on drunken women who decided as they walked to their cars that they were too drunk to drive. She had read about a more recent case where a woman alleged she was picked up by a rideshare and driven from New York into New Jersey, raped by several men, and then driven home and dropped off. It was so traumatic she blocked it out. When she saw the next morning—after waking in inexplicably horrible pain—that the cost of the ride the night before was over a hundred dollars for what should have been a fifteen-minute ride home from the bar, she looked at the map of her ride and couldn't understand how she'd been taken to another state. She sent a screenshot of the map to her friend and texted *WTF? This was my ride last night*. It was only in discussing it with a friend the next day that the memories came flooding back, and she started sobbing and went to police. The woman was now suing the rideshare for their response to her alleged attack, and for the culture that allowed a driver like that onto their workforce. Madison thought it was interesting that the victim in the case was not suing for money. She was suing for, as the woman put it, "a seat at the table"—to work on global changes so that this horrible crime didn't happen to another woman.

There were plenty of other crimes alleged against rideshare companies, and Madison couldn't help but wonder if the Gaslamp mystery would turn out to be the case of a criminal rideshare driver, or even a fake rideshare driver—someone pretending to work for a rideshare company who really wasn't—preying on women out at night alone. Madison felt like the apparent safety of the now ubiquitous rideshare was just that—an apparency. In fact, Madison felt it was more like a predator's dream, like taking candy from a baby: drunk women stumbling around getting into a car with a strange man—and not just willingly. They *paid* to get into the car with a strange man.

Every time Madison had another thought regarding what might have happened to the girls in the Gaslamp, like the rideshare angle, she would tweet about it. Sometimes another Twitter user responded, and once in a while one of the podcast's hosts, Tim or Lance, tweeted back. Twitter had created a nice community of armchair detectives and real detectives, who normally worked alone, and allowed them to share ideas and enthusiasm that kept cold cases alive. She just used the hashtag #GaslampMystery, and all the other sleuths saw it and joined the conversation.

On the one hand, Madison felt like she should probably work on finding friends in real life instead of engaging with strangers on the internet. But on the other hand, strangers on the internet could be turned off with a switch; you had to talk to real people even when you didn't feel like it.

She sat on the ground to stretch out her hamstrings.

"Even though we can't respond to everyone, we do appreciate all of your tweets with suggestions and clues and ideas," Tim said on the podcast. "We definitely forward anything that might be important to law enforcement. Not to mention that your idea might give someone else an idea that leads to a resolution. And who knows, maybe the person or persons responsible is paying attention and realizes we're getting closer. That could cause them to make a mistake."

"A slipup that gets them caught," Lance added. "You never know. That's why we bring as much attention to these cases as we can. So keep those tweets coming! And now on to the case of Maura Murray, University of Massachusetts student missing since February 9, 2004."

"I probably tweet you more than you'd like," Madison said aloud. And then she froze as an idea struck her. She jumped up, grabbed her phone, and pulled up the Twitter app. She looked at her recent tweets.

From yesterday: *@Tim: What about rideshare drivers? #GaslampMystery*

From the day before: *#GaslampMystery do you guys know if we ever found out if the same bouncers were working the nights the girls disappeared?*

From the week before: *@Lance: What does Elissa's boyfriend say? What if these are coincidences, not the work of a serial killer, and he killed Elissa? And maybe even Samantha before her? #GaslampMystery*

There were other tweets, going back months. Every time she'd had an idea, she'd tweeted it. Because Madison had a lot of downtime, she'd been listening to this podcast and using her investigative skills to try to solve this San Diego mystery casually, just as a hobby—an armchair detective like everyone else listening to true-crime podcasts. The difference was that her Twitter profile said she was a licensed private investigator. What if the killer or killers were following social media on the case and were seeing her tweets? What if she'd been getting too close?

Was this what her anonymous note person had meant when they said *Stop investigating me*? Was this the investigation she'd been doing without realizing it? But how would they have figured out where she lived? Well, her Twitter handle was her name, Madison Kelly, which took away some of the mystery. And being a PI, she knew how easy it was to find someone if you put your mind to it.

She opened up a new tweet and typed *#GaslampMystery* and then *I DON'T SCARE THAT EASILY.*

She hit *Tweet.*

"That oughta do it," Madison said.

Her adrenaline was pumping from the exercise and her epiphany. She needed to do something. She needed action. She went to the closet in the living room and pulled out the large whiteboard on wheels she kept there for big investigations. She wanted to write down each tweet she'd sent and organize her thoughts on the board. She'd spent the last three months doing nothing, and it wasn't like her. She felt best when she had a problem to work on. Well, a mystery to work on.

She didn't know if the stalker was threatening her because of her tweets or had anything to do with the Gaslamp disappearances, but it made the most sense at the moment. She didn't want to sit and wait for someone else, like Tom, to figure it all out. She was the hero in her own story and always would be. If this was all indeed connected and if she figured out who the stalker was, she might solve the disappearance of these two girls.

She needed a heading for the whiteboard. What should she call this investigation? She wrote *ANONYMOUS*, and then stepped back to look at it. Good. She returned to the board, made a column, and labeled it *Suspects*. Under that she put *Creepy P.I. John*. Until she heard back from Ted, she would keep that guy on the suspect list.

On the first day, everyone is a suspect; the only person I know for sure didn't do it is me was Madison's motto. She started to get that excitement in the pit of her stomach that she felt at the beginning of a new case.

Next she wrote a column labeled *Clues*. She started to write down all the tweets she had sent out about the case, but then just abbreviated them down to the things that would've caused "Anonymous" to react: *rideshare driver, Elissa's boyfriend, club bouncers, local transients, visiting sailors who are part of San Diego's huge military contingent, where are the girls' phones?*, and finally, *serial killer stalking the Gaslamp*. This last didn't seem specific enough to get somebody riled up enough to leave a note on her door, but who knew how the mind of a kidnapper/killer worked. It could be that the person just thought that she, a licensed PI, was working on the case, and that was enough for them to strike out at her.

Next, she wrote out leads she could follow: *family members of the victims* and *staff at the bars*. That would be where she would start. She wondered if Tom would know anything about these disappearances and if so, would he talk to her about them?

Her adrenaline rush had calmed down, and she stopped for a minute to think. She walked to the window over the front garden. There was a hummingbird hovering near the eaves above her; he was tapping his beak near the edge, looking for a hummingbird feeder that had long ago fallen in a storm.

How far was she willing to take this investigation? What was she getting herself into? She was licensed to investigate anyone or anything—but did she want to get into interviewing witnesses and family members in the disappearance of two women? How would that fit into the life path she'd been on recently? She wasn't even sure her note leaver had anything to do with Twitter; it was just an assumption at this point. This would be a huge investigation to undertake, one that the police had been working on for years. What could she even contribute?

In favor of doing it herself was the fact that no matter how seriously the police took the threatening note, it would not be as important to them as it was to her. Sure, it might be connected to two missing girls—but it also might not be. If she called the detective investigating the cases, he would probably file her idea alongside that of a psychic who'd called to say they'd had a vision of where the bodies were buried. Even if he took it slightly more seriously, he certainly wouldn't jump all over finding Madison's stalker on the off chance it was connected to his case. And even if he did—no police, the note had said. A haphazard police investigation would get her no results, except for perhaps a quicker escalation of aggressive behavior. Sometimes the old adage was true: if you want something done, do it yourself—especially if you're licensed to do so. So the only question was: Did she want to?

Her phone pinged and she reached over to grab it. A Twitter mention. It was a reply to the tweet she'd just sent where she said *I don't scare that easily*. The reply was from an account called MaddieKelly12. It said: *We'll see what it takes to scare you. The note was just the start.*

Madison felt an electric jolt in her arm and the phone dropped to the floor.

Chapter Five

~

Madison stared at her phone on the floor like it was alive and would continue the conversation on its own if she picked it up. This was no longer theoretical. "Anonymous" was connected to Twitter. And she hadn't been tweeting about anything else. If he wasn't connected to the Gaslamp mystery, he at least followed Madison on Twitter and knew where she lived—and thought that she was investigating him. What else did he know about her? Had he been following her?

Her best guess was that he was connected to the missing women and thought Madison's tweets had gotten too close to discovering him.

She went back to the whiteboard and stared at it. Her arms were shaking. She took a deep breath and tried to calm down. She wouldn't respond to Anonymous on Twitter. She'd sent the tweet to draw him out; hell, she'd sent it on a whim and hadn't thought he'd even respond. Now that he had, she wasn't going to get anywhere playing cat and mouse on Twitter. She needed to do a real investigation. And that meant doing the usual things, being meticulous and organized. And she needed to keep moving. What next?

Under *Suspects*, she put *Elissa's boyfriend*. He came across as really shady to Madison, not that it would explain the death of Samantha two years before. But she had to follow every string until it led either to the answer or to a dead end. No one knew for sure if the two disappearances were connected, and she would pursue every avenue that presented itself. How many avenues would that be? She had a stalker who was threatening to kill her. She didn't trust anyone else, even the police, to take this as seriously as she did. She wasn't going to sit and do nothing about it. She had to figure out who this guy was. Madison's head was spinning and she was still shaky from the adrenaline rush.

She opened her front door and went out onto the landing. All was quiet in the alley; no strange cars parked nearby. She could hear the waves. The sun had made its way over the top of her apartment and shimmered above the ocean in front of her. Sometimes that was all that kept her going: glimpses of sunlight like glimpses of hope. Two seagulls were fighting over part of a hamburger in a fast-food container they'd pulled out of the trash can in the alley. She took a deep breath and stretched her arms up high over her head and let the breath out in a huge sigh.

She knew that this investigation, and baiting a possible murderer to get him to come out of the woodwork and expose himself, which she'd just done with that tweet, was dangerous. But when she asked herself *Can I handle this?* her answer was yes. She refused to live her life afraid. One time she'd told Tom about ripping into a guy on the street who had catcalled her, and he'd said, "Madison, the way you talk to guys I'd think you either had a really big guy nearby or were carrying a gun." She had neither. Maybe she didn't have much to back it up, but she wouldn't be intimated by anyone. It wasn't that she was brave; she just didn't like being afraid. And she was a great investigator. She could do this.

As she released her arms and bent all the way down to put her palms flat on the sun-washed deck, she saw her neighbor Ryan walking up the path in their shared garden, surfboard under his arm. He kept his surfboard under an overhang below her apartment. As he walked toward the hutch, he stared up at her; he didn't know she could see him through her hair from her bent position.

"Hi Ryan," she said while upside down.

"Oh!" He stopped and shifted from bare foot to bare foot, his long hair full of sand and clinging to his wetsuit. "Hi there. I didn't even see you." *Right*, Madison thought. *You mean you didn't know I could see you staring at me.* She stood up and grabbed her hair to replace it into the bun it had fallen out of.

"What are you up to?" Ryan asked. He wasn't unattractive; in fact, he would normally be Madison's type. *Meaning likely a criminal*, she thought wryly. She definitely liked bad boys, and he was rugged, confident, and a surfer. But she hadn't thought it wise to date someone who lived downstairs from her, just across the neatly manicured garden that the landlord had fashioned after an English countryside. Also, even though she and Dave weren't exclusive, she didn't think he'd appreciate her bringing another surfer into the picture—one he probably surfed with every day. She hadn't asked, but Ryan and Dave likely knew each other, even if just casually. La Jolla, especially Windansea, was a *very* small town.

"Not much." Then she realized she should probably question him about anyone he might have seen hanging out around her apartment—or putting a note on her door. "Do you have a minute?" she asked.

He didn't answer for a second; he just stared up the stairs at her with his mouth open. The moment went on a little too long, to where Madison thought she might need to repeat herself.

"Right now?" he said. "With me?"

Now she was confused. He was younger than she was, maybe twenty-five to her thirty-five, and with the rapidly changing vernacular among people younger than she that made her jump to urbandictionary.com on a daily basis, she wondered if she'd just accidentally propositioned him. Was there a double meaning to "Do you have a minute?" Was it like "Netflix and chill" or something?

"I'm not sure what you think I'm asking you," she said. "I'm wondering if I can talk to you for a second. Just talk."

"Oh," he said. Then he laughed. She hadn't seen him laugh before. His laugh was disarming. "It's just you never talk to me. I . . . no I didn't think you were . . . no. Let me just get out of my wetsuit and take a shower and I'll knock on your door?"

"Awesome." She watched him stow his surfboard and then hobble down the cement path to his front door. He lived with three roommates in the front house; in the 1920s, her apartment was the carriage house for his house. His was a classic California Craftsman home, with carefully crafted built-ins like bookcases and breakfast nooks, although she hadn't seen the inside of his house specifically. Maybe that would change soon, Madison thought. She loved a guy with a great laugh. He was a bit young, which was why she'd never really paid attention to him. But these days a guy ten years younger wasn't that big a deal. That's what she would tell herself, anyway.

She went inside her apartment and started going through her tweets to see if she'd missed anything that should go on the whiteboard. She'd mentioned rideshare drivers the most in her tweets. Surely the police had checked that? Couldn't a rideshare service tell where its drivers had been on a particular day and time? She wrote that down as a lead to follow up on.

About ten minutes later there was a knock at her door.

"That was fast," she said as she let Ryan in.

"Yeah, I just had to rinse the sand off, you know." He was about six feet tall and had changed into board shorts and a green surf-competition T-shirt. He had the classic Southern California surfer accent, like Jeff Spicoli in *Fast Times at Ridgemont High.* The surfers in San Diego didn't have quite that thick of an accent, but Madison was always amused by how close they sounded to that famous surfer played by Sean Penn. The only thing Madison felt he'd gotten wrong: the surfers she knew were laid-back only up to a point. Madison had lived at Windansea long enough to see the rougher side to surfers, which for some reason hadn't made it into popular culture. When kooks—surfer terminology for someone who couldn't surf—tried to ride the notoriously difficult surf break at Windansea, they might find themselves confronted in the parking lot on Neptune Place afterward. It wasn't just territorial, although that was certainly part of it; when you didn't know what you were doing in danger-ous waves, you could get someone else killed. And surfers spent their days paddling out against heavy surf, so they were deceptively strong. The fact that they also spent time doing community service work just made them perfect men to Madison: strong, brave, and kind. Just the thought of it made her swoon.

Ryan was looking out the windows of her apartment. "Damn, you have the view alright!" he said. "I always imagined what it would look like from up here, but this is better than I thought."

Madison was standing behind him when he said this. Ryan turned around, smiling, still amazed by the view, and then he saw the look on Madison's face.

It took her a moment to find her voice. "You've 'always imagined' what it would look like from up here?"

"I just . . . sorry, I just . . ." And then he blushed.

"Do you want a beer?" she asked. She walked into the kitchen while she tried to figure out what had just happened. Why was he imagining what her view was like?

"Yeah, a beer, that's cool," he said. "I don't . . . like . . . think about being up here or anything. That sounded really weird. It just seemed like there'd be a cool view from here, and there is." He looked like he wanted to die. It was kind of cute.

"The view was definitely the selling point." She walked into the room and handed him his beer. She pointed to the wingback chair and indicated that he should sit. She sat in her office chair.

"So you know Dave Rich?" he asked.

That took her by surprise.

"Yeah, I know him," she said.

"I've seen him walking up your stairs. I figured you guys were . . . is he your . . . ?" And he blushed again.

It was really rare to meet a guy who blushed. Dave had told her that she was intimidating to guys, an observation she took offense to at first. Was she supposed to reduce her strength or power so as not to intimidate guys? "No," Dave said. "You're just beautiful and confident, and guys get stupid around you." She told him that was a nice save to get out of a feminism discussion, and they'd left it for the time being. Was that what was causing Ryan to stammer and blush?

"No, he's not my boyfriend," she said. "But we're close. So . . . anyway. I need to ask you if you saw anything weird this morning. Did you see anyone hanging around here?"

"Ummm, I don't think so," he said. "I was in the water starting at about seven AM, though. So what time would this have been?"

Madison realized that most of the people in the houses and apartments near her weren't around when she went out for her run at seven thirty that morning. Either they were on their way to work, difficult at that time of the morning to get out of La Jolla with traffic, or in the water surfing.

"Oh, right. Okay. Well, can you let me know if you see anything weird? I had something happen this morning, and I'm trying to get to the bottom of it."

"No problem," Ryan said. "If I'm not surfing I'm usually at home studying, so I can keep an eye out."

"Studying? Where do you go to school?" she asked.

"Oh I'm getting my master's in mechanical engineering at UC San Diego."

The only thing Madison liked more than surfers was smart guys. "Cool," she said. She stood up to indicate that they were done, and he stood up to be polite and knocked into her by mistake; her immovability and his trajectory caused him to fly back down onto the chair. *Nothing like knocking over a six-foot-tall guy to make you feel feminine,* Madison thought. They both laughed.

"Well I better get going," he said, and stood without falling this time. "But I wanted to ask you: do you think you'd want to have dinner with me tomorrow night?"

Madison wasn't good at being asked out. Her inclination was always to say no. In fact, she usually said no without thinking. Part of it was her attachment to Dave; part of it was that she didn't want to make small talk at dinner with a stranger: she'd rather stay home by herself and read. But Dave did not practice the same faithfulness, and she spent enough time alone as it was. It might be nice to have someone to do things with. She didn't have to marry him. And he was the kind of guy who blushed.

"Sure, why not?" Besides, going out to dinner would give her mind a break from the dangerous investigation she'd decided to pursue.

Chapter Six

～

Madison had stared at the whiteboard and her tweets for another hour after Ryan left, and she decided that was enough. She walked down to the beach for sunset, a Windansea tradition. All of the locals, and now some of the Airbnb tourists, had a tradition of walking down to the beach with their plastic cups of wine and beer or cocktails to stand on the bluff and watch the sunset together. It was one of Madison's favorite things about living there. It allowed her a sense of community without demanding too much of her. She could smile at her neighbors and acquaintances, but there was no expectation of talking to other people.

She walked out her front door, turned right, and was at Neptune Place—the place to be in the summer and every evening throughout the year. Less than a mile long, it was the demarcation for Windansea Beach. A small parking lot fit the surfers' cars during the week; on summer weekends every available parking space was taken with beachgoers who'd discovered the short stretch of beach, covered in boulders at high tide but gleaming with a mile of white sand at low tide. Named for a hotel built in 1919 along the beach that had long since burned down, Windansea Beach boasted a palm-covered shack built in 1946 as its landmark. At night Madison could hear the waves, which were sometimes too loud to sleep. The waves were always louder at night.

It was a perfect summer evening: the sun was near the horizon, shining on both the water and the gray clouds in the distance, melting a deep amethyst hue onto the entire scene. It was chilly despite being summer, and Madison had thrown a UCSD hoodie on over her tank top. She'd always wanted a Windansea Surf Club sweatshirt, but only actual members of the club, who were initiated mainly on their surfing ability, could wear the shirt. It made her want it even more.

She scrabbled down the short bluff onto the massive boulders that stood high above the sand. The tide had been high but was going back out, so there was sand available for her to sit on. She stepped and then shimmied down the boulders until she reached the sand, then sat tucked against a boulder as she faced the water. The crowd on the sidewalk above her was no longer visible; she was hidden in her own little world.

No matter how many times she sat here, she thought of her father's last days. She'd rented a condo for him in his last month of life, just a block down from her apartment. She had stayed there with him, watching the dolphins with him during the day and barbecuing on the front patio at night. They knew he was going to die—an inoperable brain tumor would take his thoughts and his life in almost exactly the thirty days the doctors had given him—so she worked on making his last few weeks memorable. He told her, right before he died, that it had been the best weeks of his life.

A surfer Madison recognized as a friend of Dave's came out of the water and grabbed his flip-flops and towel that he'd left on the beach. Madison had seen him at a Windansea Surf Club "Day at the Beach for Special Surfers," where the surf club members taught developmentally challenged children and adults to surf. Was his name Mike? She couldn't remember. It had been the last community event before he became a member of the club. Being among the best surfers in the country wasn't enough to get you in the club: you had to show considerable community involvement. The guy clambered up the path to the sidewalk, shouting a greeting to someone he saw there.

Just then Madison spotted Dave surfing in the last wave of the night. She could never figure out which of the surfers he was when he was far out in the water, but as he got closer to the shore, his silhouette was distinctive. Tall and broad shouldered, he had thick blond hair that he always kept too long.

"Hey," he said. He jumped off his board and walked the rest of the way in, flipping his wet hair out of his face as he approached her. He squinted to see her better, to assess her mood. Squinting caused his blue eyes to be even more piercing.

Emotion was like a drug to her: she couldn't have just a little, or soon she'd stop being able to function. She had perfected her equanimity. But the sight of Dave Rich always shot a thrill from her tailbone to the top of her scalp, even after all these years.

"I thought that was you," he said. "But I thought, 'Maddie wouldn't be waiting for me, would she?'"

"My God you're vain," she said. "I'm watching the sunset. I didn't even know you were in the water."

She reached her hand up for him to help her up, and he grabbed her and pulled her up and into his wetsuit—which was wet. He was so strong that her almost-six-foot body caught air as her feet came off the ground and she slammed into his chest. It had become a running gag for them; it got her every time. He looked tall and thin, maybe a little wiry, but he was stronger than any guy she'd ever met. It was like being with André the Giant. She threw her head back and laughed.

He set her back on her feet.

"What are you doing? Do you want to get something to eat?" he asked.

"No, I have work to do." She glanced up at the sidewalk and saw that quite a crowd had gathered—a lot of people for a Wednesday, watching as the sun took its final dip into the ocean. Dave knew all of them.

"Really?" He grabbed a towel he'd left in the sand before he went surfing and wrapped it around his waist. "You got a case?"

"Well, sort of." She'd been dreading this part. "Actually, after my run this morning, there was a note on my door."

Dave was doing the surfer striptease: surfers perfected changing out of their wetsuits in public without showing skin. He had wrapped a towel around his waist, and now he was easing his wetsuit off underneath the towel. "What kind of note?"

Madison explained about the threat and her idea that it had to do with tweets she'd sent out. She told him she'd given the note to Tom, a friend in the police department, and that he was looking into it.

"Okay, so the police have it. What do you have to do?"

"I have to figure out who wrote the note!"

Dave had gotten his wetsuit off and was now pulling his board shorts on under the towel.

"No, *the police* do. And I don't like that this guy knows where you live."

Madison pulled her sweatshirt off, which was now wet, and tied it around her waist. "Oh, you 'don't like it'? You're staking a claim to me now and I have to do what you say?"

Dave had gotten his shorts on and removed the towel, which he folded and set on the rock. He looked at Madison but saw something over the top of her head on the street. He looked up and waved ruefully at someone. Madison didn't turn around to see who he was waving at.

"No," he said, looking back at her. "I'm not 'staking a claim,' and you wouldn't like it if I did. But I can worry about you, can't I?" He reached out and touched the part of the scar that was peeking out from underneath her tank top. "Even if you are a badass, Madison Kelly."

She grabbed his finger. "Stop it, freak."

He bent down and kissed her. Sometimes she thought the only reason she kept him around was because of the way they kissed.

"Wow," she said. "What if one of your girlfriends sees us?"

"Oh my God Maddie, I don't have 'girlfriends.'"

"Right, Dave, save it for the judge," she said. "I have to go."

He laughed and she turned and walked up the path.

She had left Dave on the beach, grabbed something to eat, and then taken a nap. She wanted to go to the Gaslamp District late at night and get a feel for the scene. She arrived around eleven PM, when things were just starting to hop. She parked her car in the same parking lot Elissa had used the night she disappeared, around the corner from Bourbon Baby, the club where she was last seen.

Madison walked all the way down Fourth Avenue to Hank's Dive, the bar where Samantha was last seen alive. She didn't see much; she hoped this trip wasn't a waste of time.

She wouldn't try to interview the staff at the bars in the middle of a busy night. She would need to come back in the early afternoon for that. However, whenever she started a case, she needed to get a feel for the scene, and like it or not, this was the scene: music blaring out of restaurants and clubs, people walking in twos and fours and groups in various levels of intoxication, couples on first and second dates slipping into nice restaurants with cute patios on red-brick streets. Hank's was just as obnoxious as she had remembered it; in fact, there was a fight on the street in front of the bar that she deftly avoided. As she jogged to safety a block away, she wondered why she'd bothered to come down there. Sure, it was the "scene," but she'd been to the Gaslamp before and knew what it was like at night. *I had to start somewhere*, she thought. And she was trying to keep her mind off the fact that she was taking on a case that seemed insurmountable, and she wasn't even getting paid for it. She needed a starting point. A toehold. She'd thought she might find it in the Gaslamp, but she hadn't. Feeling defeated, Madison walked back to her car from Hank's.

The summer air felt soft on her face. The air feels different at night; like hope. She heard a sound—*swoosh*—and she stopped abruptly and leaned her hand on the wall next to her. Sometimes pockets of sadness came out of nowhere and took her by surprise—like a punch to the gut. If she waited, it passed.

Her father had started having seizures their last week in the Windansea condo; she'd had to admit him to a hospice for regular medication and monitoring. The hospice was in a beautiful setting on a hill overlooking Mission Valley, not far from where she stood in the Gaslamp District. Her father lay trapped in his bed and in his thoughts, the brain tumor sitting on a part of his brain making him unable to understand what he saw out of his eyes. So he kept them closed.

"What's that sound?" he'd asked.

She'd looked up from a Sue Grafton novel she was rereading for the third time. She hadn't heard anything, and she thought her father, a genius who'd ungracefully fought every loss to his senses because he missed them more than most, was imagining it.

"There it is again!" he said, and then she heard it. A swoosh. She got up from the couch in his hospice room and stepped outside to the private garden. She looked over the cliff to the Fashion Valley mall below and saw the red electric trolley pulling away from the station at the mall. *Swoosh.*

"It's a trolley," she reported when she got back in the room.

"A trolley," he said. "That's perfect." And then he fell asleep.

For the next week, as her father slipped into a coma and she waited for the inevitable, the swoosh of the trolley kept her company. It was a dreamy sound, like a train whistle: the hope of brighter days in distant places. It became the sound of her dreams.

Back in the Gaslamp District, the trolley had passed, and so had her melancholy. She lifted her hand off the wall and wiped it on her jeans. The brushing motion caused her bracelet to catch on her jeans and fly off. It landed in the crevice between two buildings. Madison at first tried to reach between the buildings to get the bracelet; she could just barely see the silver clasp where the streetlight hit it at an angle. The buildings were built as a pair, and the developers had really tried to keep them on the same lot—to the point that they were almost touching. It was no good. She couldn't reach it.

She probably would've left it, but the bracelet had been her mother's. She saw a piece of metal rebar, rusted and dirtied, lying in the gutter. She picked it up and walked back to the crevice. As she stood deciding the best way to attack it, a homeless guy walking by made a fake scream and held his hands up.

"I didn't do it! I didn't do it!"

She stood holding the rebar, waiting for him to pass. He started to let out a demonic cackle, something that probably got a satisfying reaction from most girls on the street, but as he got closer and saw Madison's expression, he broke it off abruptly.

"I was only kidding, shiiiiiit."

Madison waited until he'd cleared the area before she turned her back to the street. She decided to carefully reach the rebar much farther than where the bracelet lay to make sure not to push the bracelet farther in. She knelt on the sidewalk and placed the tip of the rebar as far as it would go, then gently scraped it back toward her. The bracelet came out—along with an iPhone 7 in a Kate Spade cover.

White hibiscus flowers on a clear background studded with crystals made to look like diamonds. *Kate Spade New York* at the bottom, with a little spade emblem. Very girly. Madison stared at it. What were the chances this phone belonged to one of the missing girls? Zero. Madison laughed that she'd even had the thought. She was standing right next to the parking lot where Elissa had parked her car, and Samantha's car had been only one block over, but still. Ridiculous. Madison had never been very good with odds, which was the reason she'd stuck to playing craps and blackjack when she went to Vegas—nothing that required her to understand statistics. But she figured that if she presented this to a bookie, she could bet one dollar and win $1,000 if it turned out to be a phone belonging to one of the missing girls.

Nevertheless, a girl could dream that she'd just found a missing piece of evidence in a major case. And having had the thought, she did not want to pick up the phone with her bare hands, in case it was a piece of evidence. She saw a trash can next to a bus stop that was overfilled and included a fast-food bag. She waited until a posse of ten girls—apparently part of a bachelorette party, given the drunken state of the revelers and the toilet-paper crown and veil worn by one of the girls—had passed on the sidewalk. Madison jumped across, grabbed the fast-food bag, tossed the leftover food, and took the napkins and bag over to her find.

She used the napkin to scoop up the phone and place it in the bag. She walked the block to her car. Madison had had a supervisor at one of her first investigation jobs tell her, "Being a good investigator is fifty percent technique and fifty percent luck. And Madison, you have good luck." She had thought about that a lot. She did have good luck. Still, it seemed unlikely that this phone belonged to one of the missing girls. But she would keep it as a juju until she figured that out.

As Madison started the car in the parking lot, her phone went off with a notification from Twitter. Prior to leaving the house she had sent a direct message to Felicity Erickson, Samantha's sister. Madison and Felicity followed each other on Twitter; Madison couldn't remember how it started, but she seemed to recall Felicity following her after one of Madison's tweets contained a suggestion for Lance and Tim on the podcast. In the direct message she'd let Felicity know that she was looking into the case, but she didn't mention why; she just said she hoped they could meet. The notification was Felicity's reply.

I would love to meet you. I will do anything to find my sister. Can you meet me tomorrow? Anywhere you say.

Madison tweeted back: *Meet me at the Pannikin in La Jolla tomorrow at 11 AM.* She pasted the Yelp review for the Pannikin with the directions.

Maybe this evening wasn't a waste after all.

Chapter Seven

~

The Pannikin in La Jolla was probably the only restaurant that catered to every group of La Jollans: the surfers living to catch the best wave and surviving on their last dollar; entitled young urban professionals who could afford a two-million-dollar beach condo the size of a postage stamp and were rushing to their high-paying jobs in downtown; and the one-percenters who lived in the multimillion-dollar mansions that peppered the coast and the hillsides in La Jolla and who stopped off before lunch or after a charity function to visit with their wealthy friends and see and be seen. Madison didn't fall into any of those categories, proving to herself that she shouldn't categorize people. But she identified most with the surfer group; otherwise she just kept to herself and watched everybody else. The Pannikin had reclaimed wood tables with broken-tile inlays, a huge tree in the patio area, and delicious coffee and baked goods. Everyone in La Jolla knew the Pannikin.

As Madison walked up she unconsciously looked around for Dave. He drove a red Jeep, the old steel kind not the new ones that look like Tonka toys made of plastic, so normally she would be able to tell if he were here. However, the restaurant was within walking distance of his cottage so he could be there without his Jeep. She didn't see him. She got a coffee in a huge white porcelain mug and grabbed a seat on the patio.

Felicity Erickson looked just like her Twitter avatar: kind and warm with a determination behind her eyes. She walked into the patio area, and Madison stood up and waved. Felicity came over and sat opposite Madison, on the bench facing the street. She was about thirty years old and wore jeans and a cardigan. She had a tattoo on her wrist in beautiful script that said *Samantha*.

"This is a nice place," she said. "I've never been here before."

"Sorry to make you drive all the way into La Jolla, but whenever someone asks me where to meet, this is the first place I think of," Madison said. "Would you like coffee?"

Felicity ignored the question. "I hope you're not going to waste my time. A lot of people have contacted me: psychics, amateur detectives, you name it. They want me to give them every last piece of information I have so that they can satisfy their curiosity, and then when they can't solve the mystery in the first week, they walk away. Well, this is not a pastime for me or a hobby. This is my sister. Samantha. This is my life." She held up the tattoo of her sister's name.

Madison realized that she was going to have to tread lightly. She did need information from Felicity, but she understood Felicity's point, and she knew exactly the type of person Felicity had been dealing with: people who looked at her tragedy and saw it as a game or as something with which to amuse themselves when they were bored. There was nothing wrong with that, to a certain degree; podcasts were made for entertainment, and even Madison listened to them for that reason. But when it came down to actually contacting the family member of a victim, you had better be doing it for the right reason.

"I completely understand," Madison said. "I am not here to waste your time. First of all, I'm not an amateur: I'm a licensed professional. But in addition, this has become personal for me. Obviously not as personal as it is for you, but I have a stake in this. I would rather not explain why just yet, if that's okay with you. But I am licensed to investigate this matter." Madison took out her PI license and showed it to Felicity. "I can explain more as we go along, but I'd like to just start off with talking about what has happened so far in the investigation of this case, if that's okay with you."

"Okay," Felicity said. "I'm sorry if I sounded rude. It's just that, since our parents died, it has only been the two of us. I miss her. I want to find her. It's been four years. And I'm tired of getting my hopes up."

"I understand."

"And the police have told me next to nothing about what they've done. I've been left in the dark. Or else they just haven't done much and don't want to admit it."

"That's okay. You probably know more than I do."

"Well, I'm going to need coffee for this."

"Let me get it for you." Madison stood up and grabbed her purse. "What would you like?"

"Black coffee would be great."

Madison walked inside to the counter. As she waited in line, she looked outside and saw Dave's Jeep pull up with a pretty blonde girl in the passenger seat. The girl got out and ran inside as Dave pulled away.

"Hi, Gabrielle!" a girl behind the counter yelled over the sound of milk being steamed on the espresso machine.

"Sorry I'm late, you guys!" The girl—Gabrielle—walked behind the counter. She was wearing really short shorts and a tank top. Madison self-consciously looked down at her own attire: baggy jeans that hung down around her hips, an English Beat concert T-shirt, a jean jacket, and black-and-white Chuck Taylors. Maybe she should make more of an effort.

"One coffee please," Madison said.

Gabrielle didn't look familiar to Madison. Dave knew everyone in La Jolla, and it was conceivable that this was just a friend. Madison knew better than to try to figure it out. This truth would not set her free.

Madison walked out to the patio and delivered the coffee to Felicity.

"There are a lot of beautiful people in this town," Felicity said.

"Yes." Madison sat down. She looked behind her to see if Dave had parked somewhere and walked back. Nope. "Unfortunately, a lot of the beauty is only skin-deep."

Felicity was emptying the contents of a stevia packet she'd brought with her into her coffee. She eyed Madison. "I think we're going to be friends."

Madison reached into her purse and took out a plastic bag containing the cell phone she had found in the Gaslamp District. "Was this Samantha's by any chance?"

Felicity took the plastic bag from her and looked at the phone closely. "No, this wasn't her phone. Where did you find it?"

"Well, it doesn't matter now." Madison threw the phone back in her purse. Why had she even asked her? *Ridiculous*, Madison thought. "So let's do it this way: you've heard every single theory, both possible and impossible. What do you think happened to Samantha?"

Felicity was warming her hands on her coffee mug, even though it was about seventy-five degrees under the umbrella on the patio. "Wow, you really cut to the chase don't you? I like that. And the answer is I just don't know."

Madison looked down at the broken-tile inlay at the table where they sat. She used her napkin to wipe a cleaner spot to rest her wrists on. "Do you think she would have taken a rideshare from the bar?"

"Sure. She definitely would not have driven drunk. And according to the videotape at the bar, she was wasted. I don't know why she walked out of the bar alone, other than the bartender cut her off and she was probably looking for her friends, or maybe she had to throw up or . . . I don't know. When a person is that drunk, it's hard to find motivation in their actions. You asked me what I thought happened, and the only thing I can think of is that she was the victim of an opportunity . . . someone saw an opportunity and grabbed her."

Madison thought for a minute. "I can see that. But something about that doesn't make sense. It was a busy night downtown. I was there last night to remind myself, and it wasn't even the weekend last night. The place is packed with people up and down the streets. If a girl had been dragged into a van kicking and screaming, someone would've noticed that. So in order to get her away from the bar she had to willingly get into a car. Whose car would she have gotten into willingly?"

"I see what you mean. Well, no one, other than a rideshare. She didn't have a boyfriend. She would've gone with a rideshare driver, or one of her friends, but they were all inside the bar and accounted for. Or she might've tried to walk to her car to take a nap and got lost on the way to her car. Maybe someone picked her up in an alley? Then there would be no witnesses. Or else she would've gotten in the car with someone that she *thought* was a rideshare driver."

Madison thought about that. It was possible and one of her initial thoughts.

"You said something on Twitter the other day," Felicity said. "You said 'I don't scare that easily.' And then someone with an account in your name said 'We'll see,' or something like that. Can you tell me what that was about?"

Madison paused. She didn't want to share details of the note yet. As an investigator, she'd found that a "need-to-know" basis was the best way to operate. "I'd rather not say, if that's okay. I might tell you later."

Felicity paused. A seagull had landed on the fence behind the bench she was sitting on. He was facing Madison; Felicity couldn't see him. He looked down at them with interest, as if he were part of their meeting.

"I do," Felicity said.

Madison's attention jerked back to Felicity. "You do . . . what?"

"I scare that easily. It's one of the reasons I agreed to meet with you even though I've been burned so many times before. I felt like it was a sign: you saying you don't scare easily, when I do."

Madison wasn't even sure that what she'd written was true; she'd tweeted it for effect.

"I'm afraid too sometimes. Everyone is."

"I feel like I can trust you," Felicity said. "I don't know why. Do people say that to you a lot?"

Madison realized that Felicity wanted to tell her something. So all she said was, "Yes, people trust me," and then she waited. As her father used to say, *the next person who talks loses.*

"He called me."

Madison said nothing. She didn't know who Felicity was referring to, but she was not about to interrupt her. If she waited, Felicity would tell her.

"Samantha has been missing for four years." Felicity stirred her coffee, although the stevia had long since dissolved. "When she had been missing for two years, I got a phone call."

Madison waited.

"It was on my house phone. I don't know whether my phone number is listed or not. I guess it is, because everyone's phone number is listed unless you pay to have it unlisted. So, he called and . . . I . . . I . . . picked up the phone."

Madison looked at her and waited.

The seagull swooped down from behind Felicity to grab a piece of bread someone had thrown on the ground for it. Felicity jumped up and knocked the table on the way up, rocking the coffee cups and spilling coffee. Madison reared back slightly but remained seated. Felicity started walking away from the table on the way to the street and stopped. She had her back to Madison.

Madison took napkins and mopped up the coffee before it dripped onto her pants and the ground. She wondered if she'd ever hear what this man had said on the phone. It was probably important. Felicity made her decision. She turned, looked at Madison, and took a deep breath. She came back and sat down.

"I haven't told this to anyone, do you understand?" Felicity said. "Not even the police." She seemed to be looking at Madison for a response.

"I understand."

"I just—I couldn't be sure if it was real or just a prank. An evil prank. I had been on Twitter a lot trying to get the police to investigate and to not forget about my sister. I also responded to people who were trying to help find out what happened to her. I didn't want to tell the police about the call because I was concerned they would tell me I had to get off social media, and it is the only thing keeping my sister's case alive . . . keeping *her* alive."

"Yes," Madison said.

Felicity started to cry.

Madison hated watching interrogators on TV pepper a subject with questions when they were trying to tell their story in their own way and in their own time. It caused them to lose their train of thought. You could always come back and ask questions when the person was done telling their story in their way. Madison said the fewest number of words possible, only enough to show Felicity that she was listening.

Madison waited.

Felicity cleared her throat and used a napkin to wipe under her mascaraed lashes. She took a sip of her coffee. She cleared her throat again. "The caller said, 'I had fun with your sister. She was a good fuck. Are you a good fuck?'"

As disturbing as this was, Madison was careful not to react.

"Then he said, 'Stop investigating me or I will hunt you down and kill you, bitch.'"

And there it is, Madison thought. *The exact same language as the note left on my door.*

Felicity had stopped talking.

"Did you ever hear from him again?" Madison asked.

"No," Felicity said. She grabbed a tissue out of her purse and wiped her nose. "But I also stopped tweeting as much. I stopped . . . I did what he said. Because I was afraid."

"That would make anyone afraid."

"But I don't want to be afraid anymore. I want to be like you and not scare easily."

Madison sighed. "Felicity, you need to tell the police about the phone call. They are going to be unhappy that you didn't tell them two years ago, but you need to tell them."

"Why? They already treat me like I'm a nuisance!"

Madison decided to tell her. She explained about the note left on her door. "It was the same wording. It is clear that the person who left that note on my door is the same person who took your sister—and then called you. You can just explain to the police that you thought it was a prank call, a mean prank call but a prank call nevertheless, and that's why you didn't tell them at the time."

This meant that the detectives handling the missing persons case were going to find out about the note left on Madison's door. They would be really upset that Tom had taken the note and processed it without putting it through normal police channels. She didn't want Tom to get in trouble, but she wasn't going to obstruct a police investigation by not reporting this phone call that Felicity had received.

Felicity's face was getting firmer. "No. I understand that the note on your door connects everything, but I don't want to tell them about this phone call. It is too late for them to do anything about it now anyway. If something happens in the future and it becomes important, I will tell them."

Madison was silent. This put her in a difficult position. She had knowledge of a crime, or at least of evidence in an active police investigation, and she had a responsibility to report it. She opened her mouth to tell Felicity that. "Felicity, I—"

Felicity stood up and put her finger in Madison's face. "You do not have permission to tell that to anyone!"

It came out in a screech, and people at tables nearby looked over at them. Felicity's face was bunched up, and there were tears streaming down her face. Her chin was quivering. It was the face of anguish.

"Sit down," Madison said quietly. "I won't say anything."

Chapter Eight

Madison walked to her car, putting her hair in a bun as she went. She got in the car and drove home with the windows rolled down. There wasn't a cloud in the sky and the temperature was a perfect seventy-five degrees, which helped to clear away her meeting with Felicity. The phone call Felicity had received was very disturbing; the fact that it showed that Madison was on the right track was only a small consolation. Madison got to a red light and leaned her head back on the headrest. There was a pretty blonde girl crossing the street, and at first Madison thought it was Gabrielle; then she realized it wasn't. Just another beautiful girl. There were always younger, more beautiful versions of Madison in La Jolla.

She had stayed with Felicity for another hour, discussing details of the investigation the police had shared and comparing notes on tweets Felicity had sent out. The police either hadn't shared much or there just weren't that many leads: they had checked the main rideshare companies and "hadn't come up with any viable evidence," which Felicity took to mean that they didn't feel like sharing what they had come up with. When Felicity asked about other things, they would just say, "We are pursuing all avenues." As far as tweets, Felicity had tweeted the same things as Madison, at least up until that horrible phone call. After the call, Felicity had stopped originating her own tweets, but she couldn't resist retweeting some of Madison's; this made Madison more of a target, since it showed that her investigative ideas were getting picked up by others—even by those who had been warned off.

A couple that used to live in the house in front of hers waved as she turned the corner onto Nautilus. They were walking to the beach with all of the accoutrements: beach chairs, cooler, small toddler struggling to carry her boogie board. Madison often took a drive by the ocean before parking at her apartment. She liked to see the beach, but also to check to see if Dave was in the water.

After comparing notes with Felicity, Madison could see no new clues or suspects to add to her whiteboard. However, she had made progress: she knew now that at least part of the Gaslamp mystery, the disappearance of Samantha, was connected to the note left on her door. The wording on the note and Felicity's phone call were exactly the same. Also, Madison had learned that Felicity had made friends with a waitress at Hank's Dive, the bar where Samantha was last seen, and this waitress was trying to help in any way she could. Felicity was going to give the waitress Madison's phone number so they could connect. Madison didn't know how she was going to reconcile not telling the police about the phone call and now the note, both likely the work of their suspect. All she knew was that Felicity had been through so much and she didn't want to add to it. Felicity was right about one thing—there was nothing the police could do about the phone call now. Nevertheless, Madison thought she might call her friend Haley, who was an attorney, just to get her advice.

Madison turned onto Neptune Place and drove slowly past the parking lot. There were several surfers in the lot watching the pattern of the waves before surfing. Dave had explained that they watched to see how many waves were coming in each set, how fast they were, and how they were breaking. This data was all needed to have a good surf session—and to not drown. *Never turn your back on the ocean*, Dave would say. That was true about a lot of things in life. *Do your due diligence. Trust everyone, but cut the cards.* Dave's jeep wasn't there.

Madison parked in her space and locked the car. She walked down the path, turned the corner of her building, and saw a woman sitting on her stairs. The woman was older than Madison: short dark hair, a little extra weight around the middle, wearing stretchy jeans, an off-label polo shirt, and Keds. The woman was reading a paperback novel and didn't see Madison approaching.

"Hi," Madison said.

The woman's head shot up and her body quickly followed. She dropped her book on the ground with the abrupt movement and left it there. She was shaking.

"I have something to say!" she shouted. She seemed to realize she was yelling and lowered her voice for the next part. "I need to talk to you."

"Okay. Who are you?"

"My name is Elaine Clark."

Oh shit, Madison thought.

"I'm Tom's wife."

"Yes, I know. Do you want to come inside?" Madison looked to her left to see if Ryan or his roommates were home. She didn't need to have a scene in the garden for the neighbors.

"That won't be necessary."

"Okay," Madison said. "We can talk here. But can you relax with the adversarial stance? We're not adversaries."

"We are when you're sleeping with my husband!"

Madison sighed and sunk into a lawn chair. She was suddenly so tired. "I'm not sleeping with your husband, and I have never slept with your husband."

"I know how often he used to come over here," Elaine said. "I used to follow him. And now it's happening again."

Madison looked at her, trying to translate what Elaine was saying into what Madison knew to be reality. Also, with all of this following going on, it was a wonder they didn't all run into each other.

"Nothing is happening *again*, because nothing happened *before*. Truly."

Elaine was still staring at Madison. "But I know he loves you."

Madison leaned back in the lawn chair and closed her eyes. This was ridiculous. She hated drama. She didn't have many friends that were women; well, to be fair, she didn't have many friends at all. But usually her friends were guys. She couldn't tolerate crying over guys, fighting over guys; frankly, she hated acting like guys were all that important to a happy life. She'd fallen for Dave and she regretted it on a daily basis; she did everything she could to avoid the drama he inherently brought with him. But what she didn't need was drama brought to her door from a guy that was just a friend, and barely that.

She opened her eyes. "He doesn't love me. He was obsessed with me because he couldn't have me. It happens. The only cure is to let them have you, at which point they realize it was all smoke and mirrors; but I didn't want to do that. However, he got over it. Right now he's just helping me with a case I have. I'm a private investigator."

"I know that," Elaine said accusatively.

"Anyway, I can't prove a negative, which is all I seem to be trying to do these days." Madison stood up. "I'm not sleeping with your husband. I barely like him."

"You'd be lucky to have him!" Elaine said.

"And with that piece of logic and reason, I'm going upstairs to my apartment." Madison walked the ten feet to her stairs, but Elaine didn't move to let her pass. There was sweat along her upper lip. Madison actually felt bad for her; she had kids. This was no kind of life.

Elaine was continuing. "He sees other women too, you know, not just you. I've followed him and seen him."

"No, I don't know," Madison said. "And dear God I don't care. Please, this is embarrassing for everyone. Just go home."

Elaine sat down on the stairs and started to sob.

Oh, great, Madison thought. *Now she's crying.* This was exhausting. She sat down next to her and handed her a Kleenex from her purse. They sat in silence for a few minutes; Elaine sobbing, Madison silent. All she wanted was to go upstairs and watch a *Friends* episode and eat popcorn. She'd had quite enough of today.

"I'm sorry," Elaine said. "I know I'm being irrational. But he's the love of my life. I've been with him since I was sixteen. He's everything to me. I get crazy when I think I'm losing him."

"It happens." That was a good phrase that applied to many things: falling in love, falling in love with the wrong person, acting crazy.

"I need to pick up my kids from school," Elaine said. She stood up. "Thank you for not laughing at me."

Madison looked at the sky and recited:

This man beside us also has a hard fight with an unfavouring world, with strong temptations, with doubts and fears, with wounds of the past which have skinned over, but which smart when they are touched.

Elaine just stared at her.

"John Watson, 1903," Madison said. "It's one of my favorites. I have my own doubts and fears and wounds of the past, they're just different than yours. So why would I laugh at you?"

"Right, well, I'd appreciate it if you didn't tell Tom I've been here."

Oh, good. Another thing I get to keep from a cop today. "I can't promise that, Elaine. But if it doesn't seem relevant, I can avoid the topic."

Elaine nodded and turned to walk down the path to the street in front of Ryan's house. She stopped a few feet along the path and turned back. "He's a good guy, you know."

"That may be. But he doesn't deserve you, Elaine."

Elaine paused. Then she turned to walk the rest of the way to her car.

Madison stood up and stretched. It was only the middle of the day, but she felt like she'd been up for a week. She walked with a heavy tread up the stairs to her apartment. She pulled out her keys and froze. Speared to her front door with a nail, typed on 8 ½" by 11" paper, was another note:

WHAT DID I TELL YOU?

Chapter Nine

Madison had called Tom three times in a row and ultimately he had put her straight to voicemail. She hadn't touched the note; she had walked past it into her apartment and tried to get Tom on the phone. She went to the windows and looked down into the alleys on both sides of her apartment. Her apartment was situated at the intersection of two alleys that made a T. She could look out her living room window at the alley between Nautilus and Bonair, and out her bedroom window at the other alley leading to La Jolla Boulevard. There were no unusual cars driving by or parked in the alleys. Nevertheless, the hair on the back of her neck was standing up. She dialed Tom's number again.

"I'm in court, Madison," Tom whispered when he finally answered. "You can't just keep calling me over and over."

"Sorry, I was a little frazzled after the visit from your wife," Madison said.

"Visit from my wife? You visited my wife? What the fuck are you doing?"

"No, dipshit. Your wife visited *me*. She was sitting on my steps when I got home."

"Oh Jesus. Look I can't deal with this right now—I'm in the middle of testifying in a murder trial." Madison could hear the echoing sounds of marble-hallway voices and footsteps.

"And then I came upstairs and there was another note from Anonymous on my front door," Madison continued. "Coincidence? Or your wife is my stalker? Keep it all in the family, right?"

"What? Oh my God Madison you've lost your mind. My wife is not your stalker. She's like . . . a housewife. Calm down."

"I am calm!" Madison realized after she said it that it had come out in a screech. She was not at all calm.

"Okay, look: I need to finish testifying today. Meet me at McGregor's tonight at seven thirty, and we will figure this out. Bring the new note."

Madison hung up. She was supposed to go out with Ryan tonight, but that no longer seemed appealing. She couldn't exactly make up an excuse when he would see her every coming and going. Accepting his invitation was seeming less and less like a good idea. Well, she could limit it. She texted Ryan, naming the restaurant around the corner from their place: *Do you want to make it happy hour at Su Casa?*

She sat in her office chair and stared at the whiteboard. Somehow yesterday it had seemed less personal or like it could still somehow be a fluke. Now it was as if she was having an actual conversation with a psychopath; someone was stalking her and knew that she was fully investigating him. It wasn't funny anymore.

The only thing to do was keep moving. The faster she figured out who he was, the faster he would be caught. If she stopped investigating out of fear, he could *still* think she was investigating; who knew how his mind worked. Nope, she had to just keep going and find him, even though she was really afraid now. She repeated the process of the day before with the note, but this time found a clear plastic sleeve to put it in; she would take it to Tom later.

She wrote on the whiteboard: *Anonymous has to be Samantha's kidnapper, because of the connection to Felicity's phone call and the exact same wording as the note.* She had nothing to write under the *Suspects* column because she still didn't have any idea who this person was. She then went to the *Clues* column and wrote down each note she had received, with the wording, along with the wording in Felicity's phone call; it was chilling to see the similarities, especially considering the violent words included in Felicity's call. Madison still didn't know if any of this tied in to Elissa Alvarez's disappearance.

According to her *Leads* column, the next thing she needed to do was talk to Elissa's mother, so maybe she would soon find out if there was a connection. Harmony Alvarez had spoken with the media early on after Elissa had gone missing; however, there hadn't been as much coverage on Elissa as there had been on Samantha, and Madison hadn't seen anything lately where Mrs. Alvarez had been quoted. Hopefully she would be willing to talk to Madison.

Madison pulled up her private investigator's database, a website that only licensed private investigators had access to, and put in the name Harmony Alvarez. It was unusual enough that there shouldn't be too many of those in the United States, and even fewer in the San Diego area. She was right: only three names came up, and only one of them was in the San Diego area. Harmony Alvarez, age fifty-five, El Cajon, California. And there was a phone number.

Yes, Madison reminded herself, *it is easy to find someone if you have the right tools.*

"Bueno?" A woman answered. Madison did not speak Spanish, but she could get by in a pinch.

"Si . . . Mrs. Alvarez? Soy Madison Kelly . . ."

"Yes?" Thank God the woman had switched to English.

"I am a licensed private investigator. I'm looking into the disappearance of your daughter. Would it be possible for me to speak with you?"

"You are in San Diego?" she asked.

"Yes, I am in La Jolla."

"Yes, this is possible. I am in La Jolla today working. I clean the house. You can come here?"

"Yes, of course. Will that be okay with your employer?"

"They are in Europe. I am alone here. I clean every two weeks while they travel."

"Okay, perfect."

Mrs. Alvarez gave her the address on a street in the hills of La Jolla. They agreed to meet in two hours.

Madison hung up. She felt a little better; she was moving forward with her plan. Now what she needed was a nap. The disturbing aspect of this case exhausted her, and she wanted to be clearheaded when she met with Elissa's mother. She went to check the windows again: no unusual cars, no one lurking in the alleys. She didn't feel safe in her home anymore. Thankfully, her wooden stairs were so rickety that the sound of someone walking up them would wake the dead. It was the built-in alarm system of an ancient dwelling. She went to the door and added a wedge lock that made it impossible to get in unless you removed the hinges from the door. Or used an ax, which would definitely get her attention.

Madison opened the windows so that there was an ocean breeze cutting across her apartment. She stripped off her clothes. As she crossed to her bed, she caught a glimpse of herself in the mirror on her antique vanity, and her breath caught in her throat. That happened sometimes. When she was living her life, she tended to forget that the bilateral mastectomy she'd had for early-stage breast cancer had taken her nipples and left her with two huge scars from her armpits to the center of her chest. Clothes allowed her to forget: the mounds under her shirt from the implants looked real. When she had the surgery, a friend had said, "At least you'll have a new rack!" She didn't talk to that person anymore. She didn't have a new rack; she had two implants placed under her pectoral muscles, huge scars, and no nipples.

Madison ran her finger along the scar that ended where her nipple used to be on her right boob. Then she did the same on the left. Her chest was permanently numb from the nerves being cut during surgery, but her finger registered the unusual texture of the scarred skin. She didn't feel pretty when she did this. She decided Dave was just being kind when he said he didn't mind. Guys liked smooth, pretty boobs, with nipples. She looked like she'd been in a knife fight.

She lay on top of the comforter and let the breeze drift across her body. The air at the beach in Southern California remained cool for most of the summer months; the feel and smell of it reminded her of every summer in her life. She remembered coming home from summer school that time she was taking drama; she was riding her bike. Her problems and worries had seemed big and real, but she was on the way home, where there was safety: Mom and Dad wouldn't let anything happen to her. That's how it felt at the time, anyway. That was so many Junes ago she'd lost count; somehow it'd had a bit more hope.

Madison was so exhausted that she easily fell asleep. Her last thought before she began to dream was: *Tom didn't ask me what the note said.*

Chapter Ten

When Madison pulled into the driveway, Mrs. Alvarez was standing on the sidewalk in front. She was wearing a uniform of some kind, sort of like scrubs in a tan pastel color. She waved. Madison eyed her as she was getting out of the car. Mrs. Alvarez looked warm and friendly; but she also looked like she'd been tired for a very long time.

"Mrs. Alvarez?" Madison got out of the car and reached out her hand to shake.

Mrs. Alvarez had to look up at Madison; she was about a foot shorter.

"Yes! You so tall!"

Mrs. Alvarez led the way into the home. It was the biggest house Madison had ever been in. As soon as you walked into the foyer, which was bigger than Madison's entire apartment, you could see the ocean. They were in the hills above La Jolla, and one entire wall of this huge house was a window. It looked like there was no seam in the glass. Madison figured they must've used a crane to get that piece of glass in place. Mrs. Alvarez pointed at the corner of a huge couch, and Madison sat down.

There was already a water bottle sitting on a coaster on the coffee table in front of her.

"You drink." Mrs. Alvarez looked encouragingly at her, as if Madison had had difficulty drinking in the past. Madison picked up the water bottle and opened it and took a small sip to be polite. She set it back carefully onto the coaster. The coffee table was glass, and she didn't want Mrs. Alvarez to have to clean again when they were done. Mrs. Alvarez sat next to the couch in an overstuffed chair that could've fit three of her.

"I'm not sure that I can help find your daughter, but I would like to try," Madison said.

Mrs. Alvarez looked out the window at the ocean. "I would like you to try. People forget. They remember the other girl, Samantha, because she was—" Mrs. Alvarez stopped and glanced back at Madison.

"Blonde?"

"I am sorry." Mrs. Alvarez's eyes went to the ground. "I upset you when you help me."

"No, you didn't. You won't ever upset me by telling the truth. I know that the media pays more attention to missing white girls than to girls of color."

"Thank you," Mrs. Alvarez said. "Other people make excuses and deny it. Thank you for saying it."

"What do you think happened to Elissa?"

Mrs. Alvarez sighed. "I no sure. I no like her boyfriend. You hear about her boyfriend?"

"Yes," Madison said. "I have heard about him. Why didn't you like him?"

"He hit her before," Mrs. Alvarez said. "But it long time ago. I tell her to leave him and she go back always. He not nice."

"Her friends said that she got in a fight with her boyfriend on the phone and she left to go home. Obviously she didn't make it to her car. Do you think she would have taken a rideshare?"

"Maybe. But her friends say she no drunk. And her car there. So why take taxi? You know?"

Madison thought about that for a minute. She had to agree. Why would Elissa have taken a rideshare when she hadn't been drinking? To get away from her boyfriend? Did her boyfriend show up that night? Was she running from him?

"I know," Madison said. "You're right, it doesn't make sense that she would take a rideshare when she wasn't drunk and her car was just a couple of blocks away."

"The police stop giving me updates." Mrs. Alvarez cleaned an invisible spot off the coffee table. She fluffed the pillows sitting behind her, then did a small karate chop into the tops of them to make a V. "They tell me what happening for the first year and a half. In the last six months? No. Nothing."

"They probably don't have any more leads," Madison said. "You realize it is not because they don't care, right? They do care. It's just . . . if they don't have any leads, they don't know where to go to find the next clue."

Mrs. Alvarez looked at Madison. "You have the lead?"

"I'm not sure. Not a clear lead, but I may be onto something. Tell me about Elissa."

Mrs. Alvarez's eyes got brighter, and she became more animated. "She smart, like you. She go to college. I no go to college. I clean houses."

Mrs. Alvarez put her chin up as if Madison were going to judge her for her occupation.

"This is hard work." Madison glanced around appreciatively. The place was immaculate. Along the wall without a window were built in floor-to-ceiling bookcases; Madison was dismayed to see that they had color-coordinated books in them: blue and yellow. Books as decoration. What a waste of good bookcases.

"Yes," Mrs. Alvarez said. "It very hard. But I pay for everything. Elissa go to college and she study hard. She no pay anything. The school gave her scholarship and I pay for everything else. By myself. Elissa going to be a social worker. She no clean houses. She going to have a better life."

Madison was silent. It had been two years since Elissa was last seen. She didn't think Elissa was going to be anything ever again. She figured Mrs. Alvarez had to hold out hope or it would be too hard to get out of bed in the morning. Madison tried to have hope against all odds too. She decided to join Mrs. Alvarez in hoping that Elissa would be a social worker and end up helping other people wounded by tragedy.

"You must be so proud of her."

"Elissa a good girl," Mrs. Alvarez said. "The news say she did drugs or met a bad man on purpose. Not Elissa. She a good girl. That is why I say she no get in car with someone."

"Did she go to that bar often? Did she know anyone there?"

"She never been there. It her friend's idea to go downtown. I say okay because her grades good. She got all As. Do you think I did wrong? I think if only I told her she no go, she be here now."

"You can't do that," Madison said. "You can't blame yourself. She was twenty-one, right? An adult. You have to let them grow up and live their lives."

"She twenty-three now. Twenty-three."

Shit, Madison thought. "Yes, sorry, twenty-three." She took another swig of water.

Mrs. Alvarez looked at her watch. "I catch the bus."

"Of course," Madison said. "Can you tell me how to reach Elissa's boyfriend? I'd like to talk to him if possible."

"I have his number. He not a nice man." She pulled out her phone and read the contact info to Madison.

"Oh, that reminds me," Madison said. She reached into her purse and took out the plastic bag containing the iPhone she had found. Before she could say anything, Mrs. Alvarez flew up and grabbed the bag out of her hand.

"*Dios mío, es su teléfono,*" Mrs. Alvarez whispered. "*Dios mío, Dios mío, Dios mío.*" She sat back down on the overstuffed chair. Big fat tears rolled down her cheeks. Her voice became so soft that Madison couldn't make out the words. Mrs. Alvarez started rocking back and forth with her eyes shut. Madison realized she was praying.

Madison had found Elissa Alvarez's phone.

Chapter Eleven

Madison started the drive home from her visit with Mrs. Alvarez. Her mind was racing so much that she pulled over on the way to think. She realized she'd stopped in front of her old apartment, the one she'd lived in when she first moved to La Jolla. *This is where I dreamed*, Madison thought.

Madison knew she had to turn over the phone to the police. Not telling them something Felicity had said was one thing; now she had actual evidence in an active investigation. She would for sure be charged with obstruction of justice if she held on to it. She had a great computer guy who could get inside the brains of this phone in no time, but anything he found would be rendered useless due to the rules regarding chain of custody. If a suspect was identified, his attorney could say that her computer guy planted the evidence. No, it had to go to the police, and quickly.

There was a white balloon floating above Madison's car. She watched its path: swirling slightly as it caught an invisible air funnel; swooping down, up, and then holding steady.

She was due to meet Tom in a few hours, so she would hand him the phone and explain how she'd found it. He could decide how best to get it to the right person involved in the investigation.

Sure, it was luck she'd found it; but whose luck? This discovery threw her smack-dab in the middle of the police investigation—if she hadn't already been there, she sure was now. The huge machine called the justice system was about to suck her into its jaws and masticate her. *Luck, shmuck*, Madison thought. She wished someone else had found the phone.

She checked her Twitter. Nothing new. Yesterday seemed like a long time ago; it was sort of fun yesterday. Today was just . . . not fun anymore.

The balloon had slipped down until it landed on her hood. She got out of the car and grabbed it. She held it up to the light and saw that there was a tiny slip of paper inside. A message to someone who had passed? A wish or a hope or a dream? Balloons could be dangerous for the environment. If you wanted a ritual like that, it was better to use paper lanterns that burned up with the message. Birds and fish could be injured by popped balloons that made it into the ocean.

She held the balloon up again and shook it. She could see the writing on the note through the thin white material of the balloon.

I'll love you all the days of my life.

She put the balloon in the back seat.

Time to go shower for her date with Ryan, who had responded that happy hour at Su Casa was fine with him.

Madison walked into Su Casa and was hit with the smell of stale beer and mustiness. *Ahhh, Su Casa, how do I love thee*, Madison thought. Su Casa had been serving Mexican food and margaritas that would put hair on the chest of surfers and the local community since 1967. The decor was ocean, but more pirate than coastal. They had a big fish tank and dark corners with red leather booths.

Ryan was already in a booth in the back.

"Hey, sorry to change the plans," Madison said as she sat down.

"No problem." Ryan was wearing a flannel button-down over a surf-contest shirt and jeans. The surfer date uniform. "I love this place, and we can fill up on half-price appetizers."

The waitress came over, and they ordered margaritas and guacamole and chips and said they would think about the rest.

"So you're a private investigator?" Ryan asked.

"Yes, I am."

"But you don't drive a red Ferrari . . . what's up with that?"

Madison cringed inwardly. Ever since Tom Selleck starred in *Magnum P.I.* in the 1980s, even guys who were way too young to have seen the TV show had talked about the red Ferrari he drove around Hawaii. And now they'd made a remake with the same stupid car. It infuriated Madison for several reasons. First, Tom Selleck and the new actor were masculinity personified, so Madison would hardly identify with them as role models; so why bring them up to her? Second, only a complete idiot would tail a subject in a bright-red foreign sports car that cost half a million dollars around a tiny island in Hawaii. The idea when tailing someone is to remain hidden, not to stand out and have people point at you. If she tailed someone in a car like that, she would be spotted in three blocks.

"I don't have a Ferrari because I'm actually a PI, not a PI on a TV show," she said.

"Oh." He looked abashed. "I love that show."

Madison knew she should give Ryan a break, but this kind of stupidity drove her insane. Her job was so difficult and nuanced, and to have it reduced to a guy driving a fancy car was infuriating.

"I've heard it was good," she said. "But it's just not realistic."

"Okay. So tell me how it really is."

He seemed genuinely interested, which caught her off guard. The waitress showed up, and they ordered more appetizers. Madison was still nursing her first drink, because she had to keep a clear head for meeting Tom later.

"I mostly investigate insurance fraud," Madison said. "A person makes an insurance claim for workers' compensation, for example. They say they were hurt at work and can no longer work. They want the insurance company to pay them a lot of money. The insurance company hires me to make sure that they are actually injured."

"So you follow them and videotape them and stuff?"

"That's right," Madison said. "I sit outside their home very early and wait for them to leave. Then I tail them to their next destination. Sometimes that is a baseball game, or the gym, and sometimes they've gotten a new job while they wait for the insurance payout. I videotape them whenever I see them."

"That is epic," Ryan said.

"So you see, I can't drive a fancy red car, or they would see me."

"Yeah," Ryan said. "I do see. The show got that part wrong, didn't they?"

"Yes, they did. I mean, I guess it made for good television. The macho guy driving the fancy car."

"Yeah, it did. But it's just like with legal shows or doctor shows: they get stuff wrong, I guess."

Madison felt he understood, which was nice. She needed to give people more chances.

"So what do you want to be when you grow up?" she asked.

"When I grow up?" Ryan laughed. "I want to go to South America and work on civil infrastructure of developing nations."

Madison snorted and shook her head.

"That's funny?"

"No. I'm laughing at myself. I'm impressed." Madison had a healthy dose of arrogance; she felt it was necessary for survival. But this guy, by his very existence, was knocking her down several pegs. She thought she was so special, but Ryan was going to go change the world.

"How have you been in the front house being all smart and ambitious and I didn't notice you?" she asked.

"I noticed you," Ryan said. And then he blushed.

Madison left Ryan at Su Casa and raced over to McGregor's Grill in the Mission Gorge area of San Diego to meet Tom. She would be a little bit late, but she figured Tom would wait. He was probably there for the night anyway.

She didn't know what to think about Ryan. He seemed nice, and smart, and he certainly was her type. But something made her hesitate. He was pretty young, but the intelligence and the career goals balanced that out. She didn't want to get involved with someone when she had this stalker and a huge investigation going on. It was stupid of her to even entertain the idea. But in the back of her mind, something was gnawing: was it just that he wasn't Dave?

She pulled into the parking lot at McGregor's and looked for a space. It was packed. There wasn't much out this way except the stadium, which didn't have an event tonight. So the streets were fairly empty and it was quiet except for the sounds coming from the bar.

McGregor's was a known cop hangout, or at least known that way to cops and their entourage. Located in a strip mall, it had fried food, cheap drinks, and televisions playing whatever game was good that night. Madison found a parking space across the parking lot and a few doors down from the bar. All the other businesses in the strip mall were closed. She walked in and saw Tom talking to another cop at the bar.

"Hey, Madison." Tom pointed to the guy he was standing with. "This is Ken."

"Hi, nice to meet you," Madison said.

"And nice to meet you, finally." Ken showed his teeth.

"Finally?" Madison said.

"Shut the fuck up, Ken." Tom signaled for the bartender.

"I'm only kidding." Ken took a swig of his cocktail. "I'm just winding you up."

"Ken was just leaving," Tom said.

"Hey, hey, hey, I can take a hint." Ken drained his drink. "But the night is young. I'll just step over here and leave you two lovebirds alone."

"Seriously?" Madison said as he walked away. "*Lovebirds?* What the hell?"

"He's just being a dick." Tom ordered another beer from the bartender, who'd finally seen him waving. "I've known him a long time. He's just giving me a hard time."

"Okay, anyway," Madison said. "Can we sit at a table?"

Tom got his beer, and Madison accepted his offer of a drink, but she got club soda. They moved to a table in the corner.

"Okay, so what's the latest?" Tom asked.

"First, I have a question for you." Madison set her glass carefully on the napkin. Beads of condensation were already forming. It was hot in the bar. "Why didn't you ask me on the phone what the new note said?"

Tom was drinking from his beer bottle. He waited until he'd swallowed and set the beer down on the table. "Didn't I?"

Is he stalling? Madison thought. That was a technique liars used: ask a question instead of answering, so you have more time to figure out what to say.

There was an explosion of yells from the other side of the bar. Madison turned and saw a bunch of guys playing darts. Someone had hit a bull's-eye and was getting congratulated, and a round was being ordered. She came back to Tom.

"No," Madison said. "You didn't."

"Look, I told you I was in court. The DA was standing right next to me, trying to get me off the phone. I didn't have time to chat."

That made sense to Madison, but it didn't make sense why he hadn't just said that instead of deflecting her question. She would file it for later. She pulled the note in its plastic sleeve out of her purse and handed it to Tom.

"A man of few words." Tom handed the note back to Madison. "What is he talking about—'What did I tell you?'"

"Okay. A lot has happened." She started shredding the cocktail napkin under her drink.

"'A lot has happened?'" Tom stared intently at her. "Don't you mean *Madison has been doing things she shouldn't be doing again*?"

"Just listen. I have to explain a lot to bring you up to speed."

She recounted how she had realized her tweets about the missing girls in the Gaslamp District might have something to do with the note on her door.

"So I went down to the Gaslamp to look around."

"And?"

"I found something."

"What did you find?" Tom was trying to stay calm.

"I found a cell phone near the parking lot where Elissa Alvarez parked her car."

Tom sighed. "Oh. Okay. You found a random cell phone. Is this story going somewhere?"

"And I carefully picked it up and put it in a bag. First I met with Samantha's sister, Felicity, at the Pannikin. She said the phone wasn't Samantha's."

"You met with a witness in an ongoing police investigation? With a piece of evidence in that investigation?" There was a vein in the middle of his forehead that was pulsing.

"I didn't know if it was evidence! You *just said* yourself that I found a random cell phone. And anyway, you knew I wasn't going to sit around and let someone else figure out who was stalking me. Oh and last time I checked? I was licensed to talk to witnesses."

Tom was shaking his head. "Okay, okay, okay. Fine. Keep going."

"Felicity said she didn't recognize the phone."

"Shocker." Tom took a drink of his beer and glanced at the game on the TV in the corner.

Madison ignored his sarcasm. "When I got home from meeting with Felicity, that second note was on my door. But first, your wife was sitting on my stairs."

Tom was quiet for a minute. "Okay, well, anyway, he is clearly following you. I don't like this."

"*He*? We don't know it's a he, now do we?"

Tom's eyes flared. "What are you implying, Madison?"

"She came to my home, Tom. She was angry. Then I walk upstairs and that note is on my door."

"It's not my wife."

"You don't know that. She said she follows you and she knows you've been coming to my apartment."

"It's not my wife."

"Do you think if you keep repeating that, it will make it so?"

Tom took a deep breath and let it out. "Madison, will you let this one go? I'm telling you, she is the sweetest person . . . I've put her through hell."

Frankly, Madison didn't think his wife was the type to leave nasty notes, but what did she know? She decided not to push it for the time being.

"Okay," Madison said. "I'll keep calling him a *he*. So he thought I was investigating him when I wasn't investigating him. Now he thinks I'm investigating him, still, and now I am investigating him. So I'm damned if I do, damned if I don't— but at least if I investigate, I might figure out who it is."

Another explosion of yells, this one louder. Madison looked over and saw big men jumping and throwing their arms around each other. *They must be betting on the darts*, Madison thought. Then she saw Ken at the other end of the bar, staring at her.

"Why is your friend staring at me?"

Tom looked over and saw Ken. Ken waved, and Tom nodded his head.

"He's a man. You're pretty. Why do you have to be such a ballbuster? Why can't you be sweet?"

Madison laughed. "Oh, I'm sorry. I forgot. My purpose in life is to be on display for men to enjoy. And to be sweet. I'll be a good statue and shut up and look pretty."

"That's not what I meant. But could you?"

"Yes, it is what you meant," Madison said. "And I'm ignoring your joke because you weren't joking when you said it. That's exactly what you meant. I'm supposed to be flattered that guys stare at me and make me uncomfortable."

"Maybe he's not staring at you. Maybe he's staring at me."

"You just said he was staring at me because I'm pretty."

"Look, I'll take this new note in, and we'll see if it tells us anything," Tom said.

"Don't change the subject."

Tom stood up. "I'm getting another beer. You make me want to drink."

"Wait, I have more to say."

"I'm coming back; calm down," Tom said. He walked away and went to the area where the restrooms were. Apparently Ken felt this was his chance, since he started to make his way to the table. Madison jumped up and walked toward the restroom. She managed to avoid Ken's arc while pretending she didn't see him.

When she came out of the bathroom, Tom was at the table with a new beer. She came back and sat across from him.

"Oh I thought you'd left." Tom kept an eye on the TV on the wall. "Too bad. Anyway, do you want to hear about the first note, or are we going to discuss how men are from Mars and women are from Venus?"

"Shut up," Madison said. "Yes, I want to hear about the note."

"Nothing, unfortunately. No DNA, no fingerprints."

"Yeah," Madison said. "That was to be expected."

"I'll take this new one in, but don't expect much."

Madison took a deep breath. "Okay, but there's more."

"Why do I feel like I'm not going to like this?"

"You're going to. It makes the fact that I'm doing an investigation on my own worth it."

"Okay, so?"

"I met with Elissa's mother. She recognized the phone. It is Elissa's phone. One hundred percent certain." She pulled the iPhone in its plastic bag out of her purse and slid it across the table to him.

Tom sat quietly looking at the phone on the table without picking it up. Madison knew that this piece of evidence was too glorious for him to get mad at her.

"Only you, Madison. Only you."

"What does that mean?"

Tom laughed. "I've told you before, I think you're a great investigator. But this is . . . only you would go out to a scene as big as the Gaslamp and find a cell phone that half the police force hasn't been able to find in two years."

Madison smiled. Sometimes her confidence annoyed people; some people thought she was full of herself. But the fact was, she only cared about doing a good job. She didn't care about being pretty or boyfriends or anything other than the pride she felt in a job well done. Having outside validation of that once in a while was nice.

"Thanks, Tom," she said.

He toyed with the bag that held the phone, thinking. "Now I'm going to have to figure out how to report this discovery. Which means I'm going to have to tell the detectives handling the missing persons about the notes on your door."

Madison thought about the phone call that Felicity had received. She really wanted to tell Tom about it. But she had promised Felicity.

"I know. Do you know anything else about the investigation? Do they have any leads?"

Tom put on his poker face. "You know I can't share details of an active police investigation."

"Disclaimer received," Madison said. "So, what do you know?"

Tom sighed. "I don't know much. If they had something, I probably wouldn't tell you. But as far as I know, they have nothing. They still don't even know if the two disappearances are connected. They don't know if the girls just ran off and it's a coincidence. I will tell you this: it might look like nothing is happening, and sometimes, for a while, it isn't. But we never give up on missing persons. Years can go by without a lead and then something will come in. Or a new set of eyes looks at the case and gets an idea. It can take a long time, especially on cases that have gone cold. But we don't give up. And hey, maybe this will help." He held up the iPhone.

Madison had hoped for more, but she understood.

"Have they checked out rideshare drivers in the area?" Madison kept coming back to this. Maybe it was because of the other cases she'd been reading about. It just seemed so easy to pick up a drunk girl and then she's gone, just like she disappeared. Because she did disappear—one minute she's walking down a crowded street, and the next minute she gets into a car that pulls up and she's gone. Quick and neat and perfect for a predator.

"As far as I know, that was one of the first things they checked. That and employees at the bars. But nothing."

Madison couldn't be sure that Tom would tell her everything the police had learned. He liked her and trusted her, but he was a cop first and foremost. He wouldn't have any qualms about lying to her if it meant protecting the integrity of a case.

"Nothing, huh? Okay." Madison looked over at a group of women sitting nearby. They were all about Madison's age, and they looked as fit as Madison. Their heads were together, discussing something they didn't want others to hear. Madison decided they were cops. Before she returned her attention to Tom, she glanced around some more. She was trying to give the appearance that they were just relaxing, having a drink, and she wasn't hanging on his every answer.

She turned back to Tom. "Nothing. Hmmmm. Okay, so . . . does that mean they weren't able to get information out of the rideshare services, or does that mean it is confirmed the girls didn't take a rideshare?"

Tom took a pull of his beer and glanced up at the TV. When his eyes returned to Madison, they had lost their humor. "Don't fucking try to question me like I'm a subject in your investigation. *Nothing* means exactly that: nothing."

Madison didn't want to push it and make him mad. She decided to try something else. "I read that Samantha's phone only pinged in the Gaslamp, so it was likely shut off or the battery went dead before it moved. I didn't know about Elissa's phone, but since I just found it in the Gaslamp, I'm guessing it didn't ping outside of that area either. Does that jive with everything you know?"

"You don't want much, do you?" He shifted in his seat. Madison sensed he didn't want to get angry either. They had just started talking again, and despite the fiery aspect of their relationship, neither of them wanted to have a real fight and go back to not speaking. "Listen, I don't know all the ins and outs of the investigation, other than what we talk about around the station. But they've wanted those phones for sure. This will be a big find."

"So I did a good job, huh?"

"Yes, you did a good job." Tom smiled at her. When he smiled like that, she wished he weren't married. "I don't suppose I can get you to stop now and let the police handle this?"

"No," Madison said. "You can't."

Someone had put a 1970s rock song on the jukebox in the corner. It was from a movie. *Deer Hunter*. A bunch of the guys threw their arms around each other and started singing at the tops of their lungs. The guys didn't sing very well, but they were committed to the song. Cops had a rough job, and it was nice to see them blowing off steam.

"Okay, well I'm going to take off." Madison stood up.

"So soon?"

"Sarcasm noted," she said.

"You take care." Tom had returned his attention to the game on the TV.

"You know, you've never said you're sorry."

Tom looked over at a game of pool that was down to the eight ball. Madison glanced that way just as the player scratched. A group on the other side yelled at the game on TV; it was hard to tell if they were thrilled or destroyed by the play. Tom gave her a sideways glance.

"Maybe I'm not sorry."

Madison wasn't expecting that. Actually, she wasn't sure what she'd been expecting.

"I got carried away." He shrugged his shoulders. "I parked outside your apartment. I wondered about you. As a cop, it's easy when you're wondering to go check something out. Maybe I did it too much. But it's not like I hurt you."

"You scared me."

"No I didn't, Madison." His eyes drilled into her. "You don't scare that easy, remember?"

Madison had been scared when she realized Tom had been sitting outside her apartment watching her, several nights a week. She had confronted him and he'd stopped. She hadn't taken it further because that kind of report could get him

investigated and demoted from what was any cop's dream job—
Robbery/Homicide. It was true, he hadn't hurt her. And as a PI,
she knew what it was like to cross the line in your personal life
because you were so used to watching people.

But she hadn't told him about her tweet where she'd said she
didn't scare easily. Had he seen it?

"What do you mean by that?" She stared at him to try to
read something from his face.

"Whaddya mean, what do I mean?"

"What you just said: 'You don't scare that easy.'"

"Are you trying to pick a fight with me? What the hell? You
say that all the time."

Madison didn't think she'd ever said that, except in that
tweet yesterday. Because it wasn't actually true. "I don't recall
saying that."

"Jesus. Okay, well, you just don't seem like the kind of girl
who scares easily. All tough and brave, all the time. But for what
it's worth, I'm sorry, I guess."

Madison rolled her eyes and turned to walk out. She wished
she hadn't brought it up. No apology was better than that half-
assed one. Ken was eyeing her from the bar, and as she walked
toward the door he started on a route to intercept her. She really
didn't want to deal with this guy right now. Tom had annoyed
her, as usual, and she just wanted to go home.

"Hey, so, anyway, nice to meet you," Ken said as he caught
up to her. She was walking fast on her long legs, but he managed
to keep up. She pushed the door to go outside and didn't hold it
for him. It was twilight on a summer night in inland San Diego:

warm and dry with a tequila sunrise–colored sunset still painting the western sky after the sun had disappeared.

"It's cool, I've got it," he said as he grabbed the door that was shutting on him and shoved it open. He pushed it so hard it slammed against the outside wall and stayed open. It startled Madison. She realized she was being rude to this guy because she was frustrated with Tom.

She turned and stopped. "I'm sorry. Yes, nice to meet you."

"No problem. So you're the PI, right?"

Madison wanted to go home. "Yep, that's me."

"I might have a job for you. Would I be able to give you a call?"

Madison kicked herself. She'd thought this guy was trying to pick her up, and he just wanted to hire her. *Vain much?* she thought. He seemed slightly socially awkward; Madison always tried harder to make a person like that feel more comfortable in social situations. She took a deep breath. "I'm kind of busy at the moment, and I usually just work for insurance companies, but I don't mind hearing about it. Sure, give me a call." She grabbed a card out of her purse and handed it to him.

He took his wallet out of his back pocket and put the card in the wallet. He was tall, with closely cut "cop hair," as Madison called it. His eyes were so blue that they were almost pastel. Madison wondered what a cop needed with a PI.

He smiled, and this time it met his eyes and made him seem less awkward. When Madison dropped the chip off her shoulder with guys, they had a tendency to get nicer.

He was thanking her. "Great. Thanks. Yeah, no obligation, just hear me out and maybe you can help me."

"Sounds good. Call me tomorrow. Have a good night." Madison turned to walk toward her car.

"Have a good night," he called out.

Madison reached her car and got in the driver's seat. She turned back and saw that Tom had come out and was talking to Ken. They laughed about something and then walked back into the bar.

Madison pulled out of the parking lot and headed back to the beach. She had a weird hangover from the margarita at Su Casa, and she just wanted her big bed. She had turned the evidence she possessed over to the police—well, Tom—and no one could say she was obstructing justice. Granted, she hadn't turned over her knowledge of the phone call Felicity had received, but she didn't feel too bad about that now. She didn't work for the police, and she'd already found a major piece of evidence in the form of Elissa's phone and handed it over. She would just keep telling herself that.

Traffic was light on a Thursday night. San Diego still had rush "hour," or maybe a few hours, unlike Los Angeles that had constant traffic night and day. She never had to give herself more than thirty minutes to get anywhere as long as it wasn't during high-traffic times.

Madison was trying not to be annoyed with Tom. She needed him for this case. She thought back to when they'd first met. She was a baby investigator and he was a baby cop (although older than she, as she liked to point out to him frequently). Madison's firm had been hired by a car rental company that had been having tons of cars stolen from tourists who'd rented them. The firm had been in coordination with the police and had assigned Madison a location and a cop; the location was the harbor area, and the cop was Tom.

When she'd met Tom down by the historic ships and the Midway aircraft carrier, there'd been an instant attraction. It was palpable. He wasn't wearing a wedding ring.

Her firm had investigators all over San Diego just watching rental cars: tourists would park and go into a tourist attraction, and the investigators would wait to see if the car was stolen while they were inside. When the tourists came back, the investigators drove to find a new rental car to watch. It was tedious work and long hours. Tom worked with her the first week: she would sit watching rental cars, and he would drive around and check on her. They talked a lot. They worked late into the night. One day he asked her to breakfast and spent twenty minutes trying to tell her something: he was married, but he was getting a divorce. Madison had been down that road before and told him she'd love to go to breakfast with him when his divorce was final.

After a week and a half, the police took Tom off the case, because they felt it was no longer worth the police man hours. Madison was on her own.

Finally, at the end of the second week, Madison's luck came through: two guys walked up to the rental car she was watching. They were not the tourist family who had parked it. They started fussing with the passenger door. Madison called 911, as was the protocol they'd worked out. The police had all been briefed and knew who she was and what she was doing. In less than three minutes the two suspects had the car started and were driving down Harbor Drive. They made a quick right and within five minutes were on the freeway heading south toward Mexico.

Madison and the suspects were only twenty minutes from the Mexican border, and she was getting nervous that the cops wouldn't get there in time. Then cop cars began entering the freeway at each entrance: one car, two cars, three cars, four. The traffic behind her began to disappear as the cops did a "round robin" technique where they swerved across the freeway to stop all traffic. Soon it was just Madison following the stolen car with about ten cop cars behind her on the freeway; she was getting instructions from the 911 operator and hadn't yet been told to pull off. Then the police helicopter came over the top of them, its magnified voice eerily clear on the empty freeway, shouting orders at the suspect vehicle: "Stop your vehicle! Stop your vehicle!" All the cop cars put their lights and sirens on at the same time, with the helicopter's spotlight shining down as bright as day. The suspects stopped in the middle of the freeway. The 911 operator told Madison on the phone to slow to a stop. The cops all jumped out of their cars, using their doors as shields, rifles pointing at the suspects. Madison was now surrounded by cops and their cars, some of them still behind her with their guns drawn. The cops had ordered the suspects out of the car and they lay facedown on the pavement. Madison had a front-row seat to a felony stop in the middle of one of the busiest freeways in California.

Madison was invited to police headquarters and got high-fives from the cops who'd been on the case for a while. A car theft ring had been busted. Tom was proud of her. He suggested they go get a celebratory drink, and she was so electrified from her night that she agreed. They went to the Aero Club, a dive bar by the freeway near the airport that had been serving stiff drinks since 1947. Madison loved a dive bar. She couldn't abide fancy places where you had to dress up and be judged by what you were wearing. She called those places "S & M" bars, for Stand and Model. So when Tom suggested the Aero Club, it confirmed that he was her kind of guy.

They sat at the bar with a bunch of mechanics who'd been out carousing all night and finally settled on a place that felt like home. Madison was doing shots of Jack Daniels, always a sign that she should go home, and ended up standing on the bar and singing Gladys Knight and the Pips' "Midnight Train to Georgia," having recruited three of the mechanics to be her Pips and sing backup. Tom was telling anyone who would listen that she was a hero, and by the end of the night the story had morphed into her single-handedly stopping the Sinaloa Cartel in Mexico.

As they stumbled out of the bar at closing and walked toward downtown, Tom grabbed her next to an abandoned storefront and kissed her. Madison was so drunk by then that she couldn't appreciate the culmination of months of brewing electricity. When she closed her eyes to kiss him, the world started spinning.

"I'm gonna hurl," she said. And then she did, in the cement alcove of Paulette's Bobbin and Stitch, your sewing supply store since 1937.

Tom turned away. He called her an Uber on his phone. When it got there, she fell into the back of the car. They'd never discussed that night again.

Tom had never gotten divorced, and Madison knew he never would. They'd kept in touch, but the air had been charged whenever they met. A few months ago he had gotten a little obsessed with her. Or, like he said, he had "wondered" about her. Madison had done some sleuthing herself when it came to boys: if you date a chef, the food is going to be really good; if you have a relationship with a cop or a PI, expect some surveillance. He'd said he was sorry. That was something. Even if he hadn't totally meant it.

She rolled down the windows and turned up the music, enjoying the open road. Sometimes driving gave her the feeling that she could conquer the world, and she could remember what it was like when she'd had her whole life ahead of her. So much hope. "Something Just Like This" by the Chainsmokers and Coldplay came on the radio, and she sang at the top of her lungs.

She drove down the alley and parked in her parking space. Ryan parked in front on the street, so she didn't know if he was home yet. Would it be awkward living so close and dating? Well, they weren't really dating yet; one happy hour did not make a boyfriend. She locked her car and walked into the garden.

Then she saw a shape sitting at the bottom of her stairs and she froze.

Chapter Twelve

❧

"It's me," Dave said. "I'm freezing."

He was sitting in his wetsuit with a towel around his shoulders. His surfboard was standing against the garden wall.

"Jesus," Madison said. She walked down the path to him. "I think I'm tired of people dropping by. What are you doing here? Have you been sitting here since sunset?"

"I figured you weren't far."

"I'm not sure I like that assumption. Anyway, come upstairs and get in the shower before you catch pneumonia."

"Thanks."

Dave started up the stairs and Madison followed him. "Why are you here?"

They got to the top of the stairs and Madison used her key to let them inside. Dave set his surfboard against the wall next to the door and then started to undress, planning to leave his sandy wetsuit outside on the landing.

"Am I charging the neighbors for the strip show?" Madison said. Dave draped his wetsuit over the railing and ran to the shower with his hands strategically placed.

"You still haven't answered my question," Madison yelled. "Why are you here?"

"Can't hear you, shower is on," Dave yelled back from the bathroom.

Madison set her purse and keys on her desk and sat in her office chair. What a day. Her phone rang, and it was a number she didn't recognize.

"Madison Kelly," she said, although normally she just said hello after business hours.

"Yes, hi," a woman said. "My name is Melissa Sands. I need a . . . I'd like to hire you to follow my husband."

Madison sighed. She hated domestic cases. When she first got her PI license, she'd thought it would be a lucrative business. Everyone she knew had been cheated on at one point or another. So it was confusing when she followed the significant others of three clients and *none of them* were cheating. Then she realized that it was so easy to catch a spouse cheating—phone numbers on scraps of paper, get into their phone or email, drive by their work when they say they're working late—that if you needed to hire a private investigator, you'd already done all of those things and hadn't found them cheating. Meaning you were just an obsessive person who couldn't let your obsession go. Her last domestic client had been a man who hid the keys to the mailbox so his wife couldn't get the mail. He made Madison follow her home from work and called every five minutes demanding to know what she was doing. "She is driving in traffic. Yes, still," Madison would say every time he called. He was so obsessive that Madison refused his offer of five thousand dollars in cash to continue the surveillance. He hadn't wanted to hire a male private investigator only because he didn't want a man following his wife. Madison could still remember the terrified expression on the woman's face in the rearview mirror as Madison tailed her in bumper-to-bumper traffic; the woman racing to get home on time to an angry and controlling husband. That poor woman. *Never again*, Madison had sworn.

"I'm sorry," Madison said. "I don't handle domestic investigations."

"It's just that . . . well . . . I really need your help," Melissa said. "I thought, with you being a woman, that you would be willing to help me."

The woman sounded older, and she spoke very clearly and distinctly, with a slight attitude. When she said the thing about helping because she was a woman, Madison thought it sounded . . . entitled. Still, she had a point. Women did need to stick together.

"What is it you need?" Madison asked.

Melissa paused. "I want to leave my husband. But he controls all of the money. Everything is in his name. He sees other women and tells me too bad. I can't go anywhere or do anything without checking with him first. I want to leave him, but there's no way I can because I would have to walk out with only the clothes on my back. He's even told me, 'Go ahead! Leave!' because he knows that I won't."

Madison was quiet for a minute. This technically wouldn't violate her rule about domestic cases, because this woman was trying to get away from a controlling spouse—she wasn't herself the controlling one. And Madison could use some money. While she'd been figuring out what to do with her life, her savings had been getting depleted. But something didn't make sense.

"How is my following him going to change the fact that he controls the money?"

Melissa's voice sped up at the prospect that Madison would agree to the job. "I met with an attorney. Even though California is a no-fault state, he said that if we take everything to a judge, the fact that my husband is abandoning me by cheating with other women, the fact that he's arranged it so that all of the assets are in his name, on and on, a judge would be sympathetic and award me immediate spousal support while we went through the court proceedings."

Madison thought that made sense. "And how would you pay me? I hate to put it so frankly, but . . . how would you do that if he controls all the money?"

"I've been taking money out of the cash he gives me for groceries. Twenty dollars here, forty dollars there. I can pay you in cash."

"Okay . . . I mean . . . I charge seventy-five dollars an hour, and for a case like this I would need at least a three-thousand-dollar retainer."

"That's no problem. I've been saving this money for a year. Money won't be a problem."

"Okay. Why don't you meet me tomorrow and I'll at least listen? I can't promise anything."

"Well, okay." Madison didn't think she sounded that appreciative.

"Where would you like to meet?"

"Don't you have an office?"

"No, I don't. I'm in the field most of the time. Do you know the La Jolla Library?"

"Yes, of course. I'm on the board."

"How about one PM tomorrow?" Madison wanted to go in the late morning to the bars in the Gaslamp to see if any of the staff would talk to her.

Melissa sounded doubtful, like she was beginning to regret calling the female PI with no office. "Alright, I guess that will work. Yes. See you then."

Madison hung up and stared at the phone. Something about Melissa Sands didn't sit right. It sounded like she was concerned about the prospect of losing a fortune rather than afraid for her life or her future. If you were really trapped, you took your thousands of dollars in cash that you'd saved from the grocery money and you left. You didn't hire a PI with it. Well, she'd made the appointment, so she'd just have to go and see.

Toward the end of the call, Dave had come out of the shower with a towel around his waist and sat in the wingback chair. Now he leaned back and stared at Madison, who was still staring silently at the phone.

"Rough day?"

Madison's head popped up, and she regarded him. When she first met Dave, she'd been struck by how comfortable she felt around him. She felt like she could drop all of her pretenses and her sometimes-false confidence. She could drop her guard. By the time she met him, it had been some time since her parents had died; she hadn't realized how much of a guard she'd had up until she met Dave. She could be herself with him.

"Such a rough day," she said. She went over to the chair and sat on his lap and put her head on his chest. His was the first face she'd seen when she woke up from her mastectomy—a surgery she'd chosen so that she wouldn't die of breast cancer like her mother had. They'd put tissue expanders under her pectoral muscles to begin the process of reconstruction; a second surgery was required to switch out the tissue expanders with the permanent breast implants, a surgery where they would cut her pectoral muscles and sew them back down a second time. She woke up with small wrinkled mounds on her chest that would eventually get bigger, but no nipples—it was too dangerous to leave even that small amount of tissue for the cancer to grow in. "You've got Barbie boobs!" Dave had said to make her laugh, even though she wouldn't let him see them for months. He'd never made her feel anything other than beautiful, despite the massive scars etch-a-sketching their way across the middle of her chest.

Dave broke the comfortable silence. "Have you heard from that guy again? The note guy?"

Madison realized this was why she'd gotten an impromptu visit in the middle of the week from Dave. But she wasn't going to tell him about the second note. She picked her head up and leaned back to eye him.

"Are you here to protect me?"

"No," Dave said. "I just thought I'd see how you were doing. You don't need protecting."

Dave knew that Madison got scared sometimes, but he never would've said it out loud. It would've been like telling another girl she was fat.

Madison stood up, grabbed his hand, and pulled him out of the chair. "Take me to bed or lose me forever."

"*Top Gun!*" he laughed. "I feel the need, the need for speed!" He picked her up and twirled her around the room as he carried her into the bedroom.

Chapter Thirteen

Madison listened to the waves for a minute before she opened her eyes. The sun was shining through her bedroom window, which faced east. It was still early. She listened to the quiet in her apartment and realized Dave must have gone to surf sunrise. Being a trust-fund kid meant all he had to do with his life was surf; nice work if you can get it. She needed coffee.

Today was the day she planned to go to the Gaslamp District and try to interview the staff at the bars where the girls were last seen. It had been four years since Samantha went missing and two years since Elissa went missing. There was normally a high turnover at restaurants and bars, so she wasn't sure she would find out anything from the staff that remained. But in order to be thorough, she had to try. She grabbed her phone from her bedside table and stood up. Her teddy bear, Harold Comfort Bear, flew across the room. He had been caught in the comforter and was catapulted as she stood. She picked him up and put him back on the bed. Some people might judge a grown woman for sleeping with a teddy bear. Madison didn't know any of those people.

She walked into the kitchen, put the coffeepot on, and then walked over and stared at her whiteboard. She was running out of leads. But she couldn't get discouraged. Her next lead could be at the end of the next string she pulled. Her phone rang. She wondered who would be calling her before eight o'clock in the morning. She didn't recognize the number.

"Madison Kelly," she answered.

"Oh, hello. This is Ken Larrabee. We met last night at McGregor's. With Tom?"

"Oh. Hi!" That's right, another job. God, she'd completely forgotten.

"Is this a bad time?"

"No, no, this is great." Madison walked over and poured herself a cup of coffee before it had finished brewing. "As I mentioned, I generally only work for insurance companies, although the fact is I've been branching out." And another job would help restore the savings account.

"Yeah, I heard from Tom about the investigation you're doing and the notes left on your door."

Madison was surprised that Tom had shared that much. He was normally more circumspect. "Oh, yeah, it's been kind of crazy," Madison said. She wasn't going to share more than that. "So how can I help you?"

"Well, the thing is, I help out with the Rescue Mission in downtown. Do you know it?"

Madison loved the Rescue Mission, and it was her charity of choice. She gave money whenever she could. In addition to a regular shelter, they had a shelter for mothers and children. Madison had taken clothes down there and seen mothers in business clothes lining up at five PM with their children to try to get a bed for the night. Madison had had some low times in her life, and she felt like *there but for the grace of God go I.*

"Yes, of course I know it. That's wonderful of you. What do you do for them?"

She stood up and looked down into the garden. Ryan's roommate was walking out the door with his surfboard, headed to the beach.

"I just help out at night getting the beds ready for turnover and assigning them as the women and children arrive. I also keep the guys out; sometimes there can be issues of domestic violence and men coming to 'get their women,' so to speak."

"Oh, wow, I bet that can be bad. It must be great for them to have a cop volunteering like that. That is really nice of you. By the way, what kind of cop are you? San Diego Police Department? Sheriff?"

Ken laughed. "I'm not a cop. I work in construction."

"Weird. I thought you were a cop. Maybe it's just because I met you at McGregor's. How did you meet Tom?"

"Yeah, there are a lot of cops in there. In fact, we met at McGregor's. Ages ago. He's a character."

"That he is. So how can I help you at the Rescue Mission?"

"I need your help with one of our clients."

"Oh, okay. What kind of help?"

Madison walked with the phone over to the window and looked out into the alley. Still no strange cars or strange people. She walked to the window in the living room and looked out onto the garden. She saw Ryan looking up at her apartment from his bedroom at the back of his house. He didn't see her at first because he was watching her kitchen window. He was squinting. Then his head turned slightly, and he saw her in the living room window. He backed up quickly into the shadows of his bedroom. *That was weird*, Madison thought.

"A woman named Sylvia stays there at night with her three kids, who are in school during the day. She's trying to get a job, and she has a final interview for one. But the interview is at three PM on Monday, right when she needs to pick up her kids from school. I'm not supposed to get that involved in people's lives . . . but if you could pick up her kids, she could make this job interview."

This was hitting Madison right where she lived. Helping a mom pull herself out of a terrible situation . . . it didn't matter that Madison was right in the middle of this huge investigation; she had to do it.

"Wow. The Rescue Mission is my favorite. I've helped them before myself."

"Yeah, Tom mentioned that. That's actually why I asked you. I want someone who is—well, frankly, female, so that Sylvia and the kids feel safe, but someone who could kick some ass if the husband showed up at the school. He hasn't been around that I can see, but she's always worried he'll try to pick up the kids. He lost custody."

"Of course I'll do it. But not as a job. I'm happy to help."

"Oh, I can pay you; it would be a job."

"No. I don't need money that badly. I want to help."

Ken gave her all of the particulars for Monday. She put it on the calendar in her phone; since it was Friday, anything could happen between now and then, and she didn't want to forget.

They hung up, and she looked at the whiteboard to focus on the matter at hand. Today she would find out what Hank's Dive and the people that worked there could tell her.

Madison found a parking space right in front of the restaurant, which was unusual for downtown San Diego. Although it was its own community, the Gaslamp District was still part of downtown. But it was late morning, and there was not as much activity in this corner of downtown at this time of day. There was an employee of Hank's hosing down bar mats in the patio area as Madison walked in. No time like the present.

"Hi. Can I ask you a question?"

The guy was in his early twenties with a sleeve tattoo on one arm and a nose piercing. He had spacers in his ear lobes creating large holes.

"Sure, what's up?" He continued to hose down the mats.

"Did you work here when that girl went missing? Samantha Erickson?"

Suddenly Madison realized that, given the guy's age and the fact that Samantha had gone missing four years ago, he probably didn't know who she was.

"Oh, I heard about her. No, man, I was in high school."

"Oh, cool," Madison said. "Do you know of anyone that was working here then?"

The guy turned off the hose and carried the bar mats inside. Madison followed him. He walked behind the bar and threw the mats down on the ground. He picked up a huge tub that Madison knew was used for carrying ice.

"You could try Josie," he said. "She was here then."

Josie was the name of the person helping Felicity. At least Madison had corroboration that Josie was in a position to know something.

"Is she around today?"

"I'm not sure," he said. "I can check the schedule. What's your name?"

"Madison Kelly."

"Cool. Give me a second." He walked into the kitchen. Madison sat down on a barstool and looked around. It didn't smell as bad as Su Casa, probably because of the airflow from the huge steel doors that were left open during operating hours. But it definitely smelled like a bar: stale beer and something musty. A girl walked out from the kitchen. She had really short hair and a tattooed sleeve to match the other guy's. She was wearing a tank top and jeans, and Madison could see a tattoo of Elvis Presley on her chest. Madison then realized that her hair was cut in a similar fashion to Elvis's: short on the sides, long on the top, and slicked back with hair gel or pomade. She was about a foot shorter than Madison and very fit.

"Madison?"

"Yes, hi, are you Josie?"

The girl looked around but didn't answer. She walked toward the sidewalk outside, looked up and down the street, and then came back in.

"I can't be seen talking to you," she said. "Felicity told me about you. I'll call you later. If anyone asks, I refused to talk to you. Okay?"

Madison thought this sounded ominous and encouraging at the same time. She wasn't about to argue. "Got it."

Josie walked back into the kitchen. Madison wasn't sure what to do next. Just then, another waitress entered the patio from the sidewalk. She was average height, with dark hair and beautiful skin. As she approached, Madison spoke to her.

"Hi, can I ask a question?"

The girl spoke with an accent. "Sure, what is it?"

"Did you work here when that girl went missing? Samantha Erickson?"

"Yes, I did." The girl seemed wary. Madison loved her accent.

"Are you from Brazil?"

"Yes. How did you know?"

"Your accent is beautiful. I like accents." Madison wasn't flattering her; she really did. "So did you work the night she was here?"

"No, I didn't." She was unfolding an apron and putting it on. "I remember everybody talking about it the next week after it came out that she had been at our bar and was now missing. But we didn't find out the next day or anything. So it wasn't like we came in and everybody said, 'Oh, a girl went missing yesterday.' We didn't find out for a week, and by then I didn't know whether I had worked or not. But when the police questioned everyone, I checked the calendar and saw I hadn't worked that night. Are you a cop or something?"

Madison figured the police would have questioned those who had been at the bar the night Samantha went missing. That would have been a normal thing to do. What Madison didn't know was why, four years later, someone connected to her disappearance had gotten so upset about Madison's tweets. What had she gotten so close to that the police had not? If anything? All she could do was keep pulling strings.

"No, I'm a private investigator. My name is Madison Kelly. I'm looking into the disappearance." Madison put out her hand.

"Sandra," she said as she shook Madison's hand. "I need to clock in. Can you give me a second?"

Madison said no problem, and the girl walked into the kitchen. A man in a crisp polo shirt and dress slacks entered the patio from the street. He was in his midthirties. He had a huge build, no neck, and a shaved head that made him look like a cop. *Actually,* Madison thought as he sauntered toward her, *this guy has a chip on his shoulder like the world owes him something that he's been unable to collect.*

Wannabe cop, Madison decided.

"Are you being helped?" he asked.

Madison figured this was the manager, and as such her days were numbered when it came to talking to the staff. He didn't seem the cooperative type. She was going to make it last as long as she could.

"Yes, thank you," she said, and smiled big.

"Okay . . . great."

Madison could tell he wanted to ask what she was doing there but couldn't think of a way to cross that social barrier of *none of your business.* He paused and opened his mouth but then closed it again and walked into the kitchen.

If he talks to Sandra about what I'm doing here I'm done, she thought. Employers were generally fussy about investigators talking to their employees. Even if it was perfectly legal for her to question people, employers ran the gamut from *I don't want to get sued and this seems like a way to get sued* to *I want to exert my power because I can*. This guy seemed like the latter type. Either way, the end result was her getting run out of places quite often.

The manager walked out of the kitchen and Madison knew she was done.

"You can't be here," he said. Even though she was ready for the concept, his phrasing irritated Madison.

"I can't be . . . where? Planet Earth? The city of San Diego?"

The manager snorted. Madison had met his kind many times before—big bruisers who were used to shoving their weight around but were not used to girls talking back to them.

"You can't be in my establishment."

"Oh! You're the owner? That's so cool! To own such a big place! Tell me, Jethro, how did you become such a success?" She had read his name tag and thought it was perfect: Jethro. *My God*, she thought. *What a name.*

Madison knew she was waving red in front of a bull. But he had pissed her off. Also, no way he was the owner; he was an hourly-wage manager who wanted to shove his lack of importance around. There were so many things he could've said to her when he came out of the kitchen: "I'm sorry, the owner doesn't like people talking to the employees without going through him first," or "Can you let me know who you're working for and why you want to talk to the employees?" She would have responded nicely to any one of those civilized communications.

Jethro walked over until he was uncomfortably close to where Madison was sitting on the barstool. In fact, he was crowding her intentionally.

"You need to leave."

"Back up and give me room to stand up and I will."

Jethro contemplated her request. He was not the kind of guy that took orders from women. Madison stared at him. He pushed his chest out further, decreasing the distance between them. Madison had to deal with guys like this every day on her job. Guys who thought they were allowed to push people around just because they were big and male. Guys who didn't think Madison had a right to ask questions, to have a job that a guy should have, to exist on the planet without their permission.

"If you were a man I would knock you on your ass right now," he said.

"If *you* were a man I'd be worried."

Jethro was so close that Madison could hear his sharp intake of breath. No, he was not used to girls talking to him like this. He was probably calculating the chances of getting fired for hitting someone at his work. His teeth clenched and the muscles in his jaw worked. Finally, he took three steps backward. Madison stood.

"You have a good day now," Madison said. She walked slowly through the patio out to the sidewalk and got in her car.

Madison drove her car toward the bar where Elissa had last been seen, Bourbon Baby. Her phone rang. She checked and saw that it was Ted calling her.

"Hey, Ted."

"Hey, Madison, how's it going?"

"Oh, you know me. Just kicking ass and taking names."

"I know you," Ted laughed. "Sounds like somebody just got what they deserved."

"Something like that."

"Well listen, I just wanted to get back to you. I spoke to that other private investigator who gave you such a hard time before."

"Oh, yeah. How'd that go?"

"Honestly, I don't think he is up to anything when it comes to you. I reminded him of you, and he just said, 'Man, she pissed me off.' And I said, 'Yeah, she has that effect on people.' And then we talked about other things. It took him a minute to remember who you were. I really don't think this is anything."

Madison trusted Ted as a private investigator. She knew he would have done his best to draw the guy out and see what his reaction was to hearing Madison's name. She could cross that old PI off her whiteboard.

"Thanks, Ted. I really appreciate it."

"You got it. Let me know if you need any help with any assignments. I'm not doing anything right now."

Madison turned into the lot where she had parked her car the other night. The same lot where Elissa had parked hers.

"I will, Ted. Talk to you soon."

She locked her car and walked over to the bar.

Bourbon Baby was a slightly more upscale establishment than Hank's Dive. It had a small patio area behind an iron railing, so that customers were technically sitting on the sidewalk like at a French bistro. The chairs and tables were ironwork, sitting atop the red brick of the Gaslamp District. Madison walked inside and was hit with refreshing air conditioning. The bar was oak. A bartender was stocking glasses.

"Hi," she said.

"Hi there." He was over six feet tall, with a strong jaw and long hair. "We're not open until two PM. Can I help you with something?"

"Yes, you can. Were you working here when that girl went missing? Elissa Alvarez?"

The bartender stopped and looked at her. "I might have been. Who's asking?"

Madison laughed. His response was such a cliché, but he pulled it off. She felt like she was in a Raymond Chandler novel suddenly, leaning on the old-fashioned bar having witty repartee with the gruff-with-a-heart-of-gold bartender. She suddenly felt like ordering a whiskey. "My name is Madison Kelly. I'm a private investigator, and I'm looking into her disappearance."

He reached his hand across the bar. "Jackson. Pleased to meet you."

Madison shook his hand and sat on a barstool. "So, may I know if you were working here then?"

"Yeah, actually I was. The police came with her credit card receipts, and I guess I served her that night. But I don't remember her at all."

Madison appreciated not being thrown out on her ear like at the last bar.

"Oh, wow, I lucked out to find you."

"Maybe," he said. "I can't really tell you anything else. She was just one of a million people here on a weekend a long time ago. A sea of faces. I wouldn't be able to pick her out of a lineup."

He finished stocking a tray of glasses, and then took the empty glass rack and walked towards the kitchen. "Excuse me I'll be right back."

Madison let her shoulders hunch forward and leaned her elbows on the bar. This seemed hopeless. She was picking over a scene that had already been picked over thoroughly by the police. Jackson came back from the kitchen with a new full glass rack. He started hanging glasses on the back of the bar.

"What was the talk at the time about what happened? What did you guys all think?" Madison had found that sometimes people close to an incident had pretty solid opinions about what went down. They could be useful in finding a theory to work off of.

"To be honest, it didn't affect us much. Other than we all had to talk to the police about a girl we'd served for maybe an hour out of our lives. I feel bad she's missing, but I don't think it caused much of a stir here. It wasn't like she was a regular or anything."

"Did you know any of the girls she was with? I guess it was a girls' night out."

Jackson finished with the glasses and picked up the empty rack and set it on the bar. He leaned on the bar. "No," he said. "The police showed us photos of the girls she was with, and I didn't recognize any of them. We have dancing here on the weekends, and it gets really packed. Seriously: no way I would recognize those girls if I saw them again. They start to all look the same."

Madison didn't care for clubbing, so she tended to agree with him. The girls did all start to look the same, which she figured the girls would consider a success: uniformity, lack of originality, must all look the same to fit in.

"Is anyone else still working here who worked here then?"

"Actually, no. We had a change of ownership, and they were like out with the old and in with the new. They kept me on because otherwise no one would know how to run the place."

"Okay, well, thank you," Madison said. "If you think of anything else, can you give me a call?" Madison handed him one of her cards.

"Sure, no problem." He walked into the back, and Madison walked out of the bar into the bright sunshine. She scrambled for her sunglasses. It was the middle of the day on a Friday and the streets were filling up with business-lunch-goers and vacationers enjoying beautiful San Diego. Watching the frivolity increased Madison's feelings of discouragement. For some reason it made her think of day drinking: wasting her life away while the rest of the world was being productive.

Well, she'd had to try. And she'd tried. Since she had nothing to lose at this point, she thought she might drop in on Elissa's boyfriend and see what he had to say. She seemed to recall that he lived nearby.

Chapter Fourteen

Frank Bronson lived in the Golden Hill section of San Diego. A historic section of San Diego, Golden Hill had nineteenth-century homes that had been gentrified and nineteenth-century homes that were in disrepair; it just depended on which part of Golden Hill you lived in. Madison loved this part of town because she loved historic houses. In addition to being originally connected to downtown by a streetcar system put in for the Panama-California Exposition of 1915, Golden Hill was within walking distance of the bar where Elissa had last been seen alive. This last part was not lost on Madison. If Frank was a viable suspect, he could have quickly walked or driven to the bar and picked up Elissa.

He lived in a duplex on 23rd near E Street. Madison had learned of his name from the podcast and had used her PI website to find his address. It was not the most run-down section of Golden Hill, but it certainly wasn't gentrified.

Out of habit, she parked her car a block away so that it wouldn't be seen from his window. She walked down the street and kept her eye on his front door. There was a porch with a rocking chair on it that had holes in the wicker back and a broken arm. There was a driveway next to the front door; in it was parked an older-model Mitsubishi that had been tricked out and painted a bright red. Madison memorized the license plate just in case. You never knew what might be useful later. The walkway up to the front door had gravel and weeds on either side of it. She knocked on the door, stepped back three steps, and waited.

Frank Bronson opened the door. She had seen his photo in a newspaper clipping online. He was wearing khaki pants with grease stains on them and a white tank top.

"Yeah?" he said.

He was about twenty-five, with long dark hair slicked back either with product or with dirt. He looked like he'd been asleep when Madison knocked. He did not look like the kind of guy who would answer questions about his missing girlfriend to a female PI who happened to knock on his door. Asking them would result in the door being slammed in her face, and she'd had enough of that today. Madison had to make a quick decision about how to proceed.

"Hi. I'm a reporter with the *San Diego Star*," Madison said, inventing the name of a newspaper. As a PI, Madison was licensed to pretend to be other people; the only rule was that she couldn't pretend to work for an actual company. For Frank, she put on her dumb-blonde persona. She made all of her sentences go up on the end as if she were asking a question. She raised the timbre of her voice a bit, while making it slightly scratchy. She smiled pretty. She gazed into his eyes as if she were stunned to meet someone so interesting and intelligent, someone so much smarter than stupid little her. It wasn't being sexual; Madison didn't care for that kind of strategy. It was just being dumb so that a guy would underestimate her.

"So?"

"So, I was just wondering what you thought about Elissa's phone being found?"

Frank's face went pale. His mouth closed into a thin line. "No, it wasn't."

"No, seriously, like I swear to God, it was." Then she giggled. "Like my dad is a cop, and he told me. He told me not to tell anyone, but I'm trying to make it as a serious journalist, you know? So I thought oh my God I have to go talk to her boyfriend and see what he thinks. I mean, maybe he knows something and then like my boss at the newspaper will finally understand that I'm like a totally serious journalist, like you know?"

Frank had been thinking while Madison was babbling. He'd found his voice and his footing. "I'm glad they found it. Maybe it will help find her. We all want her to be found and brought home safely. You can tell everyone that." He cleared his throat and ran his hand over his hair to neaten it. He pulled on the bottom of his T-shirt and tucked it into his grease-stained pants. He pulled his phone—a Motorola flip phone—out of his pants and checked the time.

"That's so cool of you," Madison said. "I will totally put that in my article."

"That's good, that's good. I've cooperated fully with the police, and I will continue to do so." This sounded completely rehearsed to Madison.

"What do you think they'll find in the black box?" she asked.

Frank stared at Madison. "In the what?"

Madison was playing craps. She was in Vegas, and she was betting it all on her roll of the dice. She would either win big or lose big. No going back now.

"The black box. You know, the iPhone 7 has a black box, like a cockpit in an airplane. It records the last phone call made on the phone. It's like so cool! Only the police can access it though, with a warrant. So the cops are doing that with Elissa's phone. As soon as Apple gets the warrant, they'll release the recording to the cops of the last phone call Elissa made—and everything that was said. I wonder what her last phone call was, don't you? Like, did she have a fight or did she ask someone to pick her up or did she arrange to meet someone? It's so exciting!"

Frank glanced past Madison at the street behind her. There were sweat drops on his forehead, and one hair had flopped down and was sticking to it. He opened and closed his mouth a couple of times and there was a smacking sound; his mouth was really dry.

"We all want her found," Frank said robotically. "She means a lot to us. I will continue to cooperate with the police." And then he shut the door in Madison's face.

"Well," Madison said as she turned to walk down the path. "That oughta do it."

Chapter Fifteen

Madison started driving to meet Melissa, the woman who wanted Madison to follow her husband. If she found parking quickly she would be on time; otherwise, she was going to be a little bit late.

She used the buttons on her steering wheel to engage the Sync system on her Ford Explorer to call Tom.

"Are you calling to tell me you have a crush on my friend?"

Madison's mind was so far past her conversation with Ken that morning that she almost didn't know what Tom was talking about. Then she remembered.

"Oh! Ummmm, no, we had a conversation about some help he needs with the Rescue Mission. I managed to have a conversation with a man without falling in love with him. Shocking, I know."

Tom laughed. "Sorry, it just happens a lot with that guy. He has a way with the ladies."

"Well, a guy who spends his spare time helping the underserved community is pretty attractive. You should try it."

"Yeah, because all I do is help the 'overserved' community, is that it?"

"Nevermind. I need to tell you something. I did something. Don't be mad."

Tom sighed. "Why do I feel like I need to buy stock in Pepto-Bismol every time I get a phone call from you? What did you do this time?"

"I had a conversation with Elissa Alvarez's boyfriend, Frank Bronson," Madison said. "That is, I went to see him and I talked to him." There was silence. "Tom?"

Tom sounded like he was speaking through clenched teeth. "What did you say to him?"

"Can I remind you that as a licensed private investigator I am allowed to interview witnesses and suspects?"

"I didn't say you couldn't. I wish you wouldn't, but I didn't say you couldn't. So what did you say to Frank Bronson?" His tone was measured, like he was trying to stay calm.

"Well, he might be under the impression that you found Elissa's phone."

Tom's reaction was immediate and explosive. "Are you out of your fucking mind? You told a possible suspect in a missing persons case about evidence that had been discovered? Are you fucking crazy? Madison, I have had your back through all of the crazy shit that you do because somehow you end up with a good result at the end of it, but you are going to get so much shit for this and there is nothing I can do about it. You think you can do things because you're not required to uphold the law like the rest of us poor fucks—"

Madison lowered the volume on the Sync system because Tom was yelling so loudly that it was distorting the sound and she was afraid he was going to blow her speakers.

"Tom! Tom! Listen to me!"

"You have probably just fucked up an investigation that has been ongoing for two years—"

Madison turned the sound all the way down so that all she could hear was a tiny little Tom coming out of the speakers, but she couldn't make out the words. She waited until there was silence. She turned the speakers back up.

"Are you fucking there?"

"Yes, I'm here. I'm trying to tell you the rest of the story. I understand you're angry but it may be okay."

Tom was silent.

"I pretended I was a journalist."

"And he talked to you?"

At least Tom wasn't screaming at her now. "Yes. He wanted to make a good impression with the media. He kept repeating that he was cooperating with the police."

Tom snorted. "He is hardly cooperating with the police. He won't give us his phone, and we can't get a warrant for his phone records because we don't have probable cause. He has refused to give a statement. He has refused us access to his house, where she spent the night a lot. He is a dyed-in-the-wool refuser."

"Okay, so then I may have helped you in the end. I made up a story and he fell for it. I told him that iPhones have a black box, like the cockpit of an airplane, and that the iPhone makes a recording of the last phone call made. But only the police can access the recording through Apple with a warrant."

Tom was silent for a moment. "That's actually pretty good."

"I know." Madison took the exit off the 5 freeway onto La Jolla Parkway. As she came down the hill into La Jolla, the ocean appeared suddenly before her; it was like traveling from black and white into color in *The Wizard of Oz*. The blue of the ocean always varied here. Madison didn't know if it was based on the temperature of the water or the sunlight or a combination of both. Right now it was a deep blue.

"And he fell for it?" Tom asked.

"He did," Madison said. "He got all sweaty and nervous and started reciting his party line about cooperating with the police, and then he shut the door in my face."

Tom was silent for a minute. "Okay. I mean, it's good, but now what?"

"Do you need me to spell it out for you? How long have you been a cop?"

"Funny. So your idea is that the one detective still working on this case, the detective who has numerous other cases, is supposed to go sit outside this guy's house to see if he gets nervous and does something interesting, all because some chick thinks she spooked him?"

"Oh now I'm 'some chick'? Thanks."

"Look, don't get all sensitive on me. You know what I'm saying."

Madison knew what he was saying. He was lucky he'd told her before what a good investigator he thought she was. She did not appreciate being called "some chick," and she wasn't going to let him live this down for a while. Either way, he was definitely communicating what the other detectives working the case would think about her suggestion, and she needed his help to convince them.

"I'm not 'some chick'; I'm a licensed professional who has a viable lead. So yes, I think someone should go sit outside his house and see where he goes."

"And you probably voted to reduce overtime for police officers, right?"

"No, I did not. I vote to increase your salary and increase the number of police officers any chance I get."

"Right. Sure you did. Look, Madison, we just don't have the manpower to do a twenty-four-hour surveillance on a suspect in a two-year-old missing persons case on the word of—"

"Do *not* call me 'some chick' again."

"Fine, on the word of a 'private investigator' who has no experience with missing persons. Not to mention it is farfetched. The guy is a dick who refuses to cooperate, but it doesn't mean he did something to his girlfriend. And also, Samantha Erickson went missing from the same area two years before. Did he do something to her and then get the itch again and do something to his girlfriend but wait until she was in the Gaslamp District to do it? When he had access to her at any other time of the day or night?"

"Well when you put it like that it sounds farfetched." Madison hated it when Tom was right. Still, she was the one who had stood there and watched the guy react to her story. There was something there. No, it didn't make sense that he would've killed Samantha two years before, but she couldn't decide where the investigation was going and push it in that direction; she had to let the investigation lead her, until it led to nothing. And this was the way it was leading her.

"Okay, Tom," Madison said. "Well, you can't say that I'm not keeping you informed of everything."

"That's true. And I do appreciate it. I don't appreciate you telling him that we found her phone."

"You mean that *I* found her phone."

"Whatever," Tom said. "Now I have to go tell this poor detective that you're messing with this part of his case."

"We have a bad connection. I have to go."

"We do not have a bad connection. And don't you do the surveillance on Frank Bronson yourself!"

"Can't hear you talk to you later bye." Madison disconnected the call.

Oh yes, Madison thought. *I* will *do the surveillance on Frank Bronson myself.*

Chapter Sixteen

❧

Madison pulled up around the corner from the La Jolla Library at one PM. Tom always made Madison laugh with his demanding this and demanding that. The fact was that while he could make requests of her, she didn't have to follow his arbitrary orders. She'd undergone a rigorous examination process and an FBI background check. It was extremely difficult to get a private investigator's license in California, for the exact reason that they did not want freaks or stalkers following people around. She was licensed to do it, and she could perform surveillance on Frank Bronson if she wanted to. And she wanted to.

When she left Frank, after he slammed the door in her face, it had been about twelve thirty PM and he had just woken up. She had to decide when Frank would get so nervous that he made a big mistake and went somewhere or did something that would give him away—assuming he had something to give away. This was when luck had to be on her side. The good news was that she was very lucky.

Madison sighed and shook her head as she took off her seat belt and prepared to meet her new client. Tom was right: this was farfetched. But Madison didn't have many leads. She had to pull on every string she found.

She figured Frank would need to wake up, get something to eat, probably smoke a lot of cigarettes or weed, and get more and more nervous. San Diego had a decent rush hour that actually lasted a few hours, starting at about three PM. He probably would wait until after seven PM to go anywhere. Madison would have her meeting with Melissa, go home and get something to eat, and then set up her car for surveillance and sit outside Frank's house and wait for his red Mitsubishi to go somewhere. Madison's fingers felt tingly; she hadn't been on a surveillance in a while and she missed it. She could sit around theorizing and looking at computer databases until she was blue in the face, but nothing beat going and sitting on someone and seeing where they led her.

Madison got out of the car and locked it with the remote. She walked up to the library and saw a middle-aged woman sitting by herself on the bench in front. She was well put together, and she was wearing about $2,000 not including her jewelry. She could've sold her clothes and jewelry and paid the deposit on an apartment, not to mention the "grocery cash" she'd saved. Madison's doubts about the case increased. Melissa's hair was done, makeup on, St. John's knit suit, pearls. She looked up and saw Madison.

"Melissa?"

"Yes, Madison?"

Madison sat down next to her.

"I'm sorry I'm a little late; I got caught up downtown."

"Oh, I just got here. No problem."

Melissa looked around. Madison loved this part of La Jolla. The library sat on a pretty street with manicured lawns. It was quiet except for some traffic noise coming from Pearl Street, which seemed far away.

"I'm afraid I have to confess something right off the bat." Melissa looked fake-sheepish. Like she was acting *Oh now don't be mad at me; I made a boo-boo.* She opened her Prada purse and then closed it. It had a clasp at the top that reminded Madison of old-time purses, the kind her mother had that Madison used to play dress-up with; it had a satisfying snap. Melissa opened it and closed it again. Rather than being indecisive about getting something out of her purse, she seemed to have a nervous tic. Open. Shut. Open. Shut. Suddenly Madison wanted to grab it out of her hands.

"Okay. Shoot." Madison thought it was a little early in their relationship for confessions, but okay. "What do you need to confess?"

"My husband saw my diary. I had written your name and phone number, and I wrote 'P.I.' next to your name. He confronted me, and I admitted I was thinking of hiring you."

Madison was floored. Her first thought was how much she disliked stupid women. It was harder for her to tolerate than a stupid man; she didn't know why. Probably because she expected more from women. She was sitting next to a domestic case—one she didn't want to take on in the first place—and this woman had thrown Madison under the bus before she'd even gotten a retainer. She almost got up and walked away without saying a word.

Madison took a deep breath. She should probably make allowances for Melissa: if you weren't used to being sneaky, something that came naturally to Madison, it was easy to make a blunder like this. Madison could also be impatient with people, a trait she'd been trying to work on.

Madison cleared her throat. "Well, that certainly makes my job more difficult. For one thing, even if someone is suspicious that an investigator has been or will be hired, they are usually looking for a man. So not only does he know there will be an investigator following him, now he will be looking for a woman."

"I'm afraid there's more," Melissa said.

Of course there is, Madison thought.

"He was very angry."

"How angry?" Madison asked.

"He said that if you investigated him, he would hunt you down and kill you."

That wording again. Was Melissa's husband Anonymous? Or were these two separate death threats in the same week? Madison didn't think she deserved such special attention; there weren't many people who had someone out to kill them, and Madison might have two.

"When did this happen?"

"About a week ago," Melissa said. "I wasn't sure I was still going to use you, but I couldn't find another female private investigator. And the men that I spoke to were so condescending I couldn't stand it."

If Melissa had told her husband a week ago about hiring Madison and he had threatened to find Madison and kill her, he could've written the note left on Madison's door. That didn't jive with the fact that the wording in Felicity's phone call was almost identical to the note. But Madison couldn't ignore it. It was a string, and she had to pull on it.

"Is your husband violent?"

Melissa involuntarily reached her hand up and touched the bone surrounding her eye socket. Madison looked closely and realized there was the faintest yellow oval under her makeup. An old bruise.

"He can be."

What had this woman brought to Madison's doorstep? She was starting to not care that she needed money to replenish her savings account or that this was a "women helping women" sort of case.

"Can you tell me what kind of car he drives?" Madison did not want this guy sneaking up on her.

"He drives a dark-blue Tesla."

"Okay. So what is the point of me following him? California is a no-fault divorce state. You can get half his assets in a divorce regardless of the reason for the divorce. I know you said something about your attorney felt the judge would be more sympathetic to your plight if he knew your husband was also cheating? I would think judges are sort of immune to that sort of thing."

Melissa looked down at her purse. At least she had stopped snapping the clasp. "I signed a prenuptial agreement. I was young and in love and I didn't know what I was signing. Or I didn't care. I basically walk out with the clothes on my back if we get a divorce. But my attorney said if I could prove he was cheating, there might be a loophole in the prenuptial agreement. And he must be cheating. I can just tell."

So that was it. A prenuptial agreement. Melissa wanted to break the prenup and get more money than she'd agreed to when she got married. "But he hits you. Can you tell me why you don't just leave him and sort this all out later?"

"It's complicated," Melissa said.

Madison knew there could come a day when you gave up on the idea of happily ever after. When you gave up on the idea that you could pull yourself out of a rough patch, a sticky situation, or have everything turn out okay. Once you lost that hope, it was hard to see a future that was anything other than more of the same. It could cause a woman to stay in a place where she wasn't safe. Madison tried to be sympathetic.

"Too complicated to try?"

Melissa ignored the question. "Will you do this for me?"

Madison sighed. "I really can't. I'm sorry. Cases like this bring a lot more trouble than they're worth. I'm sorry to reduce your life down to 'a case,' but I have to look out for my safety. And trying to catch a violent guy cheating is not something I am interested in pursuing. The cards have been stacked against me, since now he has my name and number. However, I will help you find resources so that you can leave him and be safe."

Melissa jumped up from the bench, and her purse fell to the ground. She stooped to get it. "You said you would help me." She stood up and pointed her finger in Madison's face. "You said I could trust you. But you're just like all the others!"

Madison hadn't said anything like that. She stayed seated and spoke in measured tones. "I'm sorry you feel that way. I'm just telling you that I don't feel comfortable taking this case. I told you last night on the phone that I couldn't promise you anything. I have heard you out, and I can't take this case." Madison stood up as she started to get heated and faced Melissa. This woman didn't even care that she was physically in danger—or that now Madison was—she just wanted her multimillion-dollar payout. "And frankly, you have put me at risk by doing something so stupid as to leave your address book with my name and phone number in it for your husband to find. A husband who you know is controlling and violent. You literally have put *my* life at risk."

Melissa turned to storm off, but her St. John's knit jacket caught on the reclaimed-wood bench and snagged. She grabbed the jacket and pulled, ripping a hole in it. She walked down the path to the sidewalk. Madison watched her go until she was out of sight.

"Another day of winning friends and influencing people," Madison said aloud. Time to go home and get ready for surveillance.

Chapter Seventeen

～

Madison still had several hours before she needed to be in front of Frank Bronson's house. She made herself an early dinner, leftover grilled chicken breast and a sweet potato made in the microwave, and sat at her desk and stared at the whiteboard.

She especially looked at the subject of her tweets. Something about her tweets, as her current theory went, caused Anonymous to want to punish her. But she couldn't see anything she had said that was particularly revelatory; while it was true that she could sometimes be inspired, she couldn't see that she had been in this case. She was suggesting things that everybody else was suggesting. Was it just because she was a private investigator and perhaps in a position to do something about it? That had to be it. And also she was in San Diego, so too close for comfort? Other people were tweeting from around the country, too far to do anything about their theories. Madison went back through, in between bites of chicken and sweet potato, and wrote on the whiteboard her actual tweets, not just the clues contained in them.

Do we know if the police have checked with the rideshare services regarding the drivers?

Wasn't it Fleet Week when Elissa and Samantha both went missing?

Has anyone looked into the bouncers working the night the girls disappeared?

What about the bouncers at Hank's?

This last one gave Madison pause. It was the only time she had mentioned the same thing twice. Bouncers were notoriously full of their big-shit-on-turd-hill power. Many of them couldn't make it in the police force or even in a security company that did background checks, which would reveal their criminal record, but all they had to do was be huge and mean to be a bouncer, especially at Hank's, where there were a lot of fights. A bouncer has unique access to girls, especially drunk girls, as in the case of Samantha. And most girls would trust a bouncer, thinking that he worked for the bar—not thinking he could be a thug with a criminal record and that no background check had been done before he was hired.

Madison got up from her desk and went to the sink and cleaned her plate. She was using her grandmother's butterfly china. There were only three copies of this pattern in the world. Before a fourth copy could be made in 1935, the manufacturer's facility had burned down. The set was made of beautiful ceramic with a high gloss, and each piece had delicately placed butterflies, each with a different design. It was a treat to eat on these plates; she felt like she was eating dinner with every person who'd ever used them. What had the dinner conversation been about? Who had been there? She used to keep the china set carefully packed away, until she wondered to herself, *What am I waiting for?* Best to enjoy life while you're living it. She dried the plate and carefully put it away.

Returning to the whiteboard, she realized she hadn't made an attempt to call the friends of Elissa or Samantha. More ground that had already been picked over by the police, but to be thorough she had to talk to them or at least one person from each group of friends. She looked at the names she had listed on the board and selected a somewhat uncommon one from Samantha's friends to look up in her private investigator's database: Simone Levin. The more uncommon the name, the easier it was to find in the database.

She found a Simone Levin living in Nebraska, which she discarded as unlikely. She found another one living in Ocean Beach, and that seemed more likely. She called the number listed.

"Hello?"

"Hello, Simone?"

"Yes?" There was a screaming toddler in the background. "Come here!" The sound of the screaming got louder as she apparently picked the child up. The screaming was now going directly into the phone. Madison pulled the phone away from her ear. She put it on speaker.

"My name is Madison Kelly. I'm a private investigator and I'm looking into the disappearance of Samantha. I wonder if I could speak to you for a minute about her. Maybe we could meet for coffee?"

More screaming toddler. The child was saying, "I don't want to! I don't want to!"

"I don't want to," Simone said.

Madison was confused for a minute; she thought Simone was just mimicking the child. Then she realized that Simone was answering her.

"You don't want to . . . meet with me? Talk about Samantha?"

The child had calmed down slightly and was now just sort of whimpering. "That was the worst day of my life. People say it wasn't my fault, she was a grown woman, but the fact remains that I was out with my best friend and she disappeared and has never been seen again. I let her down. I don't know how we got separated, but we did. I was drunk too. Have you ever been out with friends and gotten drunk?"

"Of course," Madison said. It had been a long time, and was mostly in high school with a fake ID, but she'd done it.

"Imagine that silly night turning into a nightmare. A harmless girls' night out turns into a tragedy I will never get over. No, I don't want to talk about it. I talked to the police and told them everything I knew at the time. I'm done."

"Even if it might help find her?"

Simone laughed. It was not a pleasant sound. "Find her? You think after four years Samantha is coming back alive? I have to go on with my life. It's either that or die wondering 'what if': What if I had stayed with her that night? What if I had seen her walking to the door and stopped her? What if I hadn't gotten drunk? What if we hadn't gone out that night? What if, what if, what if. No, sorry, I don't want to talk about it. But yes, I hope you find her." And with that, she hung up the phone.

Well, that's that, Madison thought.

She hadn't imagined she'd get much from these friends anyway; she was just trying to be thorough in her investigation. She decided to mix it up and call a friend of Elissa's. She selected Amanda Gutierrez. The name was unfortunately fairly common; however, it was less common than the other names listed on her whiteboard as being friends of Elissa's. She found thirty in the United States. There were eight in San Diego County but only one in El Cajon. Since Elissa had lived in El Cajon, Madison went with that one.

"Hello?"

"Hello, my name is Madison Kelly. I am a private investigator, and I'm looking into the disappearance of Elissa. I was wondering if I could talk to you about her?"

There were sounds of glasses and dishes and loud voices in the background. "Oh yes," Amanda said. "Her mother told me she met with you. She really liked you. You found her phone, right?"

Madison wasn't surprised that Mrs. Alvarez had shared the news that Elissa's phone had been found. It was the first break in two years.

"Yes," Madison said. "I found her phone. It was sort of a miracle."

"It is a miracle," Amanda said. "And we need those right now. I'd be happy to meet with you. Are you in East County? It's my day off, so I'm down at the beach today."

"Actually, I live at the beach," Madison said. "I have some time right now, if you're available. Or are you with friends?"

"I'm with friends, but that's okay," Amanda said. "We're at PB Cantina in Pacific Beach."

She named a fun Mexican restaurant about three miles from Madison's apartment. Too bad Madison had to do surveillance later, or she would love to drink a pitcher of margaritas on a Friday afternoon.

"Would it be okay with you if I came over? I could be there within thirty minutes."

"Sure," Amanda said. "I'm not gonna lie: we're all a little buzzed right now, and we'll be drunker by the time you get here. But two of the girls that were there that night are here, so you can talk to them as well."

"I don't mind if you're drunk," Madison said. And she didn't: people who'd been drinking had a tendency to say things they might not say otherwise. "I'll see you shortly."

Madison decided to get ready for surveillance and just stop at PB Cantina on the way to Frank's house. She changed into black yoga pants and a black tank top and brought a black hoodie in case it got cold. She would wear her jean jacket into the restaurant; that and her black-and-white Chuck Taylors made anything into an outfit. She made sure to stock her surveillance kit: a gym bag that she filled with protein bars, water bottles, a towel, a phone charger, her laptop, a laptop charger, the cigarette lighter adapter that powered her equipment, and her camera. She had a Panasonic handheld video camera that recorded onto a tiny SD disc. She had tried every brand of video camera, but Panasonic was the best. When she was waiting for someone to come out and do something worthy of videotaping, sometimes she would see the person for less than a minute; sometimes only for ten seconds. But they might do something in those ten seconds that she needed to videotape: bend at the waist, walk quickly and easily in direct contradiction to their claims of being injured, etc. If she had to wait for the camera to wake up from its sleeping state, since she had been sitting quietly doing nothing for three hours, she would lose that vital videotape. Panasonic warmed up and started videotaping with almost no delay. And her camera had pretty good night vision, which she would need for her surveillance on Frank.

The other thing she had in her surveillance kit was something that male private investigators didn't have to worry about: portable urinals that worked with a woman's body. A guy could do surveillance for eight hours and pee in a bottle if he needed to. Madison could not pee in a bottle. But she did not want to miss out on good surveillance just because she was a girl and had to drive to find a gas station. She had discovered on Amazon some small disposable plastic urinals called Travel Johns that were miraculous. She also packed ziplock bags and paper towels to dispose of them when she was done. *Oh yes*, she often thought, *surveillance is so glamorous: I'm peeing in my car.*

She brought a book just in case she would be able to read; surveillance could get very boring. Sometimes she might wait hours for something to happen. If Madison could read, she could wait endlessly. However, it didn't always work: if she was parked far away, staring at a front door the size of a postage stamp because of the distance and waiting for someone to exit, she couldn't take her eyes off the door. Looking down for even a second would mean that someone could walk out that door and she would miss them. However, if she was parked not that far away and watching, for example, a bright-red sports car, she could probably read. She would see the red sports car move over the top of her book. She hoped she could catch up on the latest Thomas Perry book. It was a new Jane Whitefield mystery, which was her favorite series.

Now Madison sat on her bed and stared at the spot of carpet under which there was a safe. In the safe were important documents like her social security card and passport. Also in the safe was a gun.

It was a Smith & Wesson double-action-trigger revolver. It was not an automatic; it didn't fire rapidly from a clip. She had to put each bullet in one at a time, and once the bullets were fired, she had to reload. Her father had gotten her the gun when she moved out at eighteen. They'd gone together to the shooting range, and the instructor had been impressed with Madison's marksmanship. Madison had always heard that women had great aim in all things target related: bowling, archery, and target shooting.

Now she was facing a dilemma. She had done all of the paperwork necessary to get a concealed-carry permit in California. She'd had to go to classes with theory and practical lessons and had taken an exam. She'd had to do extra because she was a PI, first getting an open-carry license, which made her laugh thinking that she would carry a pistol on her hip like a cowboy, and then jumping through more hoops to get a concealed-carry. She had gotten the permit. She was allowed to carry a gun in her purse. However, she had never actually done it.

On the first day of gun class, the instructor had said, "If you can't conceive of taking someone's life, then don't carry a gun." Madison had thought long and hard about that. If she was confronted with a situation where she felt it warranted pulling her gun, she would have to answer certain questions: Did the person actually intend to seriously harm her? Was she willing to actually kill someone, take them away from their parents and children and friends, and was this the moment? Despite having good aim, she had to consider what would happen if the shot went through the person she intended to kill and hit a child or other innocent victim standing behind the target, killing them as well. She would have killed two people, one of whom certainly didn't deserve to die. She could never live with herself. And she couldn't have this conversation with herself while she pulled a gun out—this all had to be figured out ahead of time. Once you pulled the gun, you'd better be ready to shoot.

Madison had decided that she would rather get herself out of dangerous situations than stay and shoot it out. She would rather run than take the chance that she would kill an innocent person. So she went to target practice once a month, kept her skills up, and kept the gun in a safe by her bed.

But things were different now. She had people threatening to kill her, and they likely meant it. This wasn't carrying a gun on the off chance something might happen; this would be carrying a gun in case the person threatening her made good on their threat. She lifted the carpet, put her code in, opened the safe, and took out the gun and a box of bullets. She put the gun in her purse and the bullets in her surveillance bag. The gun was already loaded. The good news was that since it was a revolver, the trigger had to be pulled quite hard to get it to fire, unlike the antique gun she'd found at a gun show—that one would be staying at home.

With everything set, she carried her purse and the surveillance bag out to the landing. She locked the door and walked down the stairs. Ryan came out of his house at that exact moment.

He raised his head and saw her at the top of the landing. "Hey, what's up?"

He really was a nice guy, Madison thought. She was just so consumed with everything going on right now that she didn't have time to pay attention to him. But it was things like this that caused her to be in her midthirties and alone. She always let her work and what was going on in her life interfere with relationships. Or else she was picking the wrong guy. One or the other, and likely both.

"Oh, hi."

"I was going to text you." Ryan was bouncing from foot to foot. "But you seem like you've been really busy."

"I have been." Madison got to the bottom of the stairs and paused before turning to walk to her car. "I'm actually heading out to work for the rest of the night right now."

"Wow." Ryan took a few steps on the path toward her and stopped. "On a Friday? What kind of work do you have to do on a Friday night?"

Madison kept her life compartmentalized, almost to a fault. It wasn't that she didn't trust people, it was just that . . . okay, she didn't really trust people. "A private investigator's job is never done." She took a few steps toward her car, hoping he'd take the hint, but he started to follow her. So she kept talking. "Anyway, I've got to get going." She decided to just continue walking the rest of the way to her car.

"You will probably be tired tomorrow after working all night. Maybe Sunday night, do you want to get something to eat?"

Madison's inclination was to immediately say no. *And that is why I'm alone*, Madison thought. She stopped and turned to him. "Sure. Just text me the details."

Ryan blushed. "Sounds good," he said. He turned and went back into his house as Madison walked away. She realized he'd had no reason for coming out of his house other than to talk to her. So did that mean he'd been watching her door?

Chapter Eighteen

⁓

Madison knew which table she was aiming for the second she walked into PB Cantina. The ultimate surf-shack Mexican restaurant, it had sand-covered cement floors, rattan wall decorations, and colorful surfboards hanging from the ceilings that let you know exactly what you were in for: tacos, strong margaritas, and a good time. The girls Madison had come to see were definitely having a good time; they were screaming with laughter as Madison walked in. Three dark-haired girls wearing cut off shorts and tube tops or tanks, their lightheartedness was a welcome palate cleanser to Madison's recent activities. Maybe she could have one margarita as long as she ate something with it.

She walked up to the group and said into the center of the table, "Amanda?"

The tallest girl smiled at her. "Madison! Grab a stool." She turned toward the bar, where a group of waiters were standing. "*Camarero*! Get this girl a glass!" She looked back at Madison. "We're drinking to Elissa! You have to join us." She picked up an empty pitcher and looked into it, sticking her nose a little farther than needed in order to see inside. "What the . . . ? *Camarero*! *Mas margaritas!*"

"It's okay." Madison sat down at a stool one of the girls pulled up. "I really shouldn't drink. I still have work to do tonight."

"Well, I should!" one of the other girls said. "I'm Ana. And this is Andrea. We're the three As!" They all thought this was hilarious.

Andrea had golden skin that had deepened with a summer tan and light eyes. She was striking. "Your eyes are beautiful," Madison said. "They're an unusual green . . . or are they blue?"

"Who knows," she said. "It depends on the lighting. Andrea Cohen; pleased to meet you. I know I don't look Hispanic, but I swear I am!"

"Oh, I wasn't —"

"And she's Jewish! Have you ever heard of that? A Hispanic Jew!" Ana said.

"Yeah, I'm a Hispanijew!" This caused all of the girls to gasp for breath again.

"Are your ancestors from Andalusia?" Madison asked, naming the region in Spain that at the height of its power in the Middle Ages had included the entire Iberian Peninsula.

"They totally are!" Andrea said. "I'm named after Andalusia!"

Madison loved studying different cultures, and if she hadn't become a private investigator, she thought she might have been a historian of some kind. Both professions required an investigative mind-set, so they appealed to Madison for the same reasons. But she had the current matter at hand to address; she could stalk Andrea later.

"Okay," Madison said. "Before you guys get even more drunk than you are now—"

This raised a chorus of "Woohoo!" and "Yeah, we are!"

"Let me ask you the questions I came here to ask you, okay?"

"Sounds good," Amanda said.

"Let me first ask you this: do you guys know what happened to Elissa? Do you have a theory or an idea?"

The mood at the table quickly became somber. The girls all looked at each other. Andrea spoke first.

"We think her boyfriend had something to do with it."

"I don't," Ana said. "I think it was a random stranger."

"That's because you're in love with Frank Bronson and you always have been," Andrea said.

Wow, Madison thought. *This took a turn.*

While it certainly couldn't be said that family members and friends always knew what had happened to a missing or murdered person, Madison felt like the people closest to a victim were best able to give an opinion on the matter. After all, an investigator or detective was coming in at the end of a person's life; the friends and family had been there the whole time and could see the entire picture. As such, the fact that Elissa's mother and her friends all thought it was the boyfriend was important to Madison. However, there was now a dissenting opinion, with Ana thinking it was a stranger—even if she might be prejudiced.

"It is too important to worry about what people think about you," Madison said. "If you like or liked Frank, you can just say that, Ana. No judgment."

"We used to go out before he went out with Elissa." Ana seemed defiant as she glanced around the group. "But that's not why I think it was a stranger."

"Yes, it is!"

"You know it is!"

"How can you say that?"

"Well, Andrea, you didn't have her back when she needed it! She asked you to give her a ride home that night, and you said no!" Ana said.

This caused a combined gasp around the table. Madison thought they might have just sucked all the air out of the room.

"Okay, okay," Madison said. "Please don't fight over this. You guys need each other now. So first, Andrea: Did Elissa ask you for a ride home? Why would she do that if her car was there?"

Andrea had started to cry, the kind of crying only a young drunk girl could do: big fat tears washing black streaks of mascara and eyeliner down her face, overly pink lips swollen and smearing lipstick onto her chin as she blubbered.

"She . . . she . . ."

"Okay, deep breath. Don't relive it. Just sit here right now and tell me about it," Madison said.

"She'd had a fight with Frank on the phone," Andrea said. "She wanted to go home."

Madison was silent. She wasn't about to interrupt her. She could always come back and ask questions later.

"So! *Mas margaritas* it is!" the waiter said as he dropped off a new pitcher.

There was silence at the table. The waiter, sensing that the mood had changed, gracefully switched gears. "Aaaaaand I'll leave you to it," he said as he backed away.

Madison returned to Andrea. "Go on," she said.

"Elissa wanted to go home. I was having fun, and I didn't want to leave yet. We'd come together in her car. I didn't have a way to get home if she left, so I asked her to stay longer. She asked me to go with her. She didn't ask me for a ride, *Ana*, she asked me to leave for home with her."

"Same thing." Ana tossed her head back to get the last of the drink out of her glass.

"Anyway," Andrea said. "I told her to just go home and I would get a ride with one of the girls later. She was already upset with Frank, and now she was upset with me. She left looking like she was going to cry. It was the last thing she asked of me as a friend, and I let her down."

Andrea was done talking. She took a sip of her drink and dabbed at the black streaks on her face with a napkin. *That is some industrial-grade makeup*, Madison thought. It would take more than a few swipes with a napkin to get it to come off. Madison glanced at the other girls and then back at Andrea. "Did she say what the fight with Frank was about?"

Andrea was dipping a napkin in her margarita and wiping her face with it. "He didn't like her going out in short skirts when he wasn't with her. I mean, it was ridiculous; what girl doesn't wear short skirts when she goes out these days?"

Well, I don't, Madison thought. But that was a subject for another day.

"And the argument excalated," Andrea said. Madison resisted the urge to correct her. "He started saying she was a slut and a whore and wanted to screw other guys, you know, just controlling-guy stuff. But it ruined her night. I just didn't want it to ruin mine."

"You see?" Ana said. "She could've prevented this whole thing."

Madison snapped at Ana. "Or she could've ended up missing too. You don't know what would've happened if Andrea had walked out of the club and into whatever danger Elissa met."

The girls went quiet. Ana's mouth hung open. Amanda finally broke the silence. "Wow. I never thought of that before. I always just thought, if only Andrea had walked out with her, this wouldn't have happened. But you're right: we could've lost Andrea too."

This started a round of weeping. "I'm sorry I ever said it was your fault!" Ana said, and hugged Andrea.

"Me too!" Amanda said. She piled into the hug. Their enthusiasm caused Andrea's stool to start to tip backward.

"Oh! Oh!" they all exclaimed as the stool continued to go over. There was nothing Madison could do to stop it as gravity took over. Ana and Amanda held on to Andrea on the stool and all three went down, with Ana and Amanda breaking Andrea's fall. They ended up a pile of drunken friends, hiccupping and in hysterics on the floor.

"You guys are too much," Madison said. She stood up and helped each one up from the ground. It took several tries with Ana, who was laughing really hard and couldn't get her footing.

The other patrons were looking over, but no one seemed to mind. A bunch of girls at the beach on a summer Friday afternoon. Nothing to look at here, people.

Once everyone was on their stools again, Amanda poured refills from the new pitcher. Madison still waved away a drink; that showing had reminded her why she had to stay sober for surveillance and tailing later.

Madison's phone started buzzing on the table. She glanced at it and saw it was Tom's friend Ken calling. *What does he want?* She put it to voicemail.

"So, did you guys see anyone at the bar that night that seemed especially interested in Elissa?" Madison asked.

"I mean, there was this one guy." Andrea took a swig of her new drink. "I think he was a waiter or a busboy. He kept coming up with excuses to walk over by Elissa, and we were teasing her about it."

"Yeah," Ana said. "We were like, 'Oh, someone has a crush on you!'"

"But she was still mad at Frank. And she honestly only had eyes for him," Amanda said.

"Did the waiter/busboy seem fixated on her, or just like he had a crush on her? Like, was it creepy?" Madison asked.

"I think it was just like a crush. I didn't get the creeps from it," Amanda said.

Madison thought. What could she ask that the police hadn't asked? Or that they had asked but she might get a different answer to?

"Did she know Samantha Erickson, by any chance?" Madison asked.

"Other than school, no," Amanda said.

What?

"Other than school?" Madison said. "What do you mean?"

"Didn't you know?" Amanda said. "They both went to City College."

San Diego City College was in downtown San Diego, right next to the Gaslamp and right next to Golden Hill, where Frank lived. It was one of the main community colleges in San Diego County, and both girls were of college age. It wasn't a smoking gun, but it was quite a coincidence. Madison realized that although she knew Samantha's parents were dead and even though she'd spoken to her sister Felicity, she didn't know where Samantha had lived. She would need to look that up tonight while on surveillance.

"Were they in any classes together?" Madison asked.

"I don't think so," Ana said. "When Samantha went missing, we were talking about her disappearance. I think Elissa would've said something if she'd actually known her. Then when Elissa went missing, the police asked us about the connection of them going to the same school."

Well, that was something the police knew that Madison didn't have to reveal to them at least. She would definitely need to put that coincidence, if that's what it was, on her whiteboard.

A family walked into the restaurant. Comfortable sandals, long walking shorts, hats that had good coverage, bags with souvenirs: tourists. They got a table near the big windows.

"When she left the bar, did anyone see her walk out? Can you say if she walked towards her car or away from it?"

The girls all shook their heads no. "We didn't even see her walk out," Ana said. "I think she was mad, so didn't want to say goodbye."

Madison looked at Andrea and was afraid the waterworks were going to start again. She quickly moved on.

"When did anyone first try to call her?"

Ana jumped in. "Andrea tried the next day. They were supposed to have brunch."

"I thought she wasn't answering because she was mad at me," Andrea said.

"Did it go straight to voicemail or ring?"

"It rang five times and then went to voicemail," Andrea said.

So the phone still had charge at that point. Probably sitting comfortably in its cement hiding place along the sidewalk where Madison eventually found it.

"And then we all got on a group text around one PM after Elissa's mom called Amanda," Ana said. "That's when we knew something was really wrong. By then her phone was going straight to voicemail."

"So it was decided that I should call Frank," Ana said.

"Of course," Andrea said.

"Seriously, Andrea?" Ana said.

"Oh my God you guys don't start again," Madison interjected. "Ana, what did Frank say?"

"He just said he hadn't seen her. He was pretty casual about it."

"Did you find that strange? That he would be so calm about it?"

"I mean . . . not if they'd had a fight."

"Plus, he always acted cool about Elissa when he was talking to Ana," Andrea said. "Wanted to keep his options open."

Ana glared at Andrea but didn't say anything.

"Why are you guys so sure it was Frank?" Madison asked.

"It wasn't," Ana said.

"Oh my God, don't with that! Just don't," Amanda said. "We think it was him because he was the last person she spoke to, at least that we know of. He was really controlling, and he'd hit her before when he felt like she was out of line. It just makes sense."

Madison loved a phrase that doctors used when diagnosing illness: "If you hear hoofbeats, think horses, not zebras." The point was that horses were more common and the obvious choice; don't go looking for strange explanations for things. Because of that, Madison tended to agree with these girls. But it didn't explain Samantha going missing two years before from the same area in similar circumstances. Anyway, she would know more after surveillance tonight. Hopefully.

"Can't the police see anything from her phone? Like the last phone calls and texts and also like where it pinged and stuff?" Ana asked.

"Yes, in general, they can," Madison said. "But it's limited. I found her phone in the Gaslamp, so it's doubtful it will have pinged anywhere else. I don't know if she dropped it or threw it or what, but it looks like it stayed in the Gaslamp, even if she didn't. They can figure out when the last phone call was, but even if it was Frank, it doesn't prove anything other than they had some type of conversation. The texts the police could've gotten with just her phone number, they didn't need the phone, like two years ago when she first went missing. That just requires a subpoena to the cell provider she uses. So apparently the texts didn't reveal anything useful, at least that we know of."

"Oh, so the fact that you found the phone, that doesn't help us?" Ana asked.

Madison didn't like her luck being characterized so blandly. "Well, I mean, it helps us to not worry about why her phone only pinged in the Gaslamp and nowhere else. According to what I've read, Samantha's phone only pinged in the Gaslamp too. Unfortunately, we don't know if Samantha's phone was going straight to voicemail that night or what, because no one knew she was missing until the next day. Once someone tried to call her, it went straight to voicemail, but that could've been from the battery dying."

"So like I said, it doesn't help that you found the phone," Ana said.

Andrea was definitely Madison's favorite, not Ana. "I think any evidence we find helps. It adds clues and rules things out." *It also helps us to have stuff to use to bluff the idiot boyfriend. The idiot boyfriend who you apparently have a thing for.*

"Well, I'm glad you found it," Andrea said.

"Thanks," Madison said. "So is there anything else that I should know? Anything that the police didn't ask you that you feel they should have?"

The girls all looked at each other and shook their heads no. *Picked-over ground,* Madison thought. And it had been two years. A bunch of girls out drinking and one of them didn't come home. Sometimes there was no more to be learned about a situation than that.

"I'm getting a hangover," Amanda said. "Can we go to the beach and go swimming?"

The girls all agreed that this was a good idea. It was getting close to the time that Madison wanted to start surveillance on Frank; being early would be okay too. She got up.

"I'm just going to use the restroom before I leave. It was really nice meeting you," Madison said.

Everyone smiled and said nice meeting you too. They were getting up, gathering their things, and paying the bill. Madison started for the restroom in the back. As she walked through the restaurant, which had huge arches that were open to the outside patio and Garnet Street in front, she saw a blue Chevy Blazer with tinted windows parked across the street. What caught her attention first was the tinting: in California, tinting on the front driver's and passenger's windows was illegal; the police wanted to be able to see into the car. Madison had it on her car because she needed it for surveillance. She avoided tickets in a variety of ways, including taking the tinting off, paying the fine, and putting the tinting back on. So she noticed things like that. The other thing was that she thought she saw movement in the driver's seat. It was one of the things that made Madison great at surveillance: she could hold perfectly still in a Zen-like state for hours, but especially if there were people walking by the car. Madison knew that humans were predators and noticed movement. And unless you had limo tint, which for sure would get you pulled over too frequently for it to be worth it, movement could still be seen behind tinted windows.

She walked into the bathroom, deciding to file that information for later. Just to be sure, she wrote *blue Blazer, tinted windows, PB* and the date and time in the notepad on her phone. When she came out of the bathroom if it was still there she would write down the license plate number.

When she emerged from the restroom, the Chevy Blazer was gone and so were the girls. It was probably nothing. She stepped outside the restaurant and her phone pinged; it was a text from Ken. *Call me?*

She called him as she walked to her car.

"Hey, what's up?" she asked when he picked up the phone.

"Oh, thanks for getting back to me. Two calls in one day; you're probably thinking 'What have I done to deserve this,' right?"

Madison hadn't been thinking that, but no need to be rude. "Something like that."

"Well, I have good news. When Sylvia got to the shelter today, she told me that the job had been able to do her interview today while the kids were at school. And she got the job!"

"That's great. That warms my heart. I needed that today. Glad to hear it."

"Well, I had told her how you'd been so quick to agree, and that warmed *her* heart. So you restored some faith in humanity for her."

Madison got to her car and opened the door. "Happy to help."

"Well, if you ever need my help with anything, you have my number."

Madison got in the driver's seat. She needed to get off the phone so she could get to Frank's for surveillance. As soon as she started the car, the Bluetooth would take over and interrupt their call for a minute, which was always annoying. "I sure will."

"Like if you need help with the job you're on now. How is that going?"

"Oh, you know, ups and downs." Her car was boiling, and she wanted to start it for the air conditioning.

"Well, good. The other thing is, let me know if you need help wrangling Tom. He can be a handful, but he's a good guy."

"Sure thing. Thanks so much. Talk to you soon." They disconnected, and Madison started the car. Time to go see what Frank Bronson was up to.

Chapter Nineteen

It was 7:05 PM when Madison turned the corner onto 23rd and Frank Bronson's house came into view. There was no red Mitsubishi in the driveway. Madison cursed.

If he had already left for his adventure and Madison had missed him, she was going to be furious. However, he might not have an adventure to go on and Madison could be on a wild-goose chase anyway; or he just ran to the store and would be back. Madison found a place to park at the end of his block and across the street, where she could see the front of his house and the driveway. She waited.

She didn't want to read her book in case he came back. It wasn't that she couldn't see his bright-red car drive into the driveway; she was just antsy. Plus, she felt like she didn't deserve to read her book because she'd missed him. She sat very still in the driver's seat. When she first started her career, she'd always jumped into the back seat after arriving at surveillance, behind the extra-dark tinted windows in the back, so that she wouldn't be seen by passersby. Sitting in the back, she was virtually invisible; no prying eyes of neighbors to get spooked and call the police, thereby causing Madison to get pulled out of her car and become a spectacle in the neighborhood. But this meant that when the subject left and she needed to tail them, she had to jump into the front seat, start the car, and follow them. All nearly six feet of her. On more than one occasion she'd ended up with her butt in the driver's seat and her legs stuck on the ceiling, facing backward, wedged under the steering wheel with the subject driving away. It was not ideal.

She'd since taken to staying in the front seat whenever possible. She put the sun-screen window shades up to block the view of her from the front, leaving a small spot for her to peek through, and then she just held really still when people were around. People walking by didn't notice her, although children and animals always did. She'd had adults stand right next to her car having a conversation, while a two-year-old in a stroller stared right into her eyes. Cats would jump on the roof of the car and then put their heads down along the window and stare at her. Birds, too. There was something magical about children and animals.

The red Mitsubishi came into view from the front; it turned off Broadway and came down 23rd toward where Madison was sitting in her car. It made the right into the driveway of Frank's house. Madison saw Frank's unkempt form exit the vehicle and walk into the house with a grocery bag. The store. She'd been right. Time to relax. It could be a long night of waiting for Frank to go do something interesting. *Let's hope my luck holds*, she thought.

Luck was a funny thing. She put her head back on the seat and thought about how she'd always considered herself lucky, when someone else looking at her life might not think so. A person might not think getting breast cancer was lucky, but Madison felt like hers was. Her mother hadn't caught her cancer in time to save her life; she'd died at fifty-three. But Madison's was caught early, despite being hereditary. The mastectomy had meant Madison didn't have to get chemotherapy, and she didn't have to worry about the cancer coming back. Lucky. Losing her breasts was a small price to pay for being able to leave the cancer center and never come back.

She remembered walking into the cancer center that last day and remarking that the place always felt like it was too much, like an expensive perfume bottle that had shattered on the floor. Large original artwork whose colors flashed from the light splashing through the glass walls of the atrium. Marble floors. Comfortable chairs: some in lines, some clustered for talking. Real plants. An outdoor area sprinkled with overstuffed cushions on patio love seats. Despite its beauty, it was not a place she wanted to visit. Even more, she didn't want to belong there. *You don't belong here!* screamed from the floors and the art and the greenery in the atrium; the screams echoed, and she repeated them: "I don't belong here." After that day, she wouldn't.

Sitting down, she had noticed a gaunt woman in the waiting room with her head on her husband's chest. The woman looked exhausted and defeated, the colorful bandanna covering her bald head all the cheer she could muster. Her husband was hugging her; the muscles in his arms provided the strength his words could no longer offer.

Sitting and waiting, just like she did on surveillance. Watching and observing. A woman in her eighties had been wheeled out of the office by a woman in her sixties; judging by their conversation, it had appeared they were mother and daughter. The woman in the wheelchair had an oxygen tank and a cannula under her nose. How long was it worth fighting for life? Poking, prodding, living in a wheelchair with an oxygen tank as your best friend. Then again, doctors never said, "You have cancer and you're going to die." They said, "We found something that needs to be checked out."

Then: "The something we checked out looked suspicious."

Then: "There are some malignant cells, but we have a treatment plan: we just need to cut out X and Y, then give you treatment A and B," etc., until you were over eighty sitting in a wheelchair and you didn't quite know how you'd gotten there.

A man in his fifties had walked into the waiting room. He'd stood at the check-in desk supporting an older man who was weak and having trouble standing.

I know these men, she'd realized.

They had been her neighbors four years before. The younger man used to make chili, macaroni salad, and corn bread for the neighborhood while the older man got in his car every day and went to work. Except the older man really wasn't "older"; he just looked that way now. What was the proper etiquette for meeting an old acquaintance at a cancer center? Madison hadn't wanted to intrude on what appeared to be a difficult time, but she also didn't want to ignore a kind man. She pretended not to see them.

Then they'd been taken swiftly out of the waiting room into the recesses of the building.

A man in his late forties came in with a man in his twenties; from the similarity of their noses, they appeared to be father and son. They carried identical backpacks—some brand for the serious outdoorsman, like REI or Patagonia. The son's last name was stitched into his. The son said something to the father under his breath, and they both chuckled quietly. They had an easy rapport. They were both handsome. The father looked rugged: wiry and toned, wearing a knit cap; however, he had a slightly gray cast to his skin, a just-under-healthy weight, and no hair under his cap. He looked around for a chair and spotted Madison looking at him. He quickly looked down, suddenly self-conscious.

The private investigator–as–patient presented a challenge: always an observer, Madison found it hard not to stare. Worse, she wasn't the kind of investigator who blended into her surroundings. She preferred to be behind the tinted glass of her car, where she could watch people without being noticed.

And then it was her turn. The nurse came for her and took her to the back.

"Well, your scans are all clear," the doctor said. "In fact, we caught everything so early that you don't have to come back and see me anymore!"

That made sense, because she didn't belong there.

He was trying to be nice. What do you say to a thirty-two-year-old who you've gutted like a fish?

"Ha-ha," Madison managed to chuckle. "Well, that's good." The doctor looked down at her chart, and they were both silent. She grabbed the paper robe tighter around her foobs. They were Fake Boobs, so there was no point in being modest. But the awkwardness in the room made her feel suddenly vulnerable.

"I'm not afraid anymore," she blurted out inexplicably.

The doctor looked up from the chart. He nodded and walked to the door. He stood for a moment with his hand on the knob and then turned back to her. "That's about all we can ask for, isn't it?" he said, and walked out the door.

She went to the front desk and said, "I don't have to come back again."

As she waited for the clerk to make a note in her chart, a man in his forties came out of the treatment rooms and walked toward the exit carrying a folded pink blanket, a laptop in a quilt-like cover, and a reusable lunch bag with flowers on it. He stared straight ahead and didn't pause in his path to figure out directions or turns. He looked weary but walked steadily on. He exited the building into the bright sunshine outside the glass doors, turning right toward the parking lot.

He didn't belong there either.

Madison brought her mind back to the present, to her tinted-glass SUV and Frank's house in the distance. Her cancer story would always be part of her history, but she tried so hard not to make it part of her life anymore. She had made it while her mother hadn't. So she tried to make her life worthwhile, to make those extra years that her mother didn't get worth something.

She took a deep breath and slowed her heart rate and her breathing. She hoped she wouldn't have to sit here all night. She could be very Zen when she needed to be, waiting, watching. But she wanted him to go somewhere. She needed him to. She decided to read her book. The phone rang before she could get the book out of her bag.

"Madison Kelly."

"Hi, Madison. This is Josie. The waitress at Hank's Dive? Felicity told you I'd be calling?"

"Oh, yes, great. Glad you called." Madison grabbed a pen and a notepad from the console under her elbow.

"So Felicity said that you're a private investigator?"

"Yes, I am." Madison kept her eyes on the red Mitsubishi as she talked. There was no one on the sidewalk near her car, so she didn't need to worry about being quiet or remaining still.

"I saw you at the bar. You don't look like a PI." Josie's voice was accusatory, as if Madison were lying.

Madison had long ago lost patience for that remark. "That's the point."

"What do you mean, that's the point?"

Madison was already sick of this girl, and they'd been on the phone for less than a minute. "Did you have something you wanted to tell me? Isn't that why you're calling?"

"I'm calling because Felicity asked me to call you. I didn't want to call you," Josie said.

A limo pulled up in front of the house a few houses away from where Madison was parked. The neighborhood didn't really warrant that type of ride, so Madison was intrigued. The driver got out and opened the back door, and a teenage boy in a tuxedo got out and walked up the path to the house. He was carrying a plastic container with both hands as if it were made of glass. Madison couldn't see what was in the container.

The occupants of the house he was visiting had done a lot with what they had to work with: probably a two-bedroom, one-bath home with barely a front yard. They'd put a fresh wooden fence up and landscaped with drought-tolerant plants. The house had been painted a muted gray color with green trim. The whole effect was charming.

"Okay, well then if you'd like to share some information with me, I'm happy to hear it," Madison said into the phone.

"I want to make sure you're legitimate before I just start handing you information."

Before the young man could get to the front door, a teenage girl and her parents came out of the home. The girl was wearing what could only be described as a prom dress: purple and shiny and sparkly. The boy bowed, which caused the girl's mother to put her hand to her mouth and nudge the girl's father. The boy opened the plastic container and extracted a corsage made of purple orchids; the mom helped put it on her daughter's wrist. The boy had braces and a purple bow tie to match the girl's dress. The dad beamed.

"Did Felicity tell you my last name?" Madison asked.

"Yes."

"Then you've had plenty of time to make sure I am 'legitimate.' PI licenses are public record and can be accessed online, which any Google search would have told you. Which leads me to the conclusion that you just wanted to take control of this conversation and try to put me at a disadvantage. I'm not sure why, since I'm just here to help and I've done nothing to warrant this treatment. So either tell me what you called to tell me or get off my phone line."

Josie was silent. The two kids were getting their photos taken. Both parents had their cell phones out, because what if one phone didn't save? The first photos were of the two kids, then the dad with the daughter, then the mom and dad with the daughter. Then the dad shaking the boy's hand. Madison had never gone to prom. Watching moments like this in people's lives, moments when they didn't know they were being observed, was half the enjoyment Madison got out of surveillance. It had been what made her realize that most people in the world were good: people often hide their humanity. They only let it out when they think no one is looking. Madison investigated crimes, but she found the basic goodness of human beings to be the most compelling study.

Josie found her voice finally. "I want to know if you have a thing for Felicity. All she could do was talk about how great you were."

Ohhhhhh, Madison thought. *I get it now.* "No, I do not have a thing for Felicity. I'm straight. This is purely professional." But Madison thought that was nice: she hoped Felicity would find love out of all the misery she'd been through.

"Okay, so then sorry, I guess."

"No problem."

The kids were now in front of the limo, so more photos were necessary—posing in front and then sitting with one leg out and then with the door shut waving out the open window. This was a moment these people would remember for the rest of their lives, and Madison got to be a part of it.

"Okay, so I do have stuff I'd like to talk about. Not sure if it's good stuff, but some of it might help. Can we meet, though? I don't trust the phone."

Madison thought that was a bit dramatic: a holdover from the mid-twentieth century when an operator connected phone calls and could stay on the line through the call, listening. Nowadays, unless there was a reason a government agency had probable cause to tap your phone, you didn't really have to worry about it. Then again, Madison guessed only Josie would know if that was a concern for her.

"Sure. Can you come to La Jolla tomorrow?"

"Yeah, I have the day off. Where do you want to meet?"

"Why don't you meet me at Bernini's at eleven AM?"

"Great. I will. And . . . yeah. Sorry. Felicity is just . . . I haven't met someone like her in a long time," Josie said.

"No problem. See you tomorrow."

The limo was pulling away. The parents were standing watching it with their arms around each other. They walked back up the path into the house and closed the door.

Great, now what am I going to watch? Madison thought. Sometimes on surveillance she felt like the world was a big TV screen and she wished she could flip the channel when something boring came on. Now there was nothing except an empty street and a red Mitsubishi that wasn't moving.

She remembered she wanted to look up where Samantha had lived at the time she went missing. She was sure the police had this information, but she hadn't seen it anywhere. She grabbed her laptop out of her surveillance bag and balanced it on her lap, then set her cell phone to *Hot Spot* for the internet connection. She was able to see the red Mitsubishi over the top of the laptop screen.

She put the name Samantha Erickson into her private investigator's database. There was only one Samantha in the correct age range in San Diego County. She selected this name, and the database generated a comprehensive report. Madison knew that the average citizen would be alarmed at how much information she could get about them in less than thirty seconds. This report gave her every address that Samantha had used to apply for credit, and it also made the connection between Samantha and other people who were likely relatives or associates.

Samantha had been twenty-five years old at the time of her disappearance four years before, and according to the database report, her most recent address was in Ocean Beach, which was a couple of towns south of La Jolla. It was a laid-back beach town with lots of yoga and acai bowls, but in recent years it had experienced an explosion of trendy restaurants and bars. Samantha had lived there for the two years prior to her disappearance. Madison couldn't think of any other part of this case that involved Ocean Beach, other than Samantha's friend Simone lived there, which now made sense.

Out of curiosity, Madison viewed Samantha's prior address. It was listed just below her most recent address in the report. What she saw meant nothing at first; it was just a house on a numbered street in San Diego. The realization came to her in waves: first, numbered streets were generally located only in Chula Vista and downtown San Diego; then, Madison was sitting on a numbered street right now, and Chula Vista was really far away from Samantha and the school she was going to, so it must be downtown San Diego where Samantha had lived on a numbered street; and finally, the dawning realization that Madison was sitting on the very street listed in the database. Her head flipped up as she searched the numbers on the houses next to her. And she found it. Two years before she went missing, Samantha Erickson had lived next door to Frank Bronson.

Madison felt a rush of heat start near her chest and go up to the top of her head. What did this mean? It was unlikely that the police had this information. They might have looked at a report such as this, but only in the form of a credit report obtained with a warrant at the time she went missing in order to see if Samantha had used any of her credit cards. They wouldn't have been interested at that time in where she had previously lived; it would have been irrelevant to finding her. And they were less likely to find a prior address if it wasn't an address used for a driver's license. If Samantha had still been using a childhood address for her driver's license and just staying next to Frank, the police might not have access to that information.

And now Madison knew something that the police probably didn't know: there was a connection between Samantha Erickson and Elissa Alvarez's boyfriend.

It was almost completely dark outside her car now. She was glad the Mitsubishi was so shiny, because it reflected every light that came in contact with its red paint. There weren't a lot of streetlights on this particular street, but even the ambient light reflected off the car. She didn't know what she was going to do with this new information or what the ramifications of it were. But she was really glad she'd been doing surveillance on Frank when she'd discovered it. This was the best place she could be: watching the guy who had a connection to the two missing girls.

She turned on the satellite radio to the Billy Joel channel. Some of his older songs, like "Summer at Highland Falls," infused a mood into the scene outside her windshield. It was hot; she wished she had worn shorts instead of black yoga pants. She could see there was no one on the street around her, so she started the car and ran the car air conditioning for a bit. The cold air coming out of the vents felt delicious. She turned the car off after five minutes so as not to attract attention.

She preferred to keep all of her windows up and the doors locked when she was doing surveillance. She had learned this the hard way. When she had first started out, she had done surveillance in an older car. She was sitting in the back seat one time, as she had been taught. She had the doors locked, but the front windows were down about four inches because it was summer. It was early in the morning but still baking hot. She'd been parked in a not-very-nice area in a rural part of San Diego County. All of the houses were set far back from the sidewalk. As she hid in the back seat, she saw a man walking along the sidewalk toward her car. Madison's attention was drawn to him immediately, and her pulse quickened. As he got closer to her car his pace slowed, and he started glancing at the houses, which were set so far back from the street that no one would hear if Madison yelled. He couldn't possibly see her in the car; his interest seemed to be simply in a car parked on a lonely street with the windows partly down. He was over six feet tall, with a massive head and huge hands. Madison had no weapon in the car.

As he got closer to the car, he casually walked off the sidewalk and onto the gravel next to the road. He didn't know there was a young woman in the back seat; Madison felt certain that if he'd known, it would have added to the attraction. Madison was strong and tall, but no woman had the upper-body strength of a man. It was one of the most terrifying moments of Madison's life.

With no warning, his demeanor went from casual to violent and determined: after strolling around the car, he suddenly grabbed the open window of the driver's door and started shoving it down into the doorframe with all of his strength. He made grunting noises with each shove. His intention was clear: he was going to get the window open far enough that he could reach his hand in and unlock the door. He didn't have far to go. Madison had to think quickly.

As the man was moments from getting into her car where she was hiding, Madison lowered her voice to the deepest register she could find and said just one sentence in a booming voice: "Get the fuck away from the car, motherfucker."

Confirming Madison's suspicion that this was an experienced criminal, the man did something that left Madison haunted by what could have occurred had she not acted so quickly: he casually lowered his arms and strolled away from the car. A young man looking for a joy ride in a car, who hadn't really meant much harm, would have run like the wind away from that authoritative voice; any lesser criminal would have jumped in fear. This man was so used to his violent way of life that he knew that if he ran, he would draw attention to himself. So he casually strolled away, not a care in the world.

Now Madison had a flashlight as well as a metal stick called a nightstick, which was actually illegal in California, so that she could have broken the guy's wrist when he reached inside the car. And of course today she had a gun with her. Not that she wanted to shoot a gun inside a closed car, because she liked her eardrums.

The red Mitsubishi backed out of the driveway. Madison had her left foot up on the dashboard and was lost in thought. She got her foot off the dashboard and down on the floor and the car started all in one smooth motion. Her car was an automatic start that did not require a key; she just pushed a button. However, it required that she have her foot on the brake, which lit up her taillights. She'd long ago turned off the automatic headlights on her car. She started the car with her right foot on the brake, but she quickly took her foot off the brake so there were no taillights. Madison didn't know which way Frank would turn out of the driveway.

Madison had learned long ago that someone leaving their home was on automatic pilot; they'd done it one million times before, and they usually did it fast. Madison had to stay right behind the car near their home so as not to lose them. Once they'd gotten clear of their neighborhood, she could back off. If he turned up the street toward Broadway, Madison could fall into line right behind him. However, if he came her way on the street, she would have to make a U-turn to follow him, and someone making a U-turn was noticeable in a rearview mirror.

He went toward Broadway. Madison said "Thank you" out loud. She smoothly pulled into the street to follow. She'd gotten her mind off on a tangent and hadn't figured out what it meant that Samantha Erickson had at one time lived next door to Frank. Now she had to put her entire mind onto tailing so that she didn't lose him. She'd have to come back to that new lead later.

Frank had turned right onto Broadway and was now making another right onto 25th Street. Madison had backed off slightly, but when tailing someone on city streets, it was easy to lose them at a red light. She had to stay close enough that she could make all of the stoplights he made but far enough back that he didn't notice someone was tailing him. She tried to stay in his blind spot in the right lane next to him rather than behind him. That way she could be almost even with him as they approached intersections in case the light turned red. As they got closer to the freeway entrance, she got directly behind him; she didn't want to miss seeing which direction he went on the freeway, if in fact he got on it. Madison knew that if she missed his entrance to the freeway, he would be gone in less than a minute.

Frank had been driving fairly sedately up to this point. As he made the left turn onto G Street, which was the entrance to the 94 freeway east, he picked up speed. It was a somewhat dramatic uptick in speed and made Madison concerned that he had seen her and was trying to get away. She had to make a judgment call: if she let him get on the freeway without being right behind him, she would lose him quickly, but if he knew she was following him, she would never find out where he was going. She chose to leave about six car lengths between them. As he made the left, she stayed at the stop sign for a minute, watching his car get on the freeway. Then she turned left and floored her Ford Explorer's V-6 engine.

He had jumped over into the far-left lane and was about three-quarters of a mile ahead. Madison was lucky he had a bright-red car. She gunned her engine up to ninety miles per hour and closed the distance, staying in the far-right lane. Madison loved tailing someone on the freeway: in California, the exits to the freeway were generally on the right-hand side, so her subject would have to travel from the left side of the freeway to the right side to get off of it. Madison could stay on the right so that the person looking in their review mirror saw nothing behind them, but they would have to move in front of Madison to exit the freeway.

They stayed like this for about ten miles: Frank in the fast lane and Madison in the slow lane. Madison gently passed slower cars. Frank was now keeping his speed just about five miles an hour over the speed limit; unlikely to get pulled over by a cop. Madison stayed at about the speed limit, so she was about a quarter of a mile behind him, but all the way over on the right side. There was no way he would think someone was following him, because there was no one behind him in his lane. Madison got into the familiar rhythm she had when tailing someone. She breathed deeply and enjoyed the sights. She had found that if she put her attention on the person in the car she was following, they would know it and would turn to see if someone was behind them—the same way a person could get someone in a restaurant to turn and look at them if they stared hard enough. So she concentrated on putting her attention away from the car she was tailing. Sometimes she yawned to induce a feeling of boredom in herself and to lower her heart rate and blood pressure.

About thirteen miles after they had gotten on the freeway, he transitioned to the 67 North in El Cajon. This was the city where Elissa had lived and where her mother lived. Was he going to visit someone there? Madison loved the thrill of wondering where her subject was taking her.

She didn't have any music on in the car. It required every ounce of her attention not to lose the subject while also not getting spotted. She continued to pass slower cars; she avoided any fast movement that could be seen from Frank's rearview mirror. He continued in the number-one lane for another twelve miles.

They were now officially in the boonies. They had left civilization and were traveling in the outskirts of San Diego County. There was nothing around them but rolling hills and chaparral. Madison was starting to get nervous. If he got off the freeway right here, theirs would be the only two cars getting off. It would be difficult for her to follow him, because he would wonder why another car was getting off the freeway in the middle of nowhere at night. There were no houses, there were no gas stations, they were in no-man's-land. They were traveling on the freeway in an area that wasn't even an incorporated city; it was just the wilds of San Diego County. Madison started planning how she would follow him off the freeway. She would have to slow way down while still on the freeway so that she didn't come off the exit right behind him.

It turned out she was lucky in one respect: he didn't exit the freeway at a godforsaken empty expanse of land; he continued until the freeway turned into Main Street in Ramona, a town in unincorporated San Diego County. Madison felt like it was as close to the wild, wild West as you could get in modern-day California, though she was somewhat more comfortable now that they had reached a bit of civilization. While it still had the architecture and sentiment of the old West, it also had a Jack in the Box and an Albertsons supermarket. There were people out and about even at nine at night, so she wasn't the only car behind Frank as they rolled through town.

Her relief was short-lived: it didn't take long to get through the town of Ramona at this time of night. Just a few stoplights and they were once again surrounded by chaparral; no streetlights, and just one other car to obscure Frank's view of Madison following him. Once that other car turned off, Madison would have no cover.

Now that there were no cities between them and the Anza-Borrego Desert, Madison started to get really anxious. While it was true that Frank might have needed a drive to clear his head, his route had not seemed abstract or circuitous; he had driven straight to the outback. People often thought of San Diego as being fun in the sun at the beach, and while that was true, there was probably more natural forest and desert than beach in San Diego County. Frank was currently taking her in the direction of an empty desert or the Cleveland National Forest. In just a few miles they would be deciding which way they turned, but either choice involved no other people.

He was heading right for the perfect place to hide a body.

Madison was trying not to jump to conclusions, but there was not a lot of jumping required at this point. He was a suspect in the disappearance of his girlfriend, and as far as Madison was concerned, he was now a suspect in the disappearance of another girl who used to live next door to him. He was leading Madison out into the middle of nowhere on the very day that she had scared him into thinking the police were onto him. Was he going to check to make sure that the body was still hidden? Or bodies? Should she call Tom? He had made fun of her for wanting to do this surveillance. He didn't deserve a phone call. But she also didn't want to be out in the desert alone with a murderer checking on his burial site, with no one knowing where she was. *My God*, Madison thought. *I didn't tell anyone where I was going.*

Frank turned left at a small break in the shrubs and trees that was more a path than a street. Madison couldn't see a sign indicating if it was a road with a name. She didn't dare make the turn directly after him, so she kept going straight as he made the left. As soon as he was out of sight, she made a fast U-turn and came back to the spot where he had turned. She crept her car up a few feet and looked down the road. She could see his taillights; they were bouncing because the road wasn't paved. Madison turned off her headlights so he wouldn't look in his rearview mirror and see someone stopped there. She kept checking her own rearview mirror, because this would be a perfect time for someone to come around a corner and run into the back of her, since now she had no taillights. Frank's car continued bouncing, and then the lights slowly disappeared. Had he turned? Had the road veered and there were shrubs blocking her view? There were no lights and she couldn't see what was up ahead.

This had gotten more dangerous than Madison had anticipated. She had no idea what was up that road. She had no idea if she could get out of the area if she drove in. She had no idea if there would be a place to park to see what he was doing. If she drove in there, she would be doing it completely blind. She could even get trapped in there if it was a small space and his car got behind hers. She had the bigger vehicle and could probably run him down, but that was getting a little too confrontational for what she'd planned for tonight.

It was probably time to call Tom. She backed her vehicle up so that she was not in the middle of the road and at risk of getting rear-ended. She felt safe in assuming that Frank would have to come out this same street to go home, so she wouldn't miss his exit. She took out her phone and called Tom. It didn't even ring at first. She saw she had only one bar of service. She hung up and tried again. This time it rang, but after two rings he put her straight to voicemail. She tried yet again and had the same result. She texted him:

He drove to Ramona. The middle of nowhere. He drove up a dirt road. I'm waiting at the exit to it.

At first her text didn't go through because she had no service. She had gone through several cell phone service providers until she had settled on the one that had the best service in the most obscure places, since she usually found herself in those places needing to use her phone. But apparently nobody could get her a signal in the backcountry. She held the phone up in the car, trying to get the text to go through, but it said *Failed to send*. She hit retry.

A car came around the bend behind her and drove quickly past. The text failed again, and she hit retry again. It finally went through. How long could she wait for an answer before she had to decide for herself on the best course of action?

She looked at the map on her phone, but it showed no detail on the dirt road or what lay beyond it. Her navigation system in her Ford Explorer yielded the same negative results. The only way to know what was beyond this spot was to drive up it.

There could be any amount of space up that road where a person could hide a body, and if she didn't see what area he was concentrating on they would never be able to find it. If that was even what he was doing; was she being overly dramatic? The coincidences were stacking up. Her favorite fictional detective, Nero Wolfe, always used to say, "In a world of cause and effect, all coincidences are suspect." She agreed. Samantha Erickson used to live next door to Frank. His girlfriend had gone missing in the same way as Samantha. On the day she spooked him, he'd driven to the middle of nowhere. Too many coincidences. Madison felt confident in assuming that he was checking on the burial place of a body. And if she didn't see where he was searching, they might never know where that body was buried.

She turned and drove up the dirt road.

Chapter Twenty

Madison drove slowly over the ruts, trying not to destroy her suspension system. She started steering with her knees and grabbed a black knit cap from her surveillance bag and stuffed her blonde hair up into it. In a way, she was thankful it was nighttime: the tinted windows made it almost impossible to see inside her car at night. Putting her hair up in a black knit cap meant that the only thing visible would be her face, which she could tip and turn to shield from any light coming in. And anyway, the night was slightly overcast. There was hardly any starlight or moonlight to expose her.

After about a quarter of a mile the dirt road ended. She was faced with having to turn right or left onto another dirt road. It was so dark in front of her that she couldn't tell if the road ended at a mountain or a cliff over a valley. Her headlights lit up the chaparral and high dry grass at the edge of the road and nothing beyond. She searched to the right and left but couldn't see Frank's taillights. The longer she sat here, the more chance he had to wonder why a car was coming in after him and to take evasive action. She chose right.

She drove faster than she should for the terrain. She changed the switch on her console to all-wheel drive, something she'd never needed in California before. She wanted to get to wherever he'd gone and observe his activity before he got spooked. He could certainly hear her car already; he couldn't have gotten that far on these unpaved roads. If he'd turned left at the T instead of right, he could be freaking out at the sound and leaving right now from behind her, with no chance of her seeing him or catching him.

A rabbit darted in front of her car, and she slammed on the brakes. She didn't need to kill Peter Cottontail tonight on top of everything else. She took a deep breath to try to steady the shaking that the adrenaline was causing. She continued on.

No service at all on her phone now, which was to be expected. Thank God she had an SUV, so at least the undercarriage was up high enough to handle the broken road. The carriage rocked back and forth, and she felt like she was riding a horse. If she didn't see Frank soon she'd have to figure she'd turned the wrong way and go back. In that case, she probably would've missed him, since he would've heard her car and abandoned his plan.

Suddenly his red car exploded into view, her headlights lighting it up like a fireworks display. Madison gasped and slammed on the brakes; the car wasn't there and then it was, almost right in front of her. He'd pulled it slightly to the right out of the road, but not enough so that she could get by. He probably hadn't expected other cars on this road right now. She couldn't stay here like a sitting duck. She had to decide what to do.

She decided to do the most important thing first, even before she moved her car: she used the GPS coordinates app on her phone to drop a pin on this site. The app didn't require cell service because it used satellites. She couldn't send her location to anyone, but later, assuming she made it home, she could tell Tom exactly where Frank had stopped his car.

She set the phone in the cup holder just as Frank stepped into the road in front of her. Her headlights would be blinding him so that he couldn't see into her car. He should look afraid, but he didn't; he also didn't look dumb and laid-back anymore. He looked angry. He started walking toward her car, heading for the driver's window.

Madison threw her car into reverse and started backing up the dirt road. She used her backup camera, which had good night vision, utilizing just her taillights for lighting. Frank jumped into the driver's seat of his car as soon as she took off. She concentrated on keeping the wheel as straight as possible, but there were turns in the road she had to be mindful of. Frank took the time to turn around up ahead so hadn't started after her yet. Dust and dirt were kicking up from her oversized tires; she hoped the sound kept all of the animals out of her way.

When she was getting to where she figured the exit road was, she saw Frank's headlights; they were coming straight at her. He could go faster because he was driving forward. Madison increased her speed. She planned to back up just past the exit and then turn right to head out to the main road driving forward; if he caught up to her before that, she wouldn't be able to. His speed was decreasing the distance between the two vehicles. Madison wasn't sure if she'd make it.

Because Madison's SUV sat higher, her headlights were beaming down into his car, illuminating the interior. His face looked totally different than what she'd seen earlier that day at his house; he looked crazed. His eyes were wide, and he was screaming words she couldn't hear. It almost seemed illogical for the situation: he didn't know she'd been following him, she could be a lost camper or someone who had land near here. Why this reaction? Maybe it was instinctive, a cornered rat.

Just then Madison misjudged a slight curve and ended up backing into the chaparral at the side of the road. Her wheels squealed as they tried to gain purchase to throw her up over the dune into whatever lay below. That was all Frank needed. He pulled his car up and blocked the front of her SUV. The passenger side of his car was now flush with her bumper, nearly touching it.

Frank started to get out of his car. Madison thought this was ill-advised on his part. Dave had taught her a lot about street fighting. In addition to being one of those surfers whose hang-ten casual lifestyle belied a more serious undercurrent, Dave had two black belts: one in kung fu and one in karate. And unlike others who practiced making peace with martial arts, Dave was a street fighter. So many people had misjudged Dave based on what he looked like; it had helped her to remember to never assume. And Dave had taught Madison something when she'd gotten scared by a guy who'd threatened her while she was sitting in her car: a vehicle was a four-thousand-pound weapon. You just had to be willing to use it.

Before Frank had fully gotten out of his car, Madison put her SUV in drive and slammed her foot down on the gas. The V-6 engine in the SUV shot her vehicle forward, impacting the Mitsubishi and shoving it a few feet like it was a Matchbox car.

The Mitsubishi's tires couldn't keep hold of the soft dirt and it slid; Frank almost went under the car, but he yelled and fell back into the driver's seat. Then he tried to start the car in a panic. Madison threw the SUV in reverse and backed up farther into the dried-out grass and low shrubs at the side of the road, risking the possibility that there was a drop-off right behind her; she didn't have a choice, so she hoped there wasn't one. This gave her more room to gain momentum. She shot forward again, smashing the passenger side of his car and moving it another few feet. She backed up quickly and cranked the wheel to the right hard. She floored the gas, and her SUV nipped the front right corner of the Mitsubishi, which sent shards of plastic light covers— both hers and his—flying in all directions, and spun his car out of her way. The sound was explosive. Now free and driving forward, she had just a few yards before the exit road; she turned left and flew down it to freedom.

Madison made it to the main highway and turned right. She hit speeds of a hundred miles per hour until she made it into the town of Ramona. She drove into the Jack in the Box parking lot, which thankfully was open twenty-four hours, and pulled around to the back and stopped. She switched off her lights and turned off the car.

Even if Frank drove into Ramona to look for her, he wouldn't see her black nondescript vehicle, because it was well hidden behind the restaurant. Now she had time to think.

She decided to get out of the car to survey the damage. As she set her foot on the ground, her leg almost buckled under her. Her legs were like noodles; the adrenaline had sent superhuman strength to them, and they were exhausted. She held on to the open door and took a few deep breaths. Then she was able to walk to the front of the Explorer and see what she'd done to it.

Luckily, a fight between her SUV and a tiny red car didn't leave much damage. She'd managed to hit him with her bumper for the most part. She was missing the plastic cover of the turn signal light, and she had some dings and red paint on the bumper.

"You look like a warrior now." Madison rubbed some dirt off the bumper with the bottom of her shirt. She put her hand on the hood and stood still for a moment. "Thank you."

She would have to get that damage fixed before she did any additional surveillance, so good thing she had nothing planned right now. She couldn't tail someone with damage to her car, because it made it stand out from other cars on the road and therefore made it more noticeable. She opened the driver's door to get back in and heard some sort of alarm going off on her phone. As she climbed in, she realized it was her phone pinging with all of the text messages that were coming through now that she had service again.

Who drove up a dirt road? Tom had texted first.

Wait . . . Frank Bronson?

Where in Ramona?

Why aren't you answering?

Do not follow him down a dirt road!!

Madison Kelly answer my texts!

TELL ME WHERE YOU ARE RIGHT NOW

DO NOT FOLLOW HIM ANYMORE. STAY WHERE YOU ARE. WHERE ARE YOU?

I'M HEADING OUT THERE NOW.

Maddie don't do this you're scaring the shit out of me. Answer.

None of my messages say delivered so I'm guessing you have no service. I'm heading out there now. Text me as soon as you have service. I'm calling SD Sheriff for back up.

Madison stared at her phone. *Oh God, this is going to be a scene*, Madison thought. But it had to be done. There was no good reason for Frank Bronson to be out on a dirt road at night except if there was a body out there. She had to see it through.

She knew Tom was talking about the fact that the San Diego Sheriff's Department had jurisdiction in the unincorporated part of San Diego County that was Ramona. He and other San Diego Police Department officers couldn't just march into Ramona and start doing an investigation; they had to coordinate with the department that had jurisdiction in the area. She was going to have to do a lot of explaining before the night was through.

First she made sure her GPS pin had worked; it had. She had the exact spot that Frank had parked his car. Next she texted Tom:

I'm okay. I'm parked behind the Jack-in-the-Box in Ramona.

Her phone rang immediately.

"Hi, Tom."

"I am one-zero mikes out." Madison figured the reason he'd slipped into his old military radio abbreviations was that he was scared. He was ten minutes away. "Tell me what happened."

Madison explained how the surveillance had begun and described her somewhat easy tail out to Ramona. She explained that she'd had no choice but to follow Frank down the dirt road or they never would have known where he'd stopped.

"We still don't know where he stopped, because all we know is he drove down a dirt road and parked somewhere," Tom said.

"I dropped a pin on my GPS app on my phone. I can tell you the exact coordinates where he parked his car."

"Oh."

"So anyway, I followed him down the road, found his car, and dropped the pin. Unfortunately, he was coming back to his car at that exact moment, and he saw me there."

There was a car driving down the alley behind the Jack in the Box, and the headlights belonged to a small car. Madison threw herself down onto the passenger seat. The car continued driving, and so she sat up as it passed; it wasn't Frank.

"And?"

Madison knew that this was the first of many times she would be telling the story. It wasn't that she was concerned about her story changing, because she was telling the truth. It was that as soon as the sheriff's department got there, her actions would be picked apart by men who might not like female private investigators. It was going to be a long night. "And he got in the car and tried to chase me down. I backed up as fast as I could down the dirt road, got caught in the bushes at the side of the road, and he blocked my car."

There were headlights coming from the main road through the Jack in the Box parking lot. Madison turned in her seat and watched the progress; the headlights appeared to belong to a Crown Victoria. Sure enough, it was Tom.

"That was shorter than ten minutes," Madison said. Tom disconnected the call.

Madison got out of her car and walked over to where Tom had parked. He got out and adjusted his polo shirt over the gun in his holster. Madison didn't want anyone to think of her as anything other than a tough bitch, but even she had to admit that it felt good when the cavalry arrived.

"So, your gamble paid off, huh?"

He was being nice, and it made her want to start crying as the adrenaline in her system evaporated. The last thing she wanted was to cry in front of Tom Clark. She kicked her Chuck Taylors lightly against the back tire of his car, one after the other: kick, kick, kick, kick. "I guess so."

"You're going to end up a hero before this is all over."

"Do you think the San Diego Sheriff's Department will appreciate having to come out in the middle of night to look for a body that isn't part of one their cases?"

"Oh, they'll love it. They'll get all the glory for finding a body in a missing persons case. So how did it end? Are we looking for Frank Bronson's body as well?"

"Very funny. No, I smashed the side of his car with my SUV when he tried to block me, and I got away. He is driving around somewhere with a damaged passenger door."

They were silent for a minute, standing in the parking lot. There were a lot more stars in the sky in Ramona than in the city of San Diego; fewer streetlights to obscure the view. Madison could feel the summer air on her face. The air felt different at night.

"You okay?" Tom asked. He took a few steps toward her and bent his head down slightly to make eye contact.

He had to stop being nice to her or she would be sobbing before the night was over. "I'm fine. I do this shit all the time."

"Oh. Okay. Gotcha." Tom seemed annoyed that she had not accepted his compassion. He didn't understand that Madison was never far from indulging in the grief that pervaded her life. *Sometimes if you start crying you'll never stop*, Madison screamed inside. Tom didn't hear her.

"So you got a license plate for this guy, or am I supposed to use my magic powers to find him?"

Madison gave him the license plate number from memory, and he went into his car to call it in. She wondered if Frank had raced for home or whether he was parked somewhere trying to figure out what to do. Madison knew that home could give a person a false sense of security; when the police were looking for you, your home was the last place you should go. And if he had gone back to try to move a body, he would have company very soon. The police would have the area cordoned off shortly.

Tom returned from the car. "Okay, I called it in. Right now he hasn't committed a crime that I'm aware of. But I would like to know where he is when the time comes."

Madison nodded. She shivered. Even though it was summer, it could get chilly at night in the inland areas of the county. Plus, she had a little bit of shock starting. Tom went back to the car, got a flight jacket out of the back seat, and handed it to her without saying anything. She put it on.

"I called the detective handling the case on the way here. He's waiting for me to call him back to let him know if we get anything."

"I would think he'd want to be here, just in case a body is found," Madison said.

"You operate with much more wishful thinking than we do. All we know right now is that Frank went for a drive on a dirt road and was unhappy to find you following him. That doesn't make him guilty of a crime, and it doesn't mean a body is there."

Madison walked over to her car to get her knit hat that had fallen off in the middle of her excursion. Tom followed her.

"I know you want Elissa to be out there, but that doesn't make it so, Maddie."

"I'm just following leads, pulling strings, and using my logic. I don't think Frank picked tonight to do research on nighttime flora and fauna in the San Diego desert community."

Tom shook his head and moved something invisible on the ground with the side of his shoe. "Whatever you say. Let's just wait for the sheriff's deputies to get here."

They didn't have to wait long. Within a few minutes two cop cars with San Diego Sheriff's Department decals on the doors pulled into the Jack in the Box parking lot. *And so it begins*, Madison thought. The deputies came over, and the first of Madison's many statements began.

Chapter Twenty-One

Madison stopped for the red light at La Jolla Boulevard near her apartment just past midnight. There was no one on the street this late, and she had her windows down so she could hear the waves crashing. She waited for the light to change. There was something so melancholy about a red light going through its circuit with no cars in the other direction to direct. The walk sign began flashing: *Don't walk. Don't walk. Don't walk.* The light for oncoming traffic finally turned yellow and then red so she could continue on. Like life telling her to take a moment to reflect.

She had given her statement several times to several different people, including the detective handling the missing persons case for the San Diego Police Department; he had ultimately decided to come out and join the fun. She gave everyone the GPS coordinates for the location where Frank had parked his car. They had put crime scene tape up and were securing the area until morning. When daylight came, they would see if they could figure out why Frank had decided to go off-roading on a Friday night in his souped-up street car.

She had called Dave on the way home and asked him to meet her at her apartment. She wasn't sure why, and she was choosing not to be introspective on that point at the moment. She just wanted to see him. She parked her car in her space and got out. When she came around the corner of the building, he was sitting on her steps with two bags of Mexican food from Rigoberto's Taco Shop, just up the street on La Jolla Boulevard.

"And that is why I keep you around." Madison grabbed one of the bags of food. She adjusted her surveillance pack over her shoulder so she had a free hand to eat a tortilla chip on the way up the stairs.

"So why am I getting a booty call?" Dave asked.

Madison unlocked the front door. "It's not a booty call, Dave. Don't expect me to put out just because you brought me Mexican food."

"Just for future reference, what kind of food would I need to bring to guarantee something like that?"

"If anything was going to do it, Rigoberto's probably would. But not tonight." Madison got the butterfly china plates and some utensils and brought them over to her desk/dining table. Dave sat in the wing chair, and they separated the food onto the plates. She sat in her office chair and began eating. She hadn't realized how hungry she was.

"So, any progress? Have you found a murderer yet?"

"No, but I used my vehicle as a weapon today, so you should be proud of me."

Dave finished chewing and gave her a wary glance. "And why did you need a weapon?"

"Oh, it's a long story. And you won't like it. So I'm going to spare you."

Madison knew Dave almost as well as he knew her. It took a lot to rile him up, which was surprising, considering the reaction people got from him when he was finally riled. He really did give the image of the most passive surfer you'd ever want to meet—until he'd had too much. And "too much" could take a long time, or it could be immediate. Dave had lived in a violent home. Madison thought the reason he'd started martial arts as a child was to protect himself from his mother. When he was sixteen, she'd swung back to slap him across the face, and he'd grabbed her hand and said, "No more." She'd never hit him again. One thing Madison knew for sure: the story of tonight would rile Dave up. She didn't need him going out to find Frank Bronson.

Dave knew his limitations. He knew when Madison was sparing him details that would cause him to get violent. So he left it alone and talked about surfing instead. "I caught a tube ride today! Totally in the barrel."

"Awesome!" Dave was describing the surfer Holy Grail: just after a surfer caught a wave, sometimes the wave curled over the top of them and it was as if they were surfing inside a tube or a barrel. It became difficult to keep upright with the wave overhead, and so they crouched low and tried not to get shoved forward and off the wave. Dave had told Madison that it was thrilling. Madison had never surfed but saw the reaction from the surfers, and it was fun to join in on the excitement.

Madison got up to get them water and out of habit checked the windows. Outside the bedroom window, she saw a brand-new dark-blue Tesla parked in the alley.

"Are you fucking kidding me?" She was too exhausted for this.

"What is it?" Dave asked from the living room.

"This guy whose wife wanted me to do surveillance on him is sitting in my alley right now. He is a fucking asshole who hits his wife, and apparently she gave him my name and phone number by accident. It didn't take too much longer for him to get my address, since he's downstairs right now."

"This should be fun." Dave was already on his way to the front door. He was wearing a surf-contest T-shirt, board shorts, and flip-flops. She wondered what Mr. Sands was going to think when he saw Dave walking toward his car.

"Dave, let's just let him sit in the alley and stew in his own juice for a while." Madison was talking as she followed Dave down the stairs.

"No, I want to find out what he thought was going to happen by showing up at your apartment. I'm interested. I'm just going to talk to him." Madison knew this was not true. If Dave hated anything, he hated bullies. And by revealing that this guy hit his wife, Madison knew she had just told Dave that the guy was a bully.

As they got closer to the Tesla, Madison caught up with Dave. The guy got out of his car.

"Are you Madison Kelly?" He managed to say it accusatively with a sneer on his face. He seemed like the kind of guy that always had a sneer on his face. He was wearing alligator loafers, expensive slacks, and a freshly pressed white shirt. He'd had a haircut within a week. But he was also wiry and held himself in a fighting stance that made it seem like he used to fight people for a living.

"I am." Madison wasn't surprised that Dave was silent. He was assessing the situation. Plus, he wasn't the kind of guy who took over the conversation for a girl. He knew Madison was capable of speaking for herself.

"Well, I'm Arthur Sands. I hear you think you're going to do an investigation on me?"

"You heard wrong. I'm not doing an investigation on you. I have no interest in you."

"That's a good thing. You don't want to mess with me."

"Oh really? Why is that?" Dave asked. *Don't answer that,* Madison thought. *Get back in your car.*

The guy smirked at Dave and then turned back to Madison. "Is this what you have for protection?"

"I don't need protection. Or do I? Are you threatening me?"

"I don't need to threaten you. Anything I say to you is a promise of what is to come. And this is what you've got to protect you? This pretty boy?"

Oh, God, Madison thought. *There's still time to get in your car.*

"Pretty?" Dave said. "There's a reason I don't have any marks on my face."

"Oh look, how cute: the little surfer faggot is going to protect you."

Madison thought that was probably it. Sure enough, Dave laughed. He had a laugh that sounded like the singer at the beginning of "Wipe Out," the surfer song from the 1960s: high-pitched, completely incongruous with the guy himself. Madison usually loved to hear it, except when she knew that he was laughing right before he beat the shit out of someone. For some reason, the prospect of what was about to come always made him laugh.

Dave's arm came out so swiftly that the guy didn't even see it coming. One second he was sneering, and the next he was lying on the ground. Dave literally wiped the sneer off his face.

Madison looked down at the guy, blood flooding out of his nose onto the alley.

"Did you have to hit him?" she said.

"Hey—my friend Jay is gay. That's not a nice word."

"No, it isn't." Madison sighed. "Now what?"

"Let's go back upstairs. My food is getting cold," Dave said.

Madison leaned down to get a closer look at the guy's face. His nose was all kinds of broken. "He's breathing kinda funny, Dave."

Dave leaned down and peered at the guy's face through the darkness. "He'll be fine. Well, not fine, but he's not gonna die. Let's go."

"Shouldn't we at least wait until he wakes up?" Madison said.

"Jesus, what am I, his mother? I'm getting cold. Let's go in."

They turned and walked across the alley to her garden and then up the stairs to her apartment.

Madison went to her closet to grab a clean sweatshirt; coincidentally, it was one of Dave's. It was difficult being a tall girl. Manufacturers of women's clothing thought that all women had the same arm and leg length. Most women's clothing ended at her mid forearm and midcalf. It was luxurious to put on a sweatshirt and have the arms reach down to her wrists.

"Hey! That's mine," Dave said as she returned to the living room. "I'm cold too."

"How can you be cold? You just exerted energy in order to propagate violence."

Dave grabbed a throw from behind the wing chair and put it around his shoulders. "Energy? That didn't take energy." He dug back into his Mexican food.

Madison wasn't hungry anymore. She picked up her plate and took it to the kitchen. She went back to the bedroom and looked out the window. Arthur Sands had just gotten back into the driver's seat of his car. He was looking up at her window, blood still dripping onto his freshly starched white shirt. He started his Tesla, silently of course, and flipped her off as he drove away. A car coming down the alley had to wait as he pulled in front of them; it was a Ford Fusion. Madison knew someone who had a Ford Fusion.

Thomas Clark had a Ford Fusion. Presumably his wife drove it as well. As the Ford drew adjacent to her apartment, a face looked up at her window: Tom's wife.

"Jesus," Madison said from the bedroom. "I think I'm missing out on a revenue opportunity: I should be selling my address on maps. I'll make a fortune. Apparently my home is highly sought after in some sort of macabre mystery tour." She waited until the car had turned right and driven out of sight. Just a drive-by to see if Tom was here. Madison wondered how often Elaine did that.

She walked back into the living room. Dave had stopped eating. "Who's here now?"

Madison sat in her office chair. "Nobody, it's fine."

"Are you sure?"

"She left. And anyway, it's a girl. You're not going to hit a girl."

Dave resumed eating. "That's true." He was the slowest eater Madison had ever met.

She stared at her whiteboard. She hadn't wanted to think about the ramifications of tonight until they knew what Frank was doing on that dirt road, but it was hard not to let her mind swim with the possibilities: Had Frank taken both girls? Was one or both of them buried in Ramona? She got up and wrote *Both girls went to San Diego City College* and *Samantha lived next door to Frank.*

She put Arthur Sands on the board, even though she didn't think he had anything to do with the notes or the missing girls. She thought he was just your average run-of-the-mill asshole who needed a bigger guy to smack him down to size. He was the type of guy who only picked on people smaller than he was. He never would've taunted Dave if he'd known what Dave was capable of. Madison was pretty sure she'd seen the last of him, but she'd been wrong about things before. Until he could be eliminated for sure, he would stay on the board.

But more importantly, regardless of whether he was Anonymous, he wouldn't have liked being made a fool of—and he might take it out on his wife. As much as Madison disliked Melissa for bringing this mess to her doorstep, she didn't want her to get killed. So even though it was late, she decided to call. She picked up her phone and dialed Melissa's number.

"Hello?"

"Hi, Melissa. It's Madison Kelly." Dave had finished eating finally and was rinsing off his plate in the kitchen.

"Hi, Madison. I didn't think I'd hear from *you* again. Especially this late at night."

Something about her tone made Madison want to hang up. She was just so haughty and arrogant; what an attitude to have when she could have gotten Madison seriously hurt.

"I will keep this short. Your husband paid me a visit."

Dave could tell that Madison was getting angry. He'd come back from the kitchen and was sitting in the wing chair. He grabbed her arm to try to get her to sit on his lap. She yanked her arm away.

Melissa didn't sound concerned. "Oh. Sorry about that. What happened?"

"He got what was coming to him. So much so that he might come home and give you what he thinks is coming to you. I'm calling to warn you."

"Oh. I left him. I'm at my sister's house in Palo Alto."

Madison sighed. She'd been trying to save someone who didn't even appreciate it. "Well, that's good. That's all I wanted to say." She disconnected the call.

She walked over and sat on Dave's lap.

"Too many assholes?" Dave asked.

Madison buried her head in his chest. "Way too many." Dave stood up with Madison in his lap, picking her up in one smooth motion, all six feet of her. He was literally the strongest man she'd ever met in her life. He carried her into the bedroom and laid her gently on the bed. He lay on top of her and kissed her neck and her face. She wrapped her arms around his neck and held on. He scooped his arms behind her and they lay like that, not moving, holding each other tightly for a few minutes.

"Why does it feel like someone's going to try to pull us apart?" Madison tightened her arms around his neck until she was holding her elbows.

His mouth was right next to her ear. "Never."

Chapter Twenty-Two

~

The heat of the sun beating down on her bed let Madison know she'd overslept. She was supposed to meet Josie from Hank's Dive at Bernini's at eleven AM. She grabbed her phone off the nightstand and saw it was ten thirty. She jumped up and stripped her clothes off as she walked toward the shower. Dave had left the night before; Madison had wanted her big bed to herself.

She had decisions to make this morning. While her tailing of Frank had resulted in him being on the hook like a big fat fish, her case was not over. They hadn't found a body yet, as far as she knew, and even if they did, it might only be Elissa's. The connection she'd found between Frank and Samantha was a huge string to pull, but it wasn't a smoking gun. She couldn't rest on her laurels until the girls were found and the suspect or suspects were in custody. Ultimately, she wanted to know who was leaving notes on her door; but it had become so much more.

As she washed her hair, she thought about the different ways this could go: Frank had kidnapped both women and killed them and their bodies were buried in Ramona. Or he'd kidnapped both women and they were alive somewhere. Or he'd killed Elissa and buried her body in Ramona, and somebody else altogether was responsible for Samantha's disappearance.

She got out of the shower and texted Tom. *Anything?*

She threw the phone on her bed and picked out her clothes for the day: oversized boyfriend jeans, a tank top, and a Ralph Lauren warm-up jacket from the 2016 Olympics. She had long ago stopped trying to suppress her obsession with Ralph Lauren. It was hotter than the hinges of hell outside, so she put on her Birkenstocks rather than her Chuck Taylors. Her legs looked great in heels, but that was no reason to destroy her feet and her joints—whenever possible; she wore comfortable shoes.

Tom answered: *No.* A man of few words, just like Anonymous. Madison figured the cops were systematically searching the area where Frank had parked his car. There was no rushing this process, and she would just have to wait.

She pulled up at Bernini's at 11:05 AM. Josie was sitting on the patio, and Madison could see her from the street. She seemed irritated. Madison lucked out and got a parking space right in front.

"Hey, Josie, sorry I'm late."

Josie nodded but didn't say anything. Madison sat across from her. A waitress appeared, and Madison ordered coffee and eggs and potatoes with sourdough toast.

"I don't have a lot of time. I got called into work today." Josie's lips were smashed in a tight line, accentuated by red lipstick. Madison wasn't sure it was true that she had to work. It sounded like an excuse to keep the meeting short.

"Cool." Madison wanted to like this girl. If nothing else, she had an amazing Elvis tattoo on her chest. But Josie was prickly and difficult to make friends with.

"My manager doesn't want us talking to you, or really even to the police. We were told to have short memories when we talk to the police."

The waitress brought Madison's coffee and water. "Why? What do they care?"

"Hank's has had really bad publicity for a long time. There are fights, and there was a guy that got brain damage from a fight that the bouncers took part in. They just don't want any more trouble. They are trying to run a business. I kind of don't blame them."

"That's fair. But do you think they held anything back from the police?"

It seemed like Josie was trying to decide what to say. Madison felt like she was under unwarranted suspicion. Finally, Josie spoke. "Yes, I do."

The waitress brought Madison's food. She asked Josie if she wanted anything, and Josie declined.

"Okay. What do you think they are withholding?" Bernini's made the best home-fried potatoes. Madison was starting to feel the life come back into her body.

"This is the deal. I can understand trying to keep your business going. But that could have been me leaving the bar late at night and never being seen again. We have to do everything possible to find that girl. Felicity deserves to know what happened to her sister."

"I agree. So what do you think they are withholding?" Madison was getting impatient; it took a lot for this girl to get to the point.

"The police asked for the names of all of the staff who were working the night Samantha went missing. But they didn't ask for it until about a month after she'd gone missing. By then there was a bouncer who'd quit; he'd only worked there for a couple of months, and he creeped all the girls out. I can't for the life of me remember this guy's name, and anyway, I think we called him by a nickname. It was like . . . Larry, or something like that. But I can't remember, because I just avoided him. He was the 'new guy' or the 'new bouncer' until he wasn't there anymore. But I know he was working the night that Samantha went missing, because I was working that night and I remember him being there."

Madison waved at the waitress to get more coffee. It was slow going getting up to speed this morning. "And did your manager hand over this guy's name with the other names?"

"That's the thing: I don't think he did. I specifically asked my manager, Jethro—"

"Jesus, that guy," Madison said.

"Yeah, he's a real prize. Anyway, I specifically asked him, 'Did you give them the name of that bouncer?' and he said, 'Don't worry about it. Go back to work.'"

That was hardly a smoking gun, in Madison's opinion. That sounded like the way Jethro talked to most people, most of the time, and didn't necessarily mean he was hiding something. He would definitely not like Josie questioning him as to how he was doing his job.

Josie was continuing. "So I need to get into his office and look at the personal files. I feel like if I see the guy's name, I'll know it."

Madison was glad that the breakfast at Bernini's was so good; otherwise she would be annoyed at this meeting. Josie had made it sound like she had information that would help—so much so that she hadn't wanted to talk about it on the phone. Now Madison felt like Josie was trying to be relevant so that Felicity would continue to talk to her. Madison definitely liked the bouncer angle, since that had been two of her tweets, but Hank's had more bouncers than the average restaurant, so it didn't really mean anything that Josie was interested in an employee who also happened to be a bouncer. Nevertheless, she wasn't going to burn this bridge; it could prove helpful to have an in with someone who worked at the bar where Samantha was last seen.

"Well, I would definitely love to know the guy's name. It won't help for me to call and ask Jethro for a list of employees working that night—we did not hit it off when we met."

"I'm going to be working on looking for that name during my shifts for the next week. Jethro is almost always there when I'm working, and when he's not, his office is usually locked. But I'm going to figure out this guy's name."

Madison waved at the waitress to get the check. "That sounds good. You have my phone number. Call anytime."

Madison's phone went off. It was Tom. She answered without even glancing at Josie.

"Yes?"

The connection was bad. "Well . . . right . . . meet me . . . you know?"

"Your phone is breaking up. What?"

"I said . . . And make sure . . ." And then the call dropped.

"Is everything okay?" Josie asked.

"I'm not sure. I need to go. I'm sorry." Madison stood up and met the waitress to pay. She ran to her car. She got a text from Tom just as she got in the driver's seat.

Found Elissa.

Madison sat in her car in front of Bernini's. She had watched Josie pick up her purse and walk to a blue-and-black-checkerboard Mini Cooper and drive away. Madison was waiting for Tom to call her back or give her more information. She was tapping her fingers on the steering wheel in a series of patterns that was a small indicator of her extreme agitation.

She had texted Tom back—*Alive?*—but he hadn't answered. She wanted to hope for the best, but it seemed unlikely Elissa would be alive out there in the chaparral. Madison couldn't just sit here. She had to know what was going on.

She started the car and pulled into traffic, turning left onto Pearl to leave La Jolla. Knowing Tom, he would think that his text fulfilled his obligation to keep her updated. But Madison needed a lot more information than just "found Elissa." How was she found? Alive? Buried peacefully? That was unlikely. But in what state? Where? Was it for sure Frank who had done it? It must be. Had they found Samantha as well? Had they looked for her? Tom didn't know Samantha used to live next to Frank; it hadn't come up last night, and for sure Madison had to tell him now. Her mind threatened to spin out of control. The only way to get all of this information despite bad phone service was to drive to Ramona and talk to Tom.

She planned to take the 52 until she merged onto the 67 North, which would take her straight onto Main Street in Ramona. She could text Tom to meet her somewhere. As soon as the text went through to him, she would probably be in Ramona anyway. The drive was about forty-five minutes this time of day.

She'd been on the 52 for a couple of miles when she saw the blue Blazer behind her. She first identified the headlight shape as belonging to a Chevy Blazer, approximate model year 2008, exactly like the one she'd seen parked across the street from the PB Cantina in Pacific Beach when she'd met the "three As" girls. She was driving in the number-one lane when she noticed it; he'd made the stupid mistake of driving right behind her. Perhaps not stupid in his mind, because he might not know she had seen his car in Pacific Beach the day before.

Though she thought of the driver as a *he*, she couldn't be sure it was a man. The windows were tinted dark, and it looked like there might even be some tinting on the windshield, which was so illegal that Madison couldn't believe he'd made it on the freeway farther than a mile without getting pulled over by the California Highway Patrol. The effect was such that she couldn't see who was driving the car.

She casually changed into the number-two lane; this was a small freeway with only two lanes. The idiot changed lanes right behind her at the same time rather than waiting a few minutes. Or better yet, being in the number-two lane in the first place and not following her from lane to lane. *Who is this rookie?* Madison thought. Actually, it didn't have to be a rookie. It could just be an ex-cop trying to make a living as a private investigator. Madison knew that cops didn't do surveillance with fewer than four people in a team. They preferred six. Doing surveillance by themselves? Unheard of. They didn't know how to do it. And this guy clearly did not know how to do surveillance by himself.

She was using her indignation at the bad job he was doing to cover the fear brewing in the pit of her stomach. This could be Anonymous, here to make good on his promise to kill her. She didn't want him to follow her to Ramona. She didn't want him to get her on a lonely stretch of freeway. She needed to lose him.

She exited the freeway at Genesee Avenue. She kept her movements casual so he wouldn't know that she had spotted him. He left almost no room between them as he exited behind her. He was either really bad at his job or he wanted her to know he was following her and was trying to intimidate her.

Madison rolled slowly to the bottom of the exit ramp and waited at the red light. Genesee was a large road, with several lanes in each direction, separated by a median. She had the choice of turning right or turning left and joining the traffic on the other side of the median heading south. If a U-turn were allowed at this intersection, which it was not, she would end up on the on-ramp to the 52 East, continuing on the freeway in the same direction she had been traveling. If she did that and he followed her, he would be committing the cardinal sin of tailing: doing something to remove all doubt that he was following her. If she made an illegal U-turn, that was also an illogical move since she'd just gotten off the same freeway, and if he followed her in the same illogical move, he would know that he had just revealed himself to her, making it difficult to ever do surveillance on her again. It would tell her whether he was following her to kill her or just to see where she was going; if the latter, he wouldn't want her to spot him.

As the light turned green, Madison crept slowly into the intersection and stopped. There was no oncoming traffic, so there was no reason for her to stop. The cars behind the blue Blazer began honking their horns at her in frustration. They wanted to get home, get to work, get off this damn freeway, and she wasn't moving. One by one the cars behind the Blazer started coming out from behind and passing them, honking and glaring at her as they drove past. The Blazer stayed behind her.

"My God, I hope you're just dumb." Madison still couldn't make out a person in the driver's seat.

She whipped the steering wheel to the left, punched the gas a little to complete the tight U-turn but not so much that she would spin out, and then gunned the V-6 engine up the on-ramp toward the 52 East.

Madison checked the rearview mirror as she sped up the long on-ramp. The Blazer had paused at first but then started the U-turn. Just as abruptly he gave up, altered his course, and joined the traffic making the left onto southbound Genesee. He didn't want her to know he was following her; he was just bad at tailing.

"Okay, so who the fuck are you?" Madison tried to calm her breathing. He didn't seem like someone who wanted her dead; he'd given up pretty easily for that. He seemed like someone who wanted to know where she was going. That didn't mean he didn't *also* want her dead, just apparently not right now.

If they had found Elissa, surely they'd picked up Frank already, or were about to? And anyway, Frank had a small red car with a smashed passenger side door, not a blue Blazer. And the Blazer had been following her in Pacific Beach yesterday while Frank had been at the store in his red car. This was not Frank. But Blazer man could've gotten out at the light and shot her through the glass, so he wasn't a very determined assassin, if that's what he was.

Madison kept traveling toward Ramona, checking her rearview mirror on occasion. No other cars following her. She drove with her knees and tweeted:

I see you.

She didn't use the Gaslamp hashtag. She didn't know what good that would do, but it was somewhat satisfying. As answers revealed themselves, such as Elissa being found, and as she got closer to finding the truth, Madison felt herself being pushed further away. She had found Elissa by following Frank, and yet she knew nothing else; she didn't even know if Elissa was alive, because Tom wasn't answering her texts. Was Frank connected to Samantha's disappearance as well? Who was this guy following her, and what was his connection, if any, to the disappearances?

Madison's attention was brought to the electronic sign on the freeway; there was a message on it. Common in California, these changeable-message signs were used to notify drivers on the freeway of important information, such as freeway closures and hazards up ahead, as well as persons of interest—anyone for whom a "be on the lookout," or BOLO, had been issued. She checked the sign to see if it was looking for Frank. It wasn't. The sign indicated an Amber Alert, the law passed in California to help find missing children within hours of their having gone missing. Madison grabbed a pen from the console and wrote down the license plate and vehicle information listed on the electronic sign in case she saw the kidnapper's car on her way to Ramona.

The phone pinged with a Twitter notification. The account that had mentioned her was the same one as before: MaddieKelly12. The tweet said:

NO, I SEE YOU.

Madison started to shake as a shot of adrenaline raced through her body. Her eyes shot to the rearview mirror: she was alone on the freeway. She glanced back at her phone. Frank was either in custody or hiding from the police right now; very doubtful he was tweeting her. Which meant the person leaving notes on her door wasn't Frank. She would discuss with Tom what he had learned when she saw him, but it would appear she had a lot more work to do.

And then she realized something: she had a friend, Arlo, who was a computer genius. Madison was pretty sure he'd turned down a job with the NSA. He could probably figure out at least where this Twitter account had originated. She should have done that when she got the tweet from this account three days ago. So one of the first things after Ramona would be to take her phone to Arlo and see what he could tell her about MaddieKelly12. And how did this guy know her nickname was Maddie? Not many people called her that.

She looked at herself in the rearview mirror. Her eyes were bloodshot and her pupils were pinpoints. She was so exhausted from the stress of this case. It seemed like every five minutes she was getting a shot of adrenaline. Madison wasn't much of a drinker, preferring vitamins and minerals to alcohol, but she felt like she really needed a drink right about now.

As the 67 freeway turned into Main Street in Ramona, she could tell something was up in town that day: there were cop cars everywhere. Sheriffs' cars, San Diego Police Department cars; it was like a police road show. As she approached the Jack in the Box, she saw several groups of law enforcement standing near their cars, drinking coffee in the parking lot. She figured they had discovered this was the closest place to the scene that had cell service, just like she had. Hoping to find Tom, or at least text him and let him know she was there, she pulled into a parking space next to a San Diego Sheriff's Department SUV.

She texted Tom: *Where are you? I'm at the Jack-in-the-Box on Main Street.* She wondered what the residents of Ramona thought was happening. Any that had been farther along the main highway would have seen yellow crime scene tape marking off the whole area and would've probably figured it wasn't something good.

Stay there. His immediate reply indicated that he must be somewhere with cell service now at least.

Tom must've been close by, because she saw his Crown Victoria pull into the parking lot within minutes of his text. She got out of her car and walked over to where he had parked.

"Is she alive?"

"What do you think?" Tom was not in a good mood.

"Well, when you put it like that, I guess I think she's dead."

"Give the girl a prize." Tom was gathering crushed coffee cups and fast-food wrappers from his car and walking them over to the trash can.

"So are we going to play twenty questions or can you just tell me what you discovered?"

Tom stopped and leaned against his car. He drank from a bottle of water. Madison was trying to cut him some slack; she figured he'd been up all night. "They started the search near where you saw Frank's car was parked. It didn't take long. The night that he killed her, he carried her only a few yards off that dirt road and threw her in a ravine. Then threw a blanket and some dirt down on top of her."

Madison watched a squirrel run down the tree trunk, grab a small morsel of something, and then stop to look at Madison. He turned and ran back up into the recesses of the tree. "I'm sorry, Tom."

"Yeah, well, if it weren't for you, I don't think we ever would have found her. I'm sure Frank wanted to move the body after that cat and mouse you had with him last night, but he woulda needed a crane. Bet he wishes he'd thought of eventualities the night he tossed her body down there. Anyway, it doesn't matter now, because he confessed."

This stopped Madison in her tracks. "He confessed? To both murders?"

"What do you mean, both murders? To Elissa's murder. We even used your cell phone gag: we told him we had a recording of his last phone call and how he threatened her on the way to pick her up in the Gaslamp. And then we told him that we were searching the area where he had driven into Ramona last night. That was all it took."

Madison was silent for a minute. She'd already decided that she had to tell Tom about Samantha living next door to Frank. It was too relevant to an ongoing investigation. But she was afraid that in his current mood, he would explode because she hadn't told him last night. "I need to tell you something: I found a connection between Samantha and Frank. Two years before she disappeared, she lived next door to Frank."

"You don't miss much, do you? How did you find that out?"

"You already knew that?" Madison had apparently been feeling guilty for no reason.

"Well, we do now. Frank drove to the Gaslamp and found Elissa outside the bar that night. He followed her down the street because she wouldn't come with him, and ultimately he jumped out and dragged her into the car—which is probably how you found her phone: it flew out of her hand when he grabbed her. He told some passerby she was drunk, and I guess she was too embarrassed to make a scene. They never made it into his house, because he was parked in his driveway when he strangled her. He says he has anger issues. I think he also has meth issues." That made sense: those wild eyes staring at her through the windshield the night before. Madison shuddered.

A sheriff's department car had driven into the lot and parked. Two deputies got out. They nodded at Tom, and he nodded back. They walked into the restaurant. Tom continued. "Then he drove her body out to Ramona and threw it down the ravine. When he was trying to figure out what to do, he decided on a plan to encourage the police and the media into thinking that it was the same thing that had happened to Samantha. Every time he got interviewed, he brought up Samantha. A night out in the Gaslamp and she never comes home, just like the girl two years before. 'I think it was a serial killer,' he said to the first news station, and that was all it took. The media loves a serial-killer angle. He even acted like he cared about them: 'The police need to find the man who took our girls.' The way he knew to do that was because he had known Samantha when she lived by him, and so he had followed the story of her disappearance and knew all about it."

It made sense that Frank would want to make it look like the same person had taken both Samantha and Elissa. It would take the heat off of him as a suspect. It was actually a pretty good plan, and it would've worked if Madison hadn't spooked him into doing something stupid and then followed him. That meant the person who took Samantha was still out there. And that person was probably Anonymous. And it was probably the person tweeting her today. It might also be the person following her. Elissa's case was solved, but Madison still had to figure out who'd taken Samantha so she could find out who was stalking her.

"I mean, sure, it would be easier if he had also taken Samantha and we could wrap the whole thing up. I'm willing to entertain the idea," Tom said.

Madison did a double-take. After everything he had just said, it didn't make sense that Frank had had anything to do with Samantha's disappearance. Maybe he was just being thorough and open-minded?

"Okay, but remember . . ." And then she realized she hadn't told Tom about the phone call Felicity had received, and how the wording matched her note. And she still wasn't ready to tell him.

"Remember what?" Tom said.

Madison thought fast. "That someone was leaving notes on my door. Do you really think Frank drove from Golden Hill to La Jolla to put notes on my door in a game of cat and mouse? Does he seem passive-aggressive and subtle like that to you? He seems pretty violent and aggressive, like someone who killed in the heat of passion and tried to cover it up. He doesn't seem like a sociopath who enjoys playing with his victims."

Tom had finished his water. He walked over to the garbage can to throw it out. He came back to her. "That's true. I just like to keep all options open in an investigation."

"Did you catch this case? Isn't it going to be handled by the same detective that handled the missing person? Cold case or something?"

"It's a long story, but yes, I'm handling this aspect. Although there isn't much else to handle, since he confessed. We just have to continue processing the crime scene and getting everything together for the DA."

Another oddity, but then again, Madison wasn't sure exactly how the police department worked.

"Bottom line is, you did a good job, Maddie. Everybody has been talking about you today."

"Really?" Madison couldn't help but feel proud. She had worked pretty hard and had been pretty scared in the process. But she had more work to do. "Hey listen: would you be able to get me a list of the names of the employees who worked at Hank's Dive at the time that Samantha disappeared?"

"Probably." Tom stared at her for a minute. "If you hadn't done such a good job, I wouldn't be getting it for you."

"I realize that. I appreciate it."

"I'll email it to you. I got to get back to work."

Madison walked over and got into her SUV. She decided to drive out by the crime scene; she wondered what it was like in the daylight. As she drove along the main highway, she kept an eye out for the small left turn Frank had taken, forgetting that there would be cops and yellow tape everywhere to mark the spot for her. Sure enough, as she approached it there were cops directing traffic to keep people from stopping and staring. Madison made a U-turn so that she was on the same side of the street as the crime scene. She rolled down her window to speak to the cop on duty at the entrance.

"Hi . . . I was just going to pull over here for a minute. I don't need to get behind the tape."

"Ma'am, I'm not going to be able to let you—oh. Are you Madison Kelly?"

Madison had never had her reputation precede her to law enforcement, so this was quite a step up in the world for her. "Yes, I'm Madison."

"Okay, just pull over up there and you should be out of the traffic lane."

Madison pulled over near the entrance to the crime scene and turned off her engine. She sat quietly for a minute. She thought about a girl who was going to be a social worker and take care of other people; a girl whose mother worked her fingers to the bone to give her a better life; a girl whose only crime was loving the wrong boy.

"I'm sorry he did this to you. You are not a piece of garbage to be thrown out in the trash. You mattered. And I found you because your mom needed you to come home."

Madison started the car and drove toward the beach. She needed to bring Samantha home too; but the work would have to wait. She needed a quiet night alone and a good night's sleep. Tomorrow was a new day.

Chapter Twenty-Three

Actual summer in La Jolla was starting. Not the June gloom of overcast morning skies that beach dwellers had to live through to get to the good stuff, but actual summer. Madison stood on her balcony with a cup of coffee and enjoyed the feel of the morning sun on her face. There were a few wispy clouds in the sky, a gentle breeze, and the water was a sheet of cerulean-blue glass. Since living at the beach, Madison had increased her vocabulary when it came to colors. This ocean was too beautiful not to have the proper words to describe it.

She heard her phone ring and went back inside. It was still early: she'd gotten home from Ramona, eaten a piece of toast with cashew butter and jelly, and passed out. She wanted to start fresh on Samantha's case. This had become so much more than figuring out who was stalking her.

"Madison Kelly."

"Hi, Madison, it's Felicity. Felicity Erickson. Ummm, Samantha's—"

"Yes of course, Felicity." Madison was struck again at how birdlike Felicity was. It made Madison want to protect her.

"I heard. About Elissa. Do you think he had anything to do with Samantha?"

Madison walked her apartment, checking the view out of the windows as she spoke on the phone. It had become her new routine: every so often she checked the alley and the garden in front. Nothing there. "I don't. Not really. I think Elissa's boyfriend killed her in the heat of passion and then tried to make it look like a serial killer. He didn't have to work very hard, because the media jumped on connecting the two disappearances."

"Samantha's not coming home, is she?"

Madison sat in the wingback chair. "Are you and Samantha really close?"

"Yes. We have been our whole lives. Really close."

"So then I think you know, don't you?"

There was silence on the other end of the line. Then: "I want to hope."

Madison got up from the chair and walked back to the landing. There was a ship that was visible on the water; it must've been traveling out to sea from the harbor. "I think hope is sometimes all we've got left."

"I'm so tired of being afraid, Madison. This guy has haunted me for so long. First he takes my sister, then he calls me and taunts me. I don't want to be afraid anymore. And I want to know where my sister is. Even if she's not alive."

"I will tell you this: I will do everything I can to find her and bring her home. And I will take this guy out so he can't scare you anymore."

Madison was surprised at how emphatic her words sounded. She couldn't actually guarantee any of this; after all, the police had been working on it for four years. But Madison felt determined. Sitting at the crime scene the day before, she'd felt powerful, like she had taken a wrong and made it right—Elissa was going home. Maybe she was drunk with her own power. In any event, she was going to find Samantha Erickson and bring her home too.

"Did Josie call you? She was going to call you," Felicity said.

"We spoke once, and we met yesterday. She hasn't called me since."

"Okay, well, I talked to her this morning. I think she's going to call you. And . . . I know she's sort of rough around the edges, but she cares about me."

"I understand."

They disconnected, and Madison pulled up her email on her desk computer. Tom had sent the list of employees from Hank's, which was surprising, since he'd probably been working Elissa's case all night. She printed them out and went through them.

There were forty people on the staff list the week Samantha went missing. Hank's was a big place with a lot of shifts to fill, so not all of them were working the night she disappeared. That list was shorter: about fifteen people had worked that night. Madison made an Excel document with those names. If she was going to do this, she might as well be methodical about it.

She opened her PI database and started with the first name, then ran a comprehensive report. Her database wasn't perfect when it came to criminal histories, especially when the person had lived outside San Diego County. The criminal court of each county in the United States had its own method of storing records, and not all of them were online. Madison would be especially interested in the criminal history of these employees, if any. She made columns on her Excel document headed *Name*, *Age*, *Criminal History Yes/No*, and *Comments*. Her first employee had no criminal history, and she checked the San Diego County Superior Court website separately to be sure. Her phone rang.

"Madison Kelly."

"Hi, Madison, this is Josie. From Felicity—I mean, from Hank's."

Madison had to smile. She actually had no idea if Felicity returned Josie's feelings; maybe this was unrequited love? Was Felicity even gay? Well, it didn't really matter to the case at hand. "Yes, hi Josie."

"I haven't been able to get into my boss's office. I want to get you that list of names."

Madison checked another name off her list. She wasn't spending too much time on the female names; was that sexist? This just didn't seem like a female crime. "I actually got the list of employees working that night from the police."

Josie's words came out clipped. "You're talking to the police?"

Madison was starting to feel like Josie was more trouble than she was worth. She hadn't brought Madison anything worthwhile, but she sure was annoying. "What is wrong with that?"

"The police are hiding something."

Madison knew there were bad apples everywhere; the police didn't corner the market on assholes. There could be bad police just like there could be bad PIs. But she hated when that was the default argument for why a case hadn't been solved. "What makes you think that?"

"Because it hasn't been solved in four years! This girl didn't just dematerialize off a street in downtown San Diego. And they have found nothing? No clues? I don't believe it."

Madison wanted to keep working on her spreadsheet; she didn't want to debate police conspiracy theories with this girl. She had jumped to the section of bouncers while on the phone and was checking their criminal records. "Let me read you the names I have. Maybe something will jump out. Didn't you say there was a creepy guy? Larry or something?"

"Yes. Larry or maybe Lawrence. I think we called him Larry, but that was a nickname."

Madison read her the names of the fifteen people working on the night Samantha disappeared. There weren't any with a form of the name Larry. The guy with the criminal record was named Oliver.

"I don't remember an Oliver," Josie said.

"Could that be the Larry? If my name were Oliver, I'd want a nickname. And this guy has a criminal record. It is just petty stuff like stealing; there is a battery conviction, but it's a misdemeanor, so no one was seriously injured in the fight. Either that or he pleaded down on the charge from a felony."

"I guess it could be." Josie didn't sound sure. "Do you have any other leads?"

"No, I don't have tons of leads right now. I'll tell you what. I will do a thorough background check on this guy; I'll go out to his house and see what I see. It's a start."

Madison glanced over at the whiteboard. She'd have to tidy that up now that Elissa's case had been solved. She needed to separate out what had been an Elissa clue and what might still be a Samantha clue. It felt like starting over. "I'll let you know if anything pans out. And you keep me posted, okay?"

They disconnected, and Madison went to the whiteboard and erased anything related to just Elissa. She put up Oliver's name. He lived in the East Village, a gentrified part of downtown adjacent to the Gaslamp. It just didn't feel right.

What am I missing?? she wrote across the top.

She needed to get out of her apartment. She grabbed her purse and keys and locked the door on her way out. She would go visit Arlo and see if he could figure out who had created the Twitter account that had tweeted her the day before.

With his office tucked into a strip mall across the street from the post office in Pacific Beach, it was easy to underestimate Arlo the computer guy. Madison was not a person who did so. She had seen what he could do. He was constantly getting invitations to work at Google and Yahoo, and of course there was the rumor that he'd turned down the NSA. He liked his little shop up the stairs from the parking lot with his view of the ocean and where he could keep his own hours. He liked to stay up late at night playing video games and developing software programs that he sold for more than Madison would ever make in her life.

"I haven't seen you in forever," Arlo said when Madison walked into the shop. He was tinkering with a laptop. There was classical music playing softly from the speakers set within the walls. "Have you brought me an interesting problem?"

"I have. I think you'll like this one."

"I always like the problems you bring me, Madison. What is it?"

She explained how someone had set up a Twitter account using her name and sent out subtweets in response to her subtweets. She didn't have to explain to Arlo what a subtweet was: short for subliminal tweet, a tweet sent without a name but intended for a particular person. She pulled up her Twitter account on her phone and showed Arlo the exchange.

"Can you give me your Twitter password so I can look into this?"

"Of course. If I can't trust you, I don't know who I can trust." Madison gave him all the information he needed. He said he would call her as soon as he had something.

As Madison walked down the stairs back to her car, she felt like she was walking through molasses. She had this guy Oliver's house to go look at, just to get a feel for him and where he lived, but it didn't feel right. She felt like she had gone off track somewhere and didn't know how to get back on. Right now her only leads were the tweet from the Twitter account with her name on it—and hopefully Arlo would find something out about that—and then she had the bouncer named Oliver who might or might not be the "Larry" Josie was talking about. She needed to generate some more leads, because everything she had now felt like a dead end.

She headed toward downtown where Oliver lived, taking city streets to the 5 South. She was enjoying the sun sparkling on Mission Bay to the right of the freeway when she caught sight of the blue Blazer in her side-view mirror. He had gotten smarter:

he was staying on the right side of her car, trying to remain in her blind spot. But he had failed.

This time Madison was going to take a different tack: she wasn't going to let him know that she had spotted him. Instead, she was going to make him think that he had lost her, and then she was going to follow him. This would not be easy. But she was going to do it.

As they approached the 8 freeway, Madison casually moved to the right, setting herself up to take the 8 East. The Blazer followed behind, probably feeling proud of himself for not getting spotted. After they made the transition onto the 8, Madison started to slow down—a lot. She went down to forty-five miles per hour. Then forty. Several cars started moving out from behind her and passing her. The Blazer had to do the same thing or get spotted again. He came out from behind her and then floored it. He was looking to his left over his shoulder as he passed her so she couldn't see his face, but she could tell it was a man. She gunned the engine on her SUV and exited at Taylor Street. She raced down the short ramp, barely stopping at the end, then made a sharp left turn and got straight back on the 8, utilizing the on-ramp there and accelerating onto the freeway. The Blazer didn't see her; he was up ahead about a quarter of a mile in the fast lane.

Now the tailer had become the tailed. "Okay, fucker, let's see who you are."

They continued on the 8 freeway all the way into La Mesa. His license plate was a piece of paper used to advertise dealerships, put on a new car while it awaited its actual license plates; Madison knew it was also used to hide the identity of the registered owner for as long as possible. A person could get a ticket pretty quickly for not having real license plates or the new temporary paper plates finally being handed out to new cars in California. This guy seemed to get away with a lot, considering he also had illegal tinting on his car.

He wasn't acting suspicious at all. He didn't expect her to have turned around and started following him. He drove calmly in the first lane for eleven miles. Then he transferred to the 125 South.

Ultimately they ended up in a rural part of San Diego County called Spring Valley. There was a lot of open space in this part of San Diego, named for a natural spring located there that Madison had never seen. She knew that the area had originally been settled by the Native American Kumeyaay people, who had it stolen from them by the Spanish conquerors who gave it its Spanish name: El Aguaje. Madison loved the history of places. But the interesting history did not make this part of Spring Valley a nice place. The Blazer got off the freeway at Jamacha Road and turned toward desolation and despair. If this had been nighttime instead of the middle of the day, Madison didn't think she could have continued the tail; the area was just too full of predators looking for prey. They were in a predominantly industrial part of town, with boarded-up shops that looked like they had last been in business in the 1960s. They passed a storage facility, an auto repair shop, and a low-rent apartment building. The road was large, with two lanes in each direction, but there were so few cars that they didn't really need that much room. Madison wondered if it used to be some sort of thoroughfare before the freeway was built, an area now fallen into disrepair with disuse.

Within a few minutes of leaving the freeway, the Blazer turned left into a driveway. Madison pulled over quickly so as not to drive past him. He knew her car; she couldn't be seen. She waited a few minutes and drove quickly past where he had turned in. It was some sort of storage yard with different sections full of truck parts and pieces of scrap metal, all kept behind a large gate that was closed by the time Madison drove past. She turned at the next corner and parked. There was a 7-Eleven directly across the street from the driveway where he had turned. That was a booming metropolis for this part of town. It meant witnesses. It meant that Madison felt just safe enough to get out of the car and check out the location.

This is the part in the horror movie where the audience is screaming, "Don't do it, don't do it!" She felt so determined to figure out who this person was that she was exiting the car against her better judgment. Actually, she wasn't using any judgment: she was angry and wanted to know who was following her. She got out of the car. It didn't mean she wasn't afraid. She brought her purse with the gun in it.

Her hair was tucked up in a baseball cap. Madison stood out in the best of times. Now she was going after someone who knew what she looked like, when she didn't know what they looked like. She turned the corner trying to stay close to the buildings, trying to stay in the shadows. As she got closer to the driveway she glanced around her constantly to see if anyone was following or looking at her. The street was deserted except for the 7-Eleven across the street, where the occasional shopper pulled into the lot and ran inside.

She got to the driveway and noticed there was a small stucco building next to the gate. It had bars on the windows. A sign in the window said *Cerrado*, which Madison knew meant closed in Spanish. She got up close to the window on the street side and used her hands to shield the light so she could look inside the window.

"Fancy meeting you here."

Madison whipped her head around to see Ken standing there. Her mind raced: What was Ken doing here? Was this a coincidence? Was he the one following her? She glanced to her left and saw that the gate was still closed. She scanned the yard and saw a hint of blue paint in the distance behind some stacked tires: the Blazer.

Madison planted her feet parallel with each other and a few feet apart. She held her purse loosely in her left hand. "Why have you been following me?"

"Calm down, calm down." Ken did the universal patting of the air with his hands. "I know this looks bad, but I can explain."

"I'm waiting." Madison was scared, which made her angry. A homeless person with sun-destroyed skin started shouting to himself as he shuffled past them. They both turned to look at him. Madison saw a man get out of his car at the 7-Eleven and stop to stare at her. He then turned and walked inside.

"Tom was worried about you."

Tom? This was Tom's doing?

"So he hired you to tail me? That's hard to believe."

"I know. I actually was trying to tell you about this when we talked on the phone. That's why I kept bringing up Tom. I felt like I should tell you. But I chickened out." Madison remembered him bringing up Tom, and it *had* seemed awkward. "And he will be so humiliated when he learns you found out. I know he had that issue where he was sitting outside your apartment at night, watching you, and he won't want you to think this is the same thing."

Madison was floored. "He told you about that?"

"Yeah. We're pretty close." Ken was shuffling from foot to foot. "He just wanted to make sure you didn't get in over your head with this investigation. He just wanted to make sure you stayed safe. I was only to get involved if it looked like you were in danger."

That at least explained why he hadn't done anything other than follow her. "How long have you been following me?"

"Just since you got that first note on your door."

My God. Tom had been telling this guy everything. "And you were supposed to . . . what? Jump in like Superman if I got into a scuffle?"

"Something like that. It sounds stupid now. And okay, Tom paid me. Construction work has been slow, and I needed the money. And I figured I wasn't hurting you. I was actually helping you by watching out for you, right?"

This was a lot to process. "Wow—okay. Then where were you the other night? I could've used you in Ramona."

"Yeah, I heard about that body being found. Good job on that, by the way. Sorry I wasn't there when you needed help . . . I don't follow you all the time, just when I don't have anything else going on."

This was so weird. But maybe it wasn't. Isn't that what Tom had been doing when he was sitting outside her apartment all those nights? Wondering what she was doing? If she was safe?

"You know, without a PI license you're just a stalker."

Ken shook his head. "Nah, nah, it's not like that. Don't think of it like that. It was just doing a friend a favor."

"It's not 'how I think of it'; it's a fact. I'm telling you a fact: following me without a PI license is stalking."

"Yeah, but I have friends in high places." Ken laughed. He was pretty charming, but Madison was annoyed. Ken saw that his humor wasn't working. "Look, Tom is going to be mad that I let you catch me. But more than that, he's going to be so embarrassed that you know."

Madison didn't want to deal with this. It was actually embarrassing for *her*. Tom's obsession with her was so confusing. He'd never even made a real pass at her except for that drunken night years ago; he kept his interest in her hidden, which was why, when she'd found him outside her apartment watching her, it had been so shocking. Somehow it wasn't creepy, though; it was like he was in love with her from afar, unable to act on it because he was married, so he sat and dreamed of her. While his actions were disturbing on the surface—doing surveillance on her, having someone else follow her—he never did anything other than treat her respectfully in person. She had to admit she had a soft spot for him, and she didn't want him to feel humiliated. And she didn't want to deal with an awkward conversation with Tom about obsessions when she was trying to solve Samantha's disappearance. There would be time for difficult conversations after she'd found her.

"I'm not going to say anything to him right now," Madison said. "I can't promise I won't say anything in the future. And you're going to stop following me right the fuck now."

Ken looked relieved. He took a huge breath and let it out. "That's great. I'm not gonna lie: it saves my ass, since he's gonna be pissed that you caught me. But he's my friend and he for sure would be humiliated, so that's nice of you."

"Yeah, well, don't hold me to it. I reserve the right to change my mind at any time."

"I felt like I was sort of protecting you, ya know? At least it was me he asked."

"Just . . . okay . . . whatever. Don't follow me anymore."

"That's fair, that's fair. Hey, can I buy you a cup of coffee at 7-Eleven?"

Ken seemed to be joking; at least she hoped he was. "No, I'm good. So you live here?"

"Yeah, yeah, this is my humble abode." He waved his arms like a game-show hostess. "It saves time. I keep all of my construction materials here and I sleep here, so getting to work in the morning is a breeze. Just load up and ship out."

Madison looked around. She didn't see a lot of construction materials. It seemed more like just . . . junk. But to each his own.

"Well, I have places to go and people to be, so I'll see you," Madison said. A different guy at 7-Eleven was standing outside his car staring at Madison. They probably didn't get many six-foot-tall blondes in these parts.

"You're really cool, you know that?" Ken seemed surprised. "I definitely see Tom's attraction."

"Okay, don't make it weird," Madison said. *Too late*, she thought.

"Hey, that's cool. That's cool. Okay, well, I'll see ya."

"Not soon, though, right?"

"Oh—I see what you did there." Ken laughed awkwardly. "Right. Right. No time soon."

Madison walked back to her car. So the blue Blazer turned out to be a dud lead. Just personal-life issues she could deal with when the case was solved. What a waste of time. She got in the car and punched Oliver's address into the GPS.

Chapter
Twenty-Four

By the time Madison got home from driving by Oliver's residence, it was nearly six PM. She trudged up the stairs and unlocked the door of her apartment. Maybe she would go for a run to recoup some energy. Madison felt like Sunday nights, when people were done with the beach and had given it back to the locals, were the best nights. She could be in time for sunset too. She changed into yoga pants and running shoes and put her hair in a ponytail.

Oliver's home had been a useless drive-by. He lived in a towering condo complex in the gentrified section of downtown. She couldn't get into the secure building or garage, and it wasn't worth risking getting caught sneaking in right now. She would need to develop more information about him before she went traipsing around his place.

Her phone went off with a text.

Hey! We still on for tonight? It was Ryan. Oh God, she'd forgotten she'd agreed to go out with him. She was not in the mood. She knew she should expand her dating horizons, but no more until she'd solved this case. She didn't want to be mean to him, though; she would go down and tell him in person.

Madison stuck her phone in the pocket of her Ralph Lauren warm-up jacket and walked down her steps. She went to the house's side door and knocked. His roommate—Greg? Gary? she couldn't remember—answered.

"Hey."

"Oh hey. Is Ryan here?"

"He ran to the store. You can wait in his room. That way." Greg or Gary pointed to Madison's right, toward the bay window that Madison could see from her apartment window.

Madison said thank you but he had walked away, leaving her to shut the front door. She walked into Ryan's bedroom. There was no place to sit other than the bed, and that seemed too soon. The bed wasn't made. There were some posters on the walls: a girl rock climbing, holding on to a tiny shred of outcropped rock with her bony fingers, her legs flexed and golden from the sun. Interesting way to have porn on the wall; at least it was an athletic figure. There were shelves with what Madison called "boy knickknacks": little transformer toys, different kinds of rocks and pieces of lava, some books on geology and paleontology. She wasn't trying to snoop; she was trying to remain standing without looking weird by being found stock-still in the middle of the room. There was a computer and a printer sitting on a small table near the floor and some blank photo paper in a box next to the printer.

The bay window was beautiful, and it had a windowsill that was almost something a person could sit on; well, a person smaller than Madison. She stood in the window, which started at her midthigh and went way above her head, and looked up at her apartment. You really could see right into her apartment, especially if the lights were on inside and it was dark outside. Madison brushed something with her knee that was on the windowsill and knocked it to the ground; she wasn't a klutz she always said, she was just gangly. It was a small notebook, the kind that had black-and-white dots all over the front. There was a pen stuck on the outside, and some loose papers had fallen out when it fell. She reached down to scoop it all up and saw a photo of herself. They were all photos of her: photos of her doing her everyday activities like yoga on the landing, walking up the stairs carrying groceries, going out for a run. She opened the notebook to the most recent handwritten page and saw it was a journal of her life:

Saturday 7 pm:	*Just got home. She seems tired.*
Saturday 8 pm:	*Lights out. Went to bed early. No one came over.*
Sunday 8 am:	*Just awoke. In kitchen making coffee.*
Sunday 10 am:	*Leaves home. No bag. Just purse.*

There were pages and pages of it, going back two weeks. Madison couldn't keep reading. She wanted to scream. This was her limit on fear. She'd reached it. Her skin was electrified and her hands were shaking. She dropped the book back on the floor and turned to leave. Ryan was just walking into the room. He stood between her and the door.

"Hey, hi. My roommate said you were here."

"Listen to me carefully." Madison steadied her voice and lowered it. "You need to back up slowly and let me out of this room. If you fail to do that I will fucking kill you. Do you understand?"

While she was talking, Ryan was taking in the scene that he had missed on his entrance: the notebook and photos scattered on the floor, Madison's demeanor. His face dropped all of its prior charm. "Can we talk about this?"

"I SAID BACK THE FUCK UP AND LET ME OUT OF THIS ROOM." Madison had huge lungs to match her large frame. Whenever she'd had lung X-rays, the technician had invariably had to do it twice, since they couldn't get all of her lungs on one X-ray film. It caused her voice to come out booming and very, very loud when she wanted it to.

"I—"

"Dude, what the fuck?" Gary or Greg or whatever his name was had come down the hall at the sound of Madison's yelling. His arrival caused Ryan to turn, which gave Madison enough room to get by without touching him. She walked quickly past him to the front door, opened it, and ran.

She didn't know where she was running to until she noticed she was headed in the direction of Dave's house. She had no interest in figuring out the psychology of that. She didn't think Ryan knew where Dave lived, but even if he did she doubted anyone who knew of Dave—and Ryan had already said he did—would follow her to his house.

She rounded La Jolla Boulevard and didn't slow down. The other thing her lung capacity allowed was a long run without the need to stop. Dave's house was only about six blocks away. This fear she felt was always brewing—it was why people telling her she was brave always confused her. She felt afraid all the time, and in fact she forced herself to do things to overcome that fear. She was constantly trying to prove to herself as well as others that she wasn't a coward, and in this she felt she'd failed today.

As she turned into Dave's alley, she could see his driveway was empty of his red Jeep. Great. And she didn't have a key. She slowed to a walk, breathing hard, and approached his front door. Locked. She tried the kitchen door. Same.

Dave lived in a cottage that had been built as the servants' quarters for a larger house in the late nineteenth century. It was adorable, with lots of built-ins and a kitchen and laundry room, but it was the size of a postage stamp. Most of the cool places in La Jolla were. Madison looked at the window next to the kitchen door and saw that the lock was undone. She shoved the sash window up and crawled inside, falling to the floor below.

She walked into the living room and threw herself on the couch. She grabbed her phone out of her jacket pocket—she had no wallet or keys, just what she'd walked out of her apartment with when she went to see Ryan—and dialed Dave's number. There was no answer.

Next she tried Tom. Sent to voicemail. She didn't want to call the police. Yet. She'd barely wanted to call Tom. It was just so convoluted, what with the notes on her door, the guy keeping track of her activities, and, if she were honest with herself, Tom. This news about Tom having Ken follow her had to be confronted, and it looked like it was going to be sooner rather than later. Was it hunting season for Madisons or something? Had she missed the memo? Why was she so fascinating to people that they wanted to follow her and track her movements and activities? And the biggest question of all: was Ryan the anonymous note leaver? And did that mean he had something to do with Samantha's disappearance?

She tried Dave again. No answer. She was hungry and tired and she wanted to be in her own bed. She didn't think running out of Ryan's was an overreaction, not given the death threats—and the death—connected with the case she'd been working. But she wished she had her wallet and her car with her. She walked into Dave's kitchen and opened the fridge. Yogurt and Yoo-hoos. The American surfer diet. She got a blueberry yogurt and took it to the couch with a spoon. Once she'd eaten it, she set the carcass on the coffee table next to the Silver Surfer action figure and lay back on the couch. She was so tired, but there was still too much adrenaline coursing through her veins for her to sleep.

The sound of a girl laughing woke her up. She was so disoriented at first that she thought she was at home and couldn't figure out who was at her apartment. She opened her eyes and realized two things at once: she was at Dave's, and he'd brought a girl home.

She leaped up and tried to find an escape route. There was no hope, because they were coming through the front door that had a glass window, and Dave had already seen her. The girl was Gabrielle from the Pannikin.

"I'm just leaving," Madison said. She started for the kitchen door.

"What's going on? Why are you here?"

Dave was confused, but so was Gabrielle. Clearly Madison had not been a topic of their conversations. "Dave . . . ?" Gabrielle said, the way only a confused child could. Okay, she was about twenty-one, but to Madison and everything she'd been through, twenty-one was a child.

"Right. Introductions. This is Madison. Madison, this is—"

"Gabrielle. Right. I know." Madison was standing in the kitchen doorway, wanting to flee.

"You know? How do you know?"

"Why *wouldn't* she know?" Gabrielle had found her voice.

"I'm leaving." Madison hated girl/boy drama. Hated it. Especially when she cared this much. She wanted to cry, and that made her want to kill them all in a fiery explosion.

Madison walked into the kitchen and out the kitchen door. It was dark out. She thought it might be about nine PM, based on the barest glow coming from the western sky, a leftover summery sunset that she had missed because she'd fallen asleep on her non-boyfriend's couch while running from one of her many stalkers. *How did I get here?*

Dave had never promised her he'd be exclusive. Madison hadn't expected him to: he was the elusive, handsome surfer who would never be tied down. But the farce she had just been a party to had Gabrielle cast as the girlfriend and Madison as the other woman; she did not want to be in that play. But what part did she see herself in? She didn't think she wanted to be the girlfriend or wife, the traditional "I belong to you and you're mine" trope, especially when it came time for a guy to tell her what to do; no thank you. At least, she hadn't wanted that—until she saw someone else in her part. Now she didn't know how she felt. She was in the middle of something important and didn't have time for this. Her life was more than a dime-store romance novel. It had to be.

Dave ran out of the kitchen after her. He needn't have run so fast; she was just standing in the driveway, not sure where to go.

"What is going on? Are you okay?"

"No, I'm not okay. That guy Ryan that lives below me? He's been keeping track of my movements and taking photos of me, God knows why, and then I come here because I'm afraid and you're not here, and then . . . well, this." She glanced down the alley as a car drove by on Genter. She was cold.

"He's been doing what? Okay, let's go." Dave started walking down the alley toward Madison's apartment.

"What? You're going to go punch him? That doesn't work for every problem, Dave. This guy might be an actual murderer or something. I haven't figured it out, I'm so confused. And this didn't fucking help matters."

Dave walked back toward her. "What do you mean by 'this'? Gabrielle? Are you seriously going to have a problem with this?"

She stared at him. She didn't know how to explain what she was feeling. She didn't know what she was feeling. But she thought it had been awkward for him too. "Well why wouldn't I?"

"Because you don't want me, Madison. You've made that clear in your actions. You have guys hanging around you all the time. You like me sometimes, and then you want me to go home so you can have the bed to yourself. You don't need me to help you. You don't need me to give you advice. You. Don't. Need. Me. You've made that crystal clear. So you're upset when I find someone who does?"

Madison was stunned. She hadn't known he felt that way. And the last line was like he'd stabbed her in the heart: he'd "found someone." She knew she didn't want that.

"I have a murderer to catch." She turned and walked down the alley. She didn't want to turn around to see if he was watching her. Then she heard his kitchen door bang, and she knew that he was gone.

She hadn't even made it to the mouth of the alley when her phone rang with Tom calling her back. She answered and explained everything that had happened with Ryan.

"I will handle this. Don't go home. Where will you be?"

"I have to get my car, Tom."

"No. He doesn't know where you are right now, right? So don't go home."

Madison thought for a minute. "I'll figure it out, Tom. Will you call me when you know something?"

"Yes. Be safe." And he disconnected. It was not lost on her that she hadn't mentioned the tailing he'd asked Ken to do. Any port in a storm, and Tom was a port right now. He could at least figure out Ryan while she figured out the rest.

She'd almost gotten to Genter when she saw Ryan coming down the alley. She turned and started to run back to Dave's.

"Jesus, Madison! I'm not a stalker! Someone paid me!"

The familiarity of that phrase stopped her in her tracks. Twice in one day? *In a world of cause and effect, all coincidences are suspect.* She turned around. "Who paid you?"

He kept walking toward her. "A cop. You know, he's been at your place before."

Madison had read in books where someone's blood turned cold. She'd never known what that meant until this moment. Her arms broke out in goose bumps and she started to shiver.

"What did he pay you to do?"

"He said you were working on something important for him and he just had to make sure you stayed safe. He kept saying he wanted to make sure you were safe, and also that you were reporting everything to him that happened on the case."

This was mind-blowing. Tom had gone to such lengths. She should've reported him to his superiors long ago, after the first stalking incident. She was the stupidest smartest person she'd ever met. It was guys. She was smart except when it came to guys.

"That's why I left those notes on your door."

Madison knew. But she had to ask. "What notes?"

"The one about 'Stop investigating me,' and also the one that was 'What did I tell you?' He said it was all part of the case or something. He paid me a hundred dollars every week. I needed the money. I'm a grad student."

This last sentence was said with a whine that was almost as unattractive as the information he was giving her. It was safe to say that her crush on Ryan was over.

Tom had Ryan leave the notes. To scare her? Yes. So she would call him for help. Tom had her followed so he'd know where she was. Tom was doing all of this. But why? Just obsession? Or did it have something to do with Samantha?

She picked up her phone and texted Tom: *You've been stalking me. You left the notes. Did you kill Samantha too?*

Madison put the phone back in her pocket. *That oughta do it*, she thought. She would come to regret this rash move, she figured, but it was satisfying at that moment. She'd been played. Played so, so hard.

She turned her attention back to Ryan. "Well, that cop just told me he was going to 'handle you,' so I suggest you go stay with a friend for a few nights."

"Shit."

"Exactly. I've got to go." Madison ran past him and down Genter toward La Jolla Boulevard. She needed her car. She wouldn't just report Tom; she would report him to the chief of police. And she would do it in person.

Madison made it home and went upstairs for less than a minute, just enough time to grab her purse and a sweatshirt and a protein bar. She jumped into her car and raced for the freeway, ignoring the texts and phone calls from Tom that were blowing up her phone. Apparently her text to him had touched a nerve.

The San Diego Police Department headquarters was on Broadway and 14th in downtown. She could be there in no time at this time of night. Her mind was racing, and she thought it might explode: *could* Tom be a kidnapper or a murderer? Or was he just an obsessed wannabe lover who had concocted a plan to get Madison to need him? It was Madison who had jumped to the conclusion that the notes left on her door were connected to her tweets about the Gaslamp disappearances. When she'd gotten the second note, she'd assumed it was because she'd been investigating that mystery and the person responsible didn't like it. But it had just been Tom all along. He knew what she was doing because Ken was following her and Ryan was reporting to him her every move. At least Elissa had been found as a result of Madison falling for this ruse. And what about the phone call Felicity had received? Was that the one coincidence in all of this? *Stop investigating me or I will hunt you down and kill you*, the

same wording as the note on her door. Or was Tom connected
to Samantha's disappearance, and he had made the phone call to
Felicity too? She had to admit that while Samantha would've
trusted a bouncer to help her to her car or to take her home, she
really would've trusted a cop. It made Madison sick to her
stomach.

Her phone rang again. She'd been lost in thought and had
taken the wrong freeway. No matter, all the freeways in San
Diego connected, and she could just get on the 805 South to the
163 South and she'd be in downtown. The ringing on her Sync
system was driving her insane.

She pushed the button on her steering wheel to answer.
"What?"

"Madison. I don't know what you think you've discovered,
but you need to talk to me."

"No, actually, I don't. I don't need to talk to you, Tom."

"If I heard something about you, I would ask you about it
first."

"I'm done asking. I'm done listening to excuses."

"You're in the car? Where are you going? Stop being brave
and trying to do everything yourself. Let me help you. Talk to
me."

Madison felt herself getting hysterical. Her life was falling
around her ears and she didn't know up from down; people
she'd trusted were betraying her while pointing out her character flaws. "I don't know how else to be and I don't trust you
anymore. I don't know if I trust anyone."

There was a message on the electronic freeway sign up ahead.
The cars in front of her were slowing to read the sign, which

Madison always found ironic: sometimes the sign just said *Drive Safely*, but it caused people to take their eyes off the road in order to read it. This time the sign had a license plate and a message. As she got closer, she could see that it said: *Call 911 if seen. Presumed Armed.* That was a new one to Madison. She stared at the message for ten seconds before it finally sunk in: it was her own license plate. *Black Ford Explorer, license 74BMC239.* All over California motorists were being told that Madison was armed and to call 911 if her car was seen. She was being hunted. She was prey.

Her words came out in a whisper. "My God, Tom, what have you done?"

Chapter Twenty-Five

Madison pressed the button on her steering wheel to disconnect the call. Her hysteria of a moment ago had been replaced by an eerie calm; she was in survival mode. She didn't need to go into downtown and get near police headquarters while there was some kind of warrant out for her arrest. She had no idea how Tom had managed this, but she didn't have time to figure it out. She needed to get off the road, she needed to get rid of her phone which could easily trace her location, and she needed to find a quiet place where she could think. She couldn't go to the police station now; it would be her word against Tom's. He had made the perfect move: no one would believe a word she said now.

She couldn't call Dave, not after that blowup. She didn't have anyone else she could call who would drop everything and help her while she was being hunted by the police. It took a special kind of person for that. Then she realized that wasn't exactly true: Haley would help her.

She'd met Haley when she handled her last case. Madison had underestimated Haley because she looked like Marilyn Monroe and sounded like her too. Madison could be critical of women who seemed to exploit their own sexuality. While working with her, Madison had discovered that Haley wasn't just smart—she was smarter than Madison. And she wasn't exploiting anything; she was just being herself. Now Haley was an attorney for a high-priced law firm in downtown San Diego. Haley would be able to help her figure out what to do.

Madison was well aware that someone on that freeway could be calling 911 right then to turn her in. She had to act fast. She had to get rid of the car somehow. Her mind was racing as she scanned the vehicles near her to see if anyone noticed her car or her license plate. The drivers near her seemed to be oblivious.

She didn't want to call Haley from her cell phone in case her cell phone records were obtained, and the police would then know who had helped her. She jumped off the freeway at Balboa. She needed to get a disposable phone that couldn't be traced to her. Her best bet was to put her car in a parking lot with a lot of other cars so that it wasn't as noticeable. She pulled into the lot for the Target shopping center. The parking lot served the Target store as well as tons of stores and restaurants. It was crammed morning till night, and fortunately Target was open until midnight; Madison would just make it before closing. She found a parking space up against some shrubs and backed her car in. She crawled into the back and pulled open her tool kit, grabbed a screwdriver, and got out of the car.

She glanced around. Nobody was paying attention to her; they were hurrying into Target or trying to find parking places or trying to get booze for the party that was lasting longer than they'd thought. She knelt down and quickly unscrewed the license plate on the front of her car. She grabbed the plate and threw it underneath the back seat. Tom was continuing to blow up her phone. She would only have it for a short time longer, but she needed to get phone numbers out of it before she tossed it, and the ringing and beeping were driving her insane. She opened his contact and blocked his number. She got her purse and a hat and walked into Target.

She had no idea if Tom had given a description of her as part of the BOLO, but she had to figure he had. She didn't know what he'd told them she'd done. How had he gotten a judge to sign off on a warrant when she hadn't done anything? If she tried to figure that out now, she would be paralyzed. She had to keep moving.

She put her hair up in the hat. She had sunglasses on. But nothing could disguise her height or her frame. There would be cameras everywhere in Target, but they didn't feed directly into the police station. Someone would have to know she'd been there, get a warrant to pull the tape, and look at it; and what would they see? Madison shopping. And by then she'd be long gone.

She pulled a shopping cart out and put her purse in it. She found the section with electronics and selected two prepaid phones. They would work out of the box without Madison having to give any identifying information. She didn't want to look quite so obvious at checkout—"Hi, I'm in your store because I need to make phone calls that can't be traced"—so she collected a few other things in her cart that she would need anyway: a duffle bag, some snacks, a pack of Hanes men's V-neck T-shirts, underwear, another pair of yoga pants, a black hoodie, and Lee Child's latest book—because she saw it sitting there, and it comforted her to have a new book.

She quickly checked out at the register. Fortunately, she always had a hundred-dollar bill folded up and tucked into her wallet for emergencies. She didn't want the police to know which phones she'd bought so they could get a report of the phone calls she'd made, which they would do if they traced her credit card to this store and saw her purchases. The girl at the register had hair with a pink wash in it and huge plastic baubles hanging from her ears.

"Can you activate these phones for me?"

The girl kept scanning the rest of Madison's items. "You can go to the website to do that."

Madison didn't want to go to a website, and she didn't have her laptop with her anyway. "I know, but I need to use them now, and I don't have my laptop. My sister is at Sharp Memorial in the ER, and she's going into surgery. I don't have anything with me, and I left my cell phone at home in Vista. I have to call all our relatives and make sure someone picks up her little girl from the dad's house. He's not supposed to even have the little girl without supervision, but my sister had a stroke and someone had to pick up my niece from school—"

"Okay, okay," the girl said. "Go over to the customer service counter, and they can help you."

This was way too many people that were getting a good look at Madison and hearing her voice. But she had to get the phones activated. She went over to the customer service desk. A nice guy with a tie said he'd be happy to help. He looked like he was dressing for the job he wanted, not the job he had; Madison always thought that was a good idea. He got on the store phone and plugged in numbers and pushed buttons, and the phones were activated in no time. Madison thanked him and quickly exited the store.

As long as her car was backed up against the shrubs, no one could see her license plate and she was fairly safe. She got in the car and opened her own cell phone and wrote down Haley's phone numbers. She didn't know anyone's phone number by heart. It said something about her life that there was really no one else she could call. She glanced through her recent calls list and saw names connected with this investigation, but no one who could help her in her present predicament. Well, Arlo the computer guy, who was finding out where the Twitter account originated from; it was probably Tom's Twitter account but she might need Arlo for something else, so she wrote down his number. Then she came to Ken. Could he help her? Might as well write down his number. She could figure that out later. She paused to stare at her phone. No one else to call. She turned her phone off.

She wasn't sure if her phone could be traced even if it was off, so she opened her car door and threw it in the bushes. If the phone somehow still tracked while off, they would be directed to a Target parking lot and she would be long gone.

Nothing to make you feel untethered like throwing your phone away. No one could reach her. It gave her a weird sense of freedom. She didn't want to even be parked near her turned-off, discarded phone, so she moved her car to the other side of the parking lot and backed into a space to cover her license plate. She would've removed the back plate, but that alone could get her pulled over, so she was damned if she did and damned if she didn't; and having no front plate in California could get her

pulled over as well. Law enforcement wanted to be able to identify people at all times. Madison had never thought about the
ramifications and the "Big Brother" Orwellian aspect of that, at
least not until it was she who was being sought. Again, no time
for pondering.

She called Haley from the burner phone. It was after midnight, so she was hoping the lateness of the hour would cause
enough curiosity that Haley would answer a call from a number
she didn't recognize.

Madison was right. "Hello?"

"Haley, it's Madison. Don't say my name if there's someone
with you. I'm in trouble and I need help."

"It's kind of late to be calling, Mr. Samuels. I know I'm your
attorney, but I also have a personal life, and I'd appreciate some
respect for my time."

Okay, Haley wasn't alone. "The police are looking for me,
but I didn't do anything wrong. I need a car and a place to stay."

"And I'll be in the office at eight AM as usual."

"Can you meet me in the garage of the Horton Plaza Mall
in like twenty minutes? Meet me by Macy's. And somehow I
need a car. But we can't switch, because you do *not* want mine.
The police are looking for it. I mean, if you can meet me maybe
we can figure it all out?"

"That's perfect, Mr. Samuels. I'll see you then." Haley
disconnected.

If Haley hadn't been a powerhouse attorney, Madison
would've insisted they work together as PIs. Haley had a natural
instinct for subterfuge that couldn't be taught. You either could
think on your feet or you couldn't. Madison hadn't talked to

Haley in a while, so she didn't know who she would be hanging out with at midnight; a boyfriend? God knew Haley could have any guy she wanted.

Madison decided to leave the front license plate off. She only had to drive about ten miles to Horton Plaza in downtown. She would drive it on city streets so that she wasn't on the freeway with the electronic signs blasting her license plate. She would drive sedately and not attract attention.

She exited the Target parking lot and drove south on Genesee. She made it less than a mile before a cop came out of a 7-Eleven and started driving behind her. *My God there are a lot of police in San Diego*, Madison thought. She tried to breathe and not overreact. Just because they were behind her didn't mean they were after her. It didn't mean they recognized her license plate, and it didn't mean they would even run her plate. They could be eating their 7-Eleven snacks and telling old war stories. She tried not to look in the rearview mirror or side-view mirror. She drove one mile an hour over the speed limit, because most people did, and then put her cruise control on so that her speed would be consistent. Several other cars came up behind the cop car, but no one wanted to be the one who passed a cop. So they ended up all in a train, with Madison in the lead.

Madison started to sing. The radio was off, but she figured that if she sang, she could lower her heart rate and blood pressure, and maybe the cops would sense her nonchalance. She started singing "Somewhere Over the Rainbow," because it was the first thing that came to mind. Halfway through the song, it struck her as so melancholy that she stopped abruptly; if bluebirds could fly over the rainbow, why indeed couldn't she? How had she gotten to this point in her life, where she was running through the night with the police hunting her?

There was a housing development coming up on the right up a hill; fortunately, having a job that involved driving all over meant that Madison knew every part of San Diego County like the back of her hand. She decided to take the long road that led up the hill into the development, which had pricier homes for this area. She couldn't hope to outrun a cop; the minute they realized she was running they would call the helicopter and it could be there in mere minutes. So first she had to determine if they were actually following her. She made the right, and the cop followed. This was not good. There would be no reason for a cop on regular patrol to come up the hill into this neighborhood. The road led nowhere other than into more housing developments. That meant they'd decided they were interested in Madison's car. Were they waiting for backup before pulling over the "armed and dangerous" suspect? Madison needed to lose them, and she needed to do it before ABLE, the airborne law enforcement unit helicopter, was called to watch her from the sky. She took the first left into a maze of homes, all built in the 1980s and packed into streets that began with the world *Old*: Old Bridgeport, Old Heather, etc. The cop made the turn after her. It was official: they were following her. They were just waiting for other units to arrive to make the felony stop. She had to outrun a cop, which was impossible. That meant she needed good old-fashioned luck.

Madison increased her speed slightly so that she could make the next turn without them. If she could turn right up ahead and be out of their sight even momentarily, she would have about thirty seconds to disappear before they turned after her and continued their tail. They would be expecting her to maintain her current speed after the turn. She made the right; then she floored the gas and sped up to sixty miles per hour while she was out of their view. She skipped the next right—the one they would assume she'd taken when they turned and didn't see her, just based on the speed she'd been going when they last saw her—and turned right at the second street. She raced down two blocks and made a left; they would just be turning onto that first street and wondering where she was. She accelerated fast and made the next left; now she was two streets away from them. They would be making the next right, thinking that was where she'd gone, based on the speed she'd been going. As she sped along, two streets away from them, she saw manna from heaven: an open garage door attached to a darkened house. Someone had left home and left the garage door up. She pulled into the garage just as she heard the siren begin two streets over; they'd just realized she'd ditched them. They weren't playing anymore. Another siren joined the chorus—backup had arrived. She jumped out of her car and ran to the right side of the garage door; no button to close the garage. She raced to the left wall. There it was. She pushed the button and nothing happened. She was literally a sitting duck right now. If the cops came down the street, which they would any minute, they would see her car up the short driveway and her standing right next to it, just waiting to be taken in. She pressed the button again. Nothing. What if it were broken and that's why it had been left open? She took a deep breath. She'd found that mechanical things almost had a spiritual component to them.

If you were upset or frantic, they didn't work. The sirens were getting closer.

"It's time for you to close now." She took another deep breath, let it out, and slowed her heart rate. She flowed admiration at the garage door and its opener. It was pretty. More sirens, closer now. It was loved. It would work. She pressed the button.

The door creaked and started a slow descent. "Come on come on come on come on come on," Madison chanted under her breath. "You can do it. I believe in you garage door."

The door came all the way down, and she was in darkness.

A siren came by the front of the house; she'd been moments away from capture. She stood still and listened to the silence as the siren passed. She was waiting for her eyes to adjust to the dark before she started exploring her new hiding place. Then she heard the helicopter. They had called it in to assist in the search, and it was circling the neighborhood.

She walked carefully to the door leading to the house. Unlocked. These people were pretty trusting, or maybe just absent-minded. She slowly opened the door and listened. One of her abilities was a heightened sense of sound. A guy had once told her that she had bat hearing. Normally it was just an inconvenience, since the sound of people whistling or humming could drive her around the bend. Now it helped her. She listened to the sounds of an empty house: refrigerator buzzing, undisturbed air, a kitchen clock ticking gently; no other sounds. She made kissing sounds softly to see if a dog lived here. Nothing. She stepped into the house.

Well now she had committed a crime: breaking and entering. If she got before a judge, she would argue that the door was unlocked and therefore she wasn't breaking, just entering. Right now she just needed to get a hold of Haley, since she was clearly not making it downtown to Horton Plaza. She went back to the car and grabbed the burner phone. She could hear sirens outside going up and down the streets, and suddenly there was an intense light shining under the garage door. She froze. It passed, and she realized it was a cop car driving by with the spotlight on, shining it along at the houses, looking for her or her car peeking out from somewhere. After the light passed, she went back into the house and shut the door.

When were these people coming home? First things first: she didn't need the surprise of an entire family coming home to an intruder. She went to the calendar on the refrigerator, the center of all households. The days up until yesterday were crossed off. On today's date it said *Vacation*, and the next week was blocked off. *Bingo*. She knew that often neighbors watched out for each other, but if that were the case, wouldn't someone have reached in and pushed the button to close the garage? Maybe these people weren't close with their neighbors. Unless everyone knew the garage door was "broken" and they were just watching the front of the house.

She called Haley. "Change of plans."

"Okay."

"Are you alone?"

"For a minute."

"I got spotted. The cops are really looking for me. They know they lost me in this section of town, so I can't drive my car again. I'm hiding in someone's house and my car's in their garage."

"How did you—"

"No time."

"Right."

"I'm going to give you the address. Can you meet me here and drive me somewhere so I can get a car?"

"I'm going to bring you a car."

"Okay great. Here is the address."

Madison grabbed a bunch of papers and receipts off a spindle on the counter. There was one for Tina and Jack Williams at an address that matched the street Madison knew she'd turned down. She read it to Haley.

"Thank you, Mr. Samuels. Yes, I'm sure that will be fine. Please stop calling now."

Madison disconnected. Now she just had to wait for Haley. What she didn't want to do was think. She needed to stay in action mode or her hysteria might just come back. Once she had a car, she could decide where she was going in it. She didn't think it was safe to stay here. The neighbors were a problem. It was officially the middle of the night, so Madison decided to hope the neighbors were asleep. It would keep her from getting frantic before Haley got there. But she couldn't stay here all night. And just in case, she left the lights out. Haley pulling up might attract some attention, but Madison hoped not.

Madison realized the sound of the helicopter was gone. Probably called to a more pressing matter. The police could still be in the neighborhood, though.

She wandered around the house. She found a den set up as an office with a computer. It wasn't the newest setup, but practical. It would be good if she could have access to her database if she needed it. She walked around and sat in the desk chair. The computer was off, so she hit the power switch and waited. Didn't most people have a password on their computer? She knew she did. The screen lit up, and she could see the desktop; no password needed.

Now what? She had no plan, something she wasn't used to and she didn't like. Even in the past few months while she'd been trying to decide how she wanted her life to go, she'd had a plan—the plan was to take time to figure it out. Now she had no direction and no idea of how to get one. Where would she sleep tonight? Hopefully Haley would put her IQ toward helping to figure this out, or at least talking it out with her might help.

Madison suddenly remembered another number she'd written down: Ken's. He had said to call him if she needed "help with Tom." Had he known what was brewing? Had he known Tom was going off the deep end? And if she called him, how exactly might he help her? She might as well try. But for all she knew, he was sitting next to Tom right now, so she dialed *67 before his number, thereby blocking the number of her burner phone.

"Hello?" He sounded dubious at answering an unknown number.

"It's Madison."

"Oh fuck. Oh Madison. Thank God you called. I've been worried. Where are you?"

He sounded genuinely concerned, which inexplicably made her want to cry.

"Why is Tom doing this?"

He paused before answering. "I don't know, Madison. He just . . . I don't know."

"What is his end game? Like just torture me? Or am I supposed to call him for him to save me? Is that it? Some kind of weird Munchausen's by proxy where he puts me in a situation that only he can help me out of?"

"I don't know. He's acting crazy. He was trying to call you and your phone was going to voicemail, and now I don't even know where he is. I tried to call you too just to tell you what was going on. Where are you? I can come get you and we'll figure this out."

It was tempting. She really couldn't do this by herself. It was something she'd thought she'd never feel: that she couldn't get herself out of a problem by using her wits.

"I was driving, and then these cops came behind me. I had to try to get away from them. They even brought a helicopter out! So I was—"

There was a light tapping at the front door. Could Haley have made it so quickly?

"Hang on." She ran to the door and looked through the peephole: it was Haley. She must have come from someplace nearby. Madison opened the door and scanned the street. Haley's white BMW was at the curb, but so was a brand-new black Range Rover.

"Don't be mad." Haley walked past Madison into the house, and Madison shut the door.

Madison put the phone back to her ear. "Ken, I have to go. I'll call you back."

"Wait! How will I reach you? Let me come get you—"

Madison disconnected and faced Haley. "How can I be mad? You're helping me."

"Because you will be." Madison was struck by Haley's beauty every time she saw her. It was almost painful to look at. "My boyfriend's in the Range Rover outside."

"Oh." Madison didn't want another person involved, but if Haley trusted him, she figured she could.

"And there's more." Haley went over to the sectional and sat, barely touching the edge of the sofa with her designer jeans, Prada blouse, and Louboutin heels; the middle of the night and she still managed to be better dressed than Madison on a good day. "He's a deputy district attorney."

Okay this was bad. "Haley. Why did you tell him?"

"Because you kept calling so late I didn't want him to think I was cheating on him. He's really a good guy, Madison."

Madison was sure he was. Normally Madison would consider a deputy DA to be a real catch. But not when she was running from the police.

"He insisted on making a few calls about you. So he knows you're wanted and considered armed."

Madison stood up fast. She looked around for her purse. She'd just have to run for it in her own car.

"Sit down, sit down! I got him to see that you wouldn't be asking me for help if you'd actually done something. That you know I'm an attorney and you wouldn't put me in that position. I'm right . . . right?"

Madison sighed. "Yes, you're right." She sat down. "So, he's going to give me a ten-minute head start before he calls the police, or what?"

Haley stood up and went to the window and peered out. "No, no. He's letting me give you my car, and he's going to forget the whole thing. But he won't let me help you beyond that. I'm to drop the car and we're leaving."

Letting me. Won't let me. This was why Madison didn't have a boyfriend.

"Okay. Well, I appreciate the car." Madison had hoped that she'd have a partner in crime, so to speak, and Haley would stay and help her figure out what to do. That they would do this together.

Haley stood up but lost her balance in the high heels and fell back down to the couch. "Jesus." She stood up again and gave Madison an awkward hug. "I'm on your team. I really am. I just have to be careful. You understand, right?"

Madison understood. If their situations were reversed . . . no, if their situations were reversed, Madison would help her. But Madison wasn't an officer of the court, and Haley and her boyfriend were.

"I understand."

They walked to the door together, and Haley handed her the keys to the BMW. "Just keep it. I need a new car anyway."

Madison could never do surveillance in a pearl-white BMW with red leather interior. But hey, she could sell it and buy something else. "Thank you, Haley, I appreciate it. If anything comes up . . . just tell them I stole the car."

Haley didn't say anything. Madison realized that she and her boyfriend had already come up with that plan; that was the only reason he "let" Haley give Madison her car. So this meant if Madison got caught, they would actually have a criminal offense she had committed: grand theft auto, a felony. Up until now everything that was going on had been a mistake or lies. This would be an actual crime. Was Haley helping her or hurting her right now? Well, Madison needed a car. So this was the price.

Madison opened the door, and Haley vamped down the walkway and got into the passenger seat of the Range Rover. Her boyfriend hadn't even turned off the car. The car sped away down the street. Madison was alone.

Chapter
Twenty-Six

Madison closed the door and walked back to the office. She sat at the desk. She'd always enjoyed her alone time; apparently that was a fault, according to Dave. But it was just the way she was. But this was more alone than she'd ever felt in her life. Haley had been her last lifeline, and even that had been taken away from her. She decided that if she started wallowing in her misery, the family would come home from their vacation in a week and find her sobbing on the couch. *Sometimes if you start crying you'll never stop.*

She picked up the phone to call Ken back but put it down again. She didn't consider him a lifeline at this point. He was too close to Tom. No matter how nice he was, she couldn't trust him not to give her away to Tom. In trying to help her, he might tell Tom where she was or want them to "work it out"—and thereby give her away unwittingly. No. She was on her own. He had told her all he could, and talking to him would give her a false sense of security.

She decided to check her Twitter, since anyone trying to reach her would likely try her there. Sure enough, there were a couple of direct messages for her. The first was from Arlo: *Hey what's new? Give me a call.* He must have information on the computer used to set up the Twitter account that had tweeted her. *Let me guess, a guy named Tom?* She would call him later.

The next direct message was from Josie: *I'm trying to reach you. It's urgent.*

Madison messaged back: *I don't have my phone. Call me at this number*—and she included the burner phone number.

Then she saw she had a message from Felicity. She would have checked that first if she'd seen it. She opened it and with rising panic tried to comprehend what Felicity was saying:

I know who it is. But the police won't believe me *because it's a cop.* I'm going to confront him. I know it's dangerous but I don't want to be afraid anymore. You're not afraid. I can do this. I'll get him to confess. I'll record it. I'll find out where Samantha is and bring her home.

My God, what is she doing? Madison looked at the time: Felicity had sent this message an hour ago. Madison started typing frantically.

Felicity don't do this! I lost my phone. Call me: 858-555-4278. This is not bravery this is stupidity! It doesn't make you brave to do something reckless! Please!

This was all Madison's fault. If she'd reported Tom to his supervisor when he started stalking her, he wouldn't be around for Felicity to contact. How did Felicity know who it was? Or think she knew? And something Madison had said or done had made Felicity think *this* was a brave thing to do? She was going to be brave "like Madison"?

Madison opened a new window on the browser and pulled up her PI database. She entered her password, put in Felicity's name, and requested a comprehensive report. She was looking for a pen to write down Felicity's address when the doorbell rang.

Madison froze. Should she ignore it? Someone was ringing the doorbell in the middle of the night. She tiptoed to the foyer and looked through the peephole. It was a middle-aged woman wearing a big fuzzy bathrobe and holding a cell phone with carefully manicured nails. She had permanent makeup creating eyebrows and lip liner on her sleepy face. She had obviously seen Haley and the two cars. She was pretty brave to knock on the door. Madison didn't know what the night would bring, but she wanted to at least be able to leave her car in the garage for the time being. If she could trick this woman into calming down and not calling the police, which would probably be her next move if Madison didn't answer the door, she could buy herself some time. She opened the door.

Madison put on her cheeriest face. "Hi! You're up late."

The woman was taken aback by Madison's confidence. She went for a haughty response. "I'm sorry, have we met?"

"I think so. At Jack and Tina's last party, maybe?" Madison hoped to God Jack and Tina were the entertaining type.

"That could be. They have so many parties." *Bingo.*

"Can I help you with something?" Madison managed to put the slightest tinge of irritation in her voice while still remaining polite.

"Oh. Well, I just saw cars and people, and I thought Jack and Tina were going out of town yesterday. And then there were sirens and the police helicopter . . . so I just wondered."

My God you're dumb, Madison thought. *You think some criminals that the police are looking for are in your neighbor's house, so you go knock on the door?* "I see. That makes sense. I think it's important that neighbors look out for each other." Madison was trying not to explain. Explanations sounded like excuses, which sounded like being defensive. If she had a right to be there she wouldn't be making excuses.

The woman wanted more. "Anyway . . . I just thought I would check if everything was okay . . . ?"

"Well, that was kind of you. I'll let Jack and Tina know that you were concerned. I'm sure they'll appreciate it."

The idea that the nosy neighbor was going to get a nice word put in with Jack and Tina seemed to be the thing that sealed the deal. Jack and Tina would know that she was the one who had observed unusual activity and gone across the street to check it out. Jack and Tina would be happy that she had been nosy. "Alrighty then. Well, you have a good night. Sorry to disturb you." She still sounded a little bit confused, but her doubt seemed to have turned toward herself: *Did I come over here for no reason? I think maybe I did.*

"You too, dear. Have a good night, hon." Madison found that if you called middle-aged woman dear and hon, they naturally felt you were older and more knowledgeable, even if you were clearly thirty years younger. They seemed to relax into being patronized. Madison shut the door.

She ran back to the office and checked to see if Felicity had responded to the direct message. She had not. What on earth was she doing? And where was she going to meet Tom? Was she just going to call him? Or try to meet him somewhere? Or have him come over? Madison didn't have Felicity's phone number in the burner phone, and no phone number came up in the comprehensive report. Madison had to rely on the direct message to reach her—or else she would just have to go to Felicity's house and see if she was home; if not, Madison would track her from there. She finished writing down Felicity's address. She erased the history from the browser and turned the computer off.

She went back to the living room and grabbed her purse and the keys to Haley's BMW. She suddenly remembered her bag of belongings from Target; she might need that. She went into the garage and grabbed the Target shopping bags from the back of her SUV—and saw the balloon. The white memorial balloon with the message inside. She got a utility knife from the console and popped the balloon; she put the message in her pocket. Back inside, she took one last look around. She hadn't turned on any lights, so there was nothing to turn off.

The dilemma would be how she was going to get back into the house. She checked out the lock on the front door: if she shut the door, it would lock automatically. She went back to the kitchen and dining area and searched for a garage door opener. If she made it back, the main thing she would need would be her car. She could access the house from the garage, so a garage door opener handled all of her problems. She just had to find one.

She finally found it on the kitchen counter in a bowl that had some mismatched screws and nails, a plastic part to some unknown plastic item, and a set of keys. She took the keys and ran to the front door, opening it slightly. The keys didn't fit. The garage door opener would have to do; she would have to pray that it worked. She didn't dare test it out, because she didn't need the garage door opening right now and her car being visible.

She gathered all of her belongings, walked out the front door, and got into the BMW. She had to move the seat back to accommodate her legs; Haley was tall, but not as tall as Madison. She started the car and took off. Her Ford Explorer was fast, with a lot of power, but nothing beat the pickup of a BMW. If she was being hunted and it was the worst night of her life, at least she was driving a BMW.

She drove out of the neighborhood slowly and entered Felicity's address into the BMW's navigation system. Felicity lived in North Park, another suburb of downtown that was full of architecture that Madison loved: California Craftsman homes like Ryan's, built in the early part of the twentieth century, many of them since certified as historic homes.

Madison decided to call Arlo on the way; he was a night owl, so she knew he'd be up.

"Hello?"

"Hi, Arlo, it's Madison."

"I wondered what had happened to you."

"I know, it's been rather hectic. This is my phone number for the time being."

"Cool. Anyway, I wanted to ask you: what have you gotten me into?"

It was hard for anything to shock Madison at this point. But she honestly didn't know what was coming next. "What do you mean?"

"I was able to find out which computer was used to open the Twitter account MaddieKelly12. I can't tell you where the person ended up tweeting you from, but I can tell you where the account was opened."

"Okay. I'm ready. What computer was used to open that Twitter account?"

"A computer in the lobby of the San Diego Police Department headquarters on Broadway in San Diego."

Madison shouldn't have been surprised at this point. She would have thought Tom wouldn't use a computer at the police station, but he was always there. He was smart enough not to use the computer at his desk. And he probably didn't know that Madison would try to figure out who had opened the account, or if she did, that she had someone like Arlo who could find out so much that he scared the government.

"Thank you, Arlo. I haven't gotten you into anything. No one can tell you traced that, right?"

"Oh, don't be silly."

"That's what I thought. I'll talk to you soon." They disconnected the call. Madison didn't consider telling him what was going on; they didn't have that kind of relationship. If she needed something specific from him later, she would call back.

Madison got off the freeway at the exit for North Park. She drove through the not-great part of town on her way to Felicity's house. Madison had noticed that most communities surrounding the entrance and exits to freeways were not very nice. Probably because nobody with money wanted to live next to a freeway.

Madison turned onto Felicity's street. It was a quiet neighborhood of small bungalows, some of them Craftsman and some of them just imitating the Craftsman style. Felicity's was small, probably two small bedrooms and one small bathroom, on the corner of Myrtle Avenue and an alley. One whole side of her little bungalow was along an alley. Madison was looking for Tom's Crown Victoria or his Ford sedan but didn't see them on her approach. She didn't have time to make a search of the neighborhood. She had to make sure Felicity was okay, if she was even home.

She parked two doors down. She took off the Ralph Lauren Olympics jacket and threw it in the back of the car; she didn't need to stand out more than she already did. She ran to Felicity's front gate, through it, and up the steps to the front door and started banging on the door. She yelled through the door. "Felicity! It's Madison! Open the door!" She cupped her hands to the curtained window in the door but couldn't see through. There was a light on near the back of the house. She walked down the steps and around the corner into the alley. There was a long fence, six feet high, protecting the house and the backyard. Madison grabbed a milk crate next to a trash can and propped it next to the fence. The milk crate wasn't tall enough for her to get all of her core muscles utilized to help her over the fence. She ran back and got the actual trash bin and brought it over to the fence. She used the fence to pull herself up on the trash bin, onto her knees. It was plastic and nearly empty, so it wasn't steady or prepared to hold her weight. She needed to get over the fence before the trash can collapsed.

Her pectoral muscles had never been the same since the plastic surgeon sliced through them in order to put implants underneath. She regretted getting the plastic surgery, especially in moments like this. Who cared if you had pretend boobs if you had no strength in your upper body? She yanked and pulled and used every muscle in her upper back and torso and managed to yank herself over the fence and fall to the other side, landing on her hip. It really stung, but she had to keep moving.

She jumped to her feet. She had made a huge racket trying to get over the fence. She was surprised Felicity had not come to the back door, and if someone were inside with her, he must have heard her. Tom. *Why can't I say "Tom?"* She made it to the back door, which was two French doors with tiny pains of beveled glass. She could see that this was the room the light was coming from. She could see movement but not much else. She heard a sound from inside. It sounded like a dove cooing. The door was locked.

She looked to her right and saw gardening tools: gardening gloves and a metal trowel and other implements. She put the gloves on and grabbed the trowel and smashed it through one of the small panes of glass. She reached her arm through the broken glass and unlocked the door.

Felicity was lying in a pool of blood on the floor, staring straight at Madison. She was trying to indicate something with her eyes, which were huge and round.

"Is he still here?" Felicity couldn't talk. She couldn't communicate at all. She just stared at Madison like she wanted to say something but couldn't. There was blood gushing out of her neck.

Madison had left her purse with the gun in it in the car. She didn't make a very good outlaw. She grasped the trowel in her hand, which was at least metal and sharp, and raced through the house, searching. She made it to the front door; it was standing open. He must have heard Madison coming over the fence, stabbed Felicity, and left.

Madison went back to Felicity and tried to assess the situation quickly. Her arms were tied behind her; her legs had been tied but had been loosened. Her clothes were on, but her jeans were undone and halfway down her hips; it looked like he'd tried to pull them off but had stopped. Madison must have interrupted him; *at least there's that.* Madison wasn't going to think about what would've happened if she hadn't interrupted. Madison took the gardening gloves off and lifted Felicity's hair and saw that the blood was coming from a wound in her neck: he had stabbed her with a letter opener that was still protruding from her neck. It seemed to Madison that she had interrupted his plans, so he had grabbed the nearest weapon to end Felicity's life quickly so she wouldn't be a witness. But she wasn't dead yet.

Madison grabbed the house phone from the bedside table and called 911.

"Nine-one-one, what is your emergency?"

"A woman has been stabbed in the neck. She is bleeding profusely. There isn't much time." Madison gave the address.

"Who stabbed her? What's your name?"

Madison knew that 911 operators could dispatch the fire department and the police on a keyboard while keeping the reporting person on the phone talking. These were important questions that would be recorded and listened to later. But Madison wasn't going to discuss anything other than getting Felicity help.

Madison dropped the phone, but she left it off the hook so they could continue to trace the call and use GPS to find Felicity if needed. Madison jumped up and went to the bathroom and grabbed a towel. She came back to Felicity and held the towel to her throat. She knew better than to remove the letter opener; it could be the only thing keeping Felicity from bleeding to death. She ran over to a small desk and opened the drawers, looking for scissors; found them. She sat on the floor behind Felicity to cut her bindings. They seemed to be drapery cord, tied using intricate knots. Felicity groaned as her arms and legs fell down into a more natural position. Madison left the scissors and cut cords on the floor behind Felicity. She cradled Felicity's head in her lap, trying to keep her neck straight and the handle of the letter opener from causing any more damage. She pressed the towel into Felicity's neck, trying to slow the bleeding.

"Just stay with me, Felicity. You were very brave. Don't give up now."

Felicity had been watching Madison, but now her eyes didn't seem to be focusing.

"Think of all you have to do in your life. Think of Josie. How much she loves you. Or did you not know that? She does.

Even if you don't love her, she wouldn't make it through without you."

Felicity's eyelids fluttered; it seemed she was straining to keep them open.

"I know you have dreams, Felicity. Think of your dreams; they didn't die with Samantha. You have your whole life ahead of you. But you have to stay here and stick it out with the rest of us. We are so close to catching the guy. You helped—he made a lot of mistakes tonight, and you will help catch him. You have to stick around and see this through."

Felicity had closed her eyes, and Madison felt like she was slipping away. "Do not leave me, Felicity! Stay with me!" Madison started crying. She was rubbing Felicity's forehead and trying to hold pressure on the wound in her neck at the same time, without pushing the letter opener in further. She could hear the sirens now; they were getting closer. When the piercing shrill stopped in front of the house, Madison set Felicity's head gently on the ground and leaped up. She was covered in Felicity's blood. She ran out the back door and dragged a patio table to the fence. She climbed up onto the table and jumped over, landing on her feet in the alley.

She ran to the mouth of the alley but stopped abruptly and stood against the fence before she got to the street. She peered around the corner. It was one paramedic unit and one fire truck. The paramedic unit members had gone inside the open front door, and the firemen were gathering supplies and getting ready to go in. She waited. The firemen went inside. She assumed the driver was still in the driver's seat, but he was way on the other side of the truck and wouldn't see Madison. She could hear more sirens; the police would be here in moments. She stepped out of the alley and turned left. She had two doors to walk past, and then she got in the BMW. She made a U-turn so that she did not drive past Felicity's house again. She was out of the neighborhood in thirty seconds.

Chapter
Twenty-Seven

Madison drove down 30th until she was out of North Park. Even though the police were not looking for a white BMW, she didn't need to tempt fate by staying near Felicity's house. She turned a few corners until she was once again in a quiet neighborhood. She pulled over and parked in front of some bushes between two homes. Whenever she was doing surveillance, she found that parking between houses was the best bet; one house thought she was visiting the other house and vice versa. This was a nice neighborhood, and there were other BMWs parked on the street. She turned off the car and put her hands in her lap.

Madison had been through a lot in her life. She had lost both her parents—nursed them and then watched them slip away and die of cancer. She'd had breast cancer. But she could honestly say that this was the lowest moment of her life.

She had held Felicity while the blood drained out of her. She had known Tom for ten years; she could not believe he would stab a girl in the neck with the closest sharp instrument because he was about to get caught. She couldn't believe that

Tom would kill anyone in cold blood, ever, but this was so bar-baric that it held everything she knew about Tom in stark relief, like a map of a mountain range. The things sticking up were the things she could imagine Tom doing, in his worst moments in the worst of times of his life; this was not one of them. She remembered reading a book about Ted Bundy, the infamous serial killer, written by a journalist who had been close friends with him. The journalist had not known that he was the serial killer they were all looking for; they had even discussed it between them. But that seemed like such an unusual and rare occurrence. Madison knew she could be dumb when it came to guys, but she didn't have feelings for Tom—not the kind of feelings that made her ignore red flags. And yet everything pointed to him. Every single thing. Arthur Conan Doyle had Sherlock Holmes say, "When you have eliminated the impossi-ble, whatever remains, however improbable, must be the truth." Had she eliminated the impossible? Tom had had her followed. Tom had had her activities monitored. Tom had left the notes. And who else but Tom could have access to the BOLO system of law enforcement?

She had eliminated every other possibility, at least. And what remained, Tom, was improbable, but it must be the truth.

She sat in the driver's seat unmoving while Felicity's blood dried on her clothes and her hands and arms. She was afraid to go back to the house where her car sat in the garage, because she was afraid the neighbor would see her and decide it was just too weird: Tina and Jack hadn't told her someone was going to watch her house, and now this strange girl was coming and going at all hours of the night. With blood all over her. If she went back, it needed to be in the morning and in the daylight when people might be at work. She would have to run in before anyone saw her. Then she remembered she had a bag of clothes she had bought at Target. Thank God. She grabbed the bag and changed her clothes in the front seat: a brand-new T-shirt and a brand-new pair of yoga pants. She balled up her bloody clothes and threw them in the back seat. She still had blood on her arms and her hands, but she could stop at a fast-food place and wash them in a sink, hopefully before anyone noticed her. And then what?

The burner phone rang. She had forgotten that she had given anyone the phone number and so it caused her to jump in her seat. She grabbed it and answered it.

"Hello?"

At first she couldn't figure out who it was or what they were saying. It was a woman crying. Hysterical.

"Who is this?"

More crying. And then, "It's Josie."

Apparently Josie knew about Felicity. The police must have hit redial on Felicity's cell phone, or else maybe they'd found Josie's name and number somewhere in the house.

"Okay, calm down. I know."

"You know? How do you know?"

Madison did not want to get into the fact that she'd been there. Frankly, she didn't want Josie to know she was in trouble right now. Josie was suspicious enough, and it was hard to explain things to her in the best of times. And right now, Madison didn't even understand what was going on.

"Yes, the police called me. I think they went through Felicity's phone, and she had called me yesterday."

"Oh, yes, that's how they got my number." Josie started crying again.

Madison tried to get her to talk. "Did they give you any idea of her condition?"

"No, they wouldn't tell me. They just said that she'd been stabbed."

"Do you know who she was planning to see? She sent me a DM on Twitter saying that she knew who it was and that it was a cop and she was going to confront him. Do you know what she was talking about?"

More crying. "It's all my fault."

"Josie. You need to calm down. I want to understand what's going on and I want to help. But I can't understand you when you're crying. What do you mean, it's your fault?"

Madison had found that if you gave someone sympathy when they were upset, it just made them cry harder. But if you told them kindly to knock it off, they generally did. Sure enough, Josie got it together. "I got Jethro to tell me what he did."

For a minute, Madison couldn't remember who Jethro was. It felt like she had lived two years in the last week. But how could she forget Jethro? The ape who was the manager at Hank's Dive. What did he have to do with this? "And? What did he do?"

"I got him drunk. I made him think I was going to sleep with him. He's such an idiot; he is so convinced of his manhood that he thinks a lesbian is going to sleep with him. Fucking asshole."

Madison was silent, wanting her to finish without interruption.

"I started talking about who was working there when Samantha went missing. I asked him about the bouncer that was creepy, and I said, 'What was his name? Larry?' And he said yes. And then I asked if Larry was short for Oliver."

Someone turned on a porch light near where Madison was parked. She had such a loud voice that she wondered if it had carried in the silence of the night in this quiet neighborhood. She started the BMW and drove two streets over while Josie continued to talk.

"He laughed at me and said Oliver was a dweeb who got fired for stealing. He wasn't the bouncer. Then he said, 'You thought the bouncer was creepy? I liked him,' and I knew I had him."

Madison found another space between two houses to park. She pulled over and turned off the engine. She kept her voice soft and low. "So what was the bouncer's name? Was it on the list that I read you?"

"No! That's the thing. He told me that the bouncer wasn't creepy, because he was an ex-cop."

An ex-cop? Who in this scenario was an ex-cop? Tom was a current cop, and he certainly had never worked at Hank's as a bouncer. Madison had been doing all of her figuring assuming that the only current or former law enforcement connected to this case was Tom; if there were another, it would mean there was someone else who could've done all the things she'd been attributing to Tom.

"But was his name on the list of employees that they gave to the police?" Madison had been through the list that Tom had given her over and over, and she didn't remember seeing anyone who even seemed old enough to have been an ex-cop at some point.

Josie had picked up steam. "No, the guy's name was not on that list. The ex-cop/bouncer guy called Jethro on the phone after it hit the news that Samantha had been at the bar that night, and he told Jethro that he was helping the police on the investigation of Samantha's disappearance. He actually asked Jethro to compile that list of names and to have it ready for when the police called for it. I think the guy figured that the police would call for it, and Jethro was too stupid to see that he was being played. Because then the guy told him, 'Obviously, you don't need to put *my* name on the list, because I'm helping the police and they know that I worked there.' So Jethro left his name off the list of employees that he gave to the police."

This was it. Madison could feel it. Her skin was electrified. An ex-cop would explain everything: they might still have contacts within the police department and could get a BOLO put out on her. They could convince Ryan they were a cop—Ryan had never actually said Tom's name, had he? Had he? Hadn't he just said "a cop," and Madison had assumed he meant Tom?

Madison's heart was pounding. She turned on the car so she could roll down the window and get some air. "What was the guy's name?"

"His last name was Larrabee. Remember how I said we called him Larry? That's because of his last name. Larrabee. Larry."

Madison didn't remember anyone connected to this case with that last name. Could this be somebody completely new that she'd never heard of? Someone who hadn't come up in the investigation? That would explain why she hadn't figured it out so far.

"What was his first name?"

"Ken."

Madison sucked air in so fast that it caused her to inhale some saliva and she started coughing.

"Are you okay, Madison?"

Madison kept coughing, trying to get control of her breathing diaphragm and her nerves. My God, how could she have been so stupid? She had taken Ken's word for it that Tom had asked him to follow her. When Madison first met Ken, she'd thought he was a cop. And Madison was pretty familiar with cops. So if she'd thought he was a cop, probably other people had thought that as well, like Ryan. Which would mean that it was Ken who'd hired Ryan to document Madison's activities and to leave the notes on her door. It was Ken who'd made the phone call to Felicity, the wording of which matched the note left on Madison's door. Arlo had said that the MaddieKelly12 Twitter account had been opened on the computer in the lobby of the police department. Ken loved hanging out with cops at the cop bar; there was no reason to suspect that he wouldn't also hang out with his friends at headquarters and use the computer in the lobby. Everything that Madison had assigned to Tom worked for Ken as well, now that she knew Ken was an ex-cop.

Madison got her coughing under control. "I'm okay. So I guess you told Felicity all of this?"

Josie started to cry again. "Yes, I told her. Jethro gave me the application for this Larrabee guy from his personnel file, and I gave Felicity his address and phone number. I thought she wanted to see if she knew him. I didn't know she was going to try to confront him. I mean, how stupid? Why did she do that?"

"Because she wanted to be brave," Madison said to herself.

"What?"

"Nevermind. Right now, you need to go stay with a friend. You have been tweeting me, and you tweeted me asking me to call you. He follows me on Twitter, and he will have seen that. You need to get yourself to safety. Will you do that?"

"But what about Felicity?"

"I'm sure they are taking care of her at the hospital, and I'm sure that there's nothing you can do right now for her. You can, however, save yourself. He might be watching the hospital for either you or me, so don't go there, okay?"

It all made sense now, but Madison wasn't willing to completely buy it without some outside corroboration. She needed to talk to Ryan, to find out if he'd meant Tom or Ken when he said "a cop" had paid him to document Madison's activities. She didn't have his phone number in the burner phone. This meant that she had to go back to her apartment to see him. It was dangerous, but she had to confirm this theory before she was willing to call Tom.

"Yes, I will go to my friend's house. What are you going to do?" Josie asked.

"I'm going to catch him."

Madison disconnected the call and started the BMW. She still had blood all over her arms and hands, but she didn't want to stop to clean up. If it all went according to plan, she could get in the shower when she got home. What would that be like? A shower in her own apartment. The thought of it made her want to cry—the thought of her life before two weeks ago, before someone started stalking her, before her home didn't feel safe anymore. Back when she still had Dave.

She passed by the large homes on the eastern and then southern edge of Balboa Park. They were huge, built at the beginning of the twentieth century in the Spanish Colonial style, but late at night they looked spooky. Like haunted houses. She leaned over to get a glimpse into their second floors and saw no lights on, no toys in the front yard, no individual style other than the historic architecture. Madison loved historic homes, but these seemed to have no soul. Then she realized that anyone looking out the window at her would see a woman covered in blood staring up at their windows. She was the one who was spooky tonight.

She didn't know how Ken could have gotten a BOLO put out on her, getting her license plate put on electronic signs on the freeway, without being current law enforcement. But he had a lot more chance of doing it then someone who didn't used to be a cop. It was conceivable that he could've done it. And it made so much more sense than Tom.

As she took the exit onto La Jolla Parkway from the 5 freeway, she thought back to her dealings with Ken. He had seemed so charming. It was hard for her to believe even now that he was the stalker and the killer. She normally would have noticed a red flag with a guy like this, but not this time. She had totally trusted him. She tried not to beat herself up: if he were a true sociopath, she wouldn't have been able to tell. They didn't have the remorse or shame that was normally the thing Madison picked up on. Sociopaths could lie with abandon, and when it came down to it, they could even admit their crimes freely and fully with no sense of responsibility. Madison didn't think she'd ever met one before. There was always a first time.

She didn't park in her parking space. She pulled up on Bonair and parked in front of Ryan's house. She went to the front door but then realized everybody would be asleep and she'd have better luck tapping on his window. She went to the back of his house, cautiously, and tapped. It took a minute, and then Ryan's face appeared in the window. He looked afraid at first; his eyes got really big, and he started to back away from the window. Madison realized she had blood all over her arms and hands. She waved at him to say *it's okay*, but waving your bloody hands at someone was not exactly the way to reduce their fear.

"I need to talk to you. Can you come to the door?" she said through the window. She put her arms down by her side and tried to look nonthreatening. He nodded and walked away from the window.

She walked over to the side door, and he opened it slightly. He looked like he had his foot up against it so she couldn't rush the door.

"Hi. Excuse my appearance. I was trying to save someone's life earlier and I haven't had a chance to clean up."

"Sure. I figured," Ryan said. How did he figure that she was trying to save someone's life? Madison decided he was trying to be polite, and she probably would have laughed if the circumstances had been different.

"You told me that a cop hired you to document my movements."

"That's right. I said I was sorry. Can't we get past this? I really needed the money—"

"No, I'm not here to stab you for documenting my activities, Ryan. I want to know which cop hired you. Did you get his name?"

Ryan stood still for a moment. "Wow. I don't think I did. I think he showed me a badge. Or did he?"

Madison wasn't sure why she'd ever thought Ryan was smart. *Some guy walks up to you and says he's a cop and you don't even ask for ID? You don't even ask his name?*

"What did he look like? Was he big with a huge chest, sort of Italian looking, with slicked-back hair?" She was leading the witness, but she was describing Tom. He was very different from Ken. If it was Tom, she wanted to know right now.

"No, not at all. That's the other cop that comes to see you. I'm talking about the other one."

Now Madison did want to stab him. The other cop? There was no "other cop" that ever came to see her.

"I'm not sure what you're talking about, Ryan. There is only one cop that has ever come to see me. His name is Tom, and he looks Italian like I just described."

"No, this guy is medium build, kind of wiry, bald head and blue eyes."

Ken.

Ryan started to look worried. "I fucked this up, didn't I?"

"Yeah, Ryan, you kind of did. He's a murderer. If you see him, call 911. Okay?"

Madison didn't want to walk into her apartment until she had straightened things out with Tom. She went back to the BMW and sat in the driver's seat. She didn't have Tom's cell phone number with her. She called dispatch and told them she needed to talk to him urgently and that he would want to talk to her. She said her name was Maddie.

She sat listening to the waves as she waited for them to find Tom on his cell phone and connect the call. She was so exhausted. She was trying not to think about whether or not Felicity was going to make it; if she thought about that too hard, she wouldn't be able to keep doing what she had to do to bring this case to a conclusion. She could fall apart later.

She remembered the memorial slip of paper in her pocket and pulled it out. "I'll love you all the days of my life."

Madison liked the way that surfers memorialized their fallen soldiers with a "paddle out": when a surfer died, all of his surfer friends paddled out past the breaking point of waves and sat on their surfboards in a circle with joined hands. After a moment of silence, they threw flowers into the center of the circle. It was a hallowed event in surfing and breathtaking to observe. She set the note in the console. Madison decided that tomorrow, when this was all over, she would take the note to the beach and toss a flower into the ocean for the loved one who had passed, finishing the delivery of this message without endangering wildlife with a popped balloon.

But what if the message has already been delivered? she thought. *What if the message was for me?*

Suddenly Tom's voice came through the phone. "Maddie? Where are you?"

"Tom. I'm sorry, Tom."

"What did you do? There's a BOLO out for you for assaulting a police officer! What did you do?"

So that was how he did it. An assault on a police officer warranted a "blue alert," which was shared with all of law enforcement throughout California and got put on the electronic message boards on the freeway. Somehow Ken had gotten someone to report her for assaulting a police officer.

"I didn't, Tom. This is Ken. This is all Ken. I thought it was you, but it was Ken."

"Ken? What are you talking about?"

Madison explained everything from the beginning. She told him about the phone call to Felicity from the anonymous caller and how the wording matched the note left on her door. She explained about Ryan documenting her activities at the request of someone who fit Ken's description and claimed to be a cop. She explained about Felicity and Josie and how Felicity had said she was confronting him and he was a cop.

"I'm covered in blood, Tom. Did Ken used to be a cop?"

Tom's voice was getting darker as it dawned on him what had occurred. "Yes, he used to be. In Sacramento. A long time ago. I never really checked into it. He was just a guy at the bar."

"But you told him that you had stalked me?"

"What? No! I would never share that kind of information with a guy I know from a bar. I mentioned you, that you were a cool person or something, but it was just guys talking at a bar."

This part could wait, but Madison wondered if Ken had been tailing Tom as well and if that's how he knew Tom had stalked Madison.

"Did you guys talk about Samantha's disappearance?"

"Probably; that was a pretty big story in the news. Other people asked me about the disappearance too. You asked me about it."

Madison thought for a minute. Some of these details would have to get sorted out later, but they would bug her until they made sense. "Did you tell him I was investigating it? About the notes left on my door?"

"No, not at all. I'm telling you: he's a guy in the bar. I don't talk about my personal life."

"You said you'd known him a long time. How long is a long time?"

"Did I? I've known him for a couple of years. I guess sometimes it's just something you say; I've known him for a while."

So Ken could have been stalking Madison since she first started tweeting about the case, to see how much she knew, and he could have seen Tom sitting outside her apartment. That must have been a bonus. San Diego was a pretty small town, when it came down to it. People knew each other. And bad guys could have good luck too.

"What do we do now?" Madison said.

"I'm going to cancel the BOLO on you, and then I'm going to find out who put it out on you in the first place. We don't need a warrant from a judge for a BOLO, but we should have a good goddamn reason for it. Then I'm going to put an actual BOLO out on Ken. So wait . . . you thought this was me? That I had put the BOLO out on you?"

"Not my finest hour, Tom, but we can go over that later. Can we catch a murderer first?"

"Okay. Where will you be?"

Where would she be? That was an excellent question. She didn't have to hide from the police anymore. She should probably get her car out of the garage at that house pretty quickly before she found herself charged with breaking and entering. But she had to get this blood off her. It was starting to make her skin crawl.

"I'm going to be at home. I'll be careful."

"Okay. Is this number you're calling me from a good number to reach you?"

Madison missed her phone. She would have to get a new one. "Yes, this is fine. I can get texts on it. Can you text me when the BOLO is canceled?"

"Sure." They were silent on the phone for a minute. So much to say. Not the time. They said goodbye and disconnected.

Madison couldn't sit in this filth any longer. She figured that if there was an odd patrol officer who happened to drive by and check her apartment based on the BOLO—unlikely anyway—she could have them call Tom and she wouldn't get arrested. She wanted to be back in her apartment.

She locked the BMW and left it on the street. She walked through the garden and up the stairs. The Santa Ana winds had picked up during the night, and it was dry and breezy. She had a painted wooden plaque hanging from the overhang: it had a moon face on one side and a sun face on the other. It was twisting in the wind and scraping against a piece of wood. She unlocked her front door and went inside, shutting and locking it behind her. She turned on the lamp sitting on her desk and threw her purse down. She didn't want to sit on any of her furniture while covered in blood. She stripped off her clothes and walked into the shower.

Her life had changed so much in forty-eight hours. She felt a little bit like she was going into shock. She washed her hair and scrubbed her arms and fingernails. She wanted to hear from Tom that the BOLO had been canceled, but she figured it was just a matter of paperwork at this point. What she really wanted was for Tom to find Ken. Now that she knew what Ken was capable of, she had to take seriously the note he had left on her door. It wasn't just a threat.

She got out of the shower and put on a clean pair of yoga pants and a white T-shirt—her uniform when she was at home. Her hair was wet, so she had it up in a towel. She could hear the wind outside, mixed with the waves. The scratching of the sun/moon plaque on her front porch was starting to creep her out. Maybe she shouldn't have come home alone. Maybe she should have asked Tom to send a patrol car; but of course, when she was talking to Tom, she had still been wanted by the police, so that would've been a little bit like putting a fox in charge of the hen house. Normally she would call Dave to come over, but she didn't even know his phone number by heart, and anyway he had a girlfriend now. She took her hair out of the towel and hung the towel up. She was starving. She walked out of the bedroom, and Ken was standing in her living room.

"You really need to get a better lock on that front door."

Chapter
Twenty-Eight

If Madison screamed really loudly, it was possible Ryan would hear her. But there was so much wind tonight, and the waves were so loud, that she didn't think her screams would make it over there. And then she would have lost her one chance to save her life. Ken would certainly kill her immediately to shut her up, just like he had tried to do with Felicity. She needed to figure out how to keep herself alive as long as possible.

She knew instinctively that she couldn't act scared. She'd fallen apart when she saw Ryan's journal of her activities; now was the time for steely calm and determination. Her life depended on it. Ken was a monster that thrived on fear. It was part of the high that he got. It was the power over another.

"Good locks are only necessary as long as there are people like you."

He ignored her. "You are a busy little girl. I was looking for you everywhere, and then you turned up at the *wrong place*"—he shouted the last two words—"and messed up the fun I was about to have." Ken was looking behind her desk along the wall.

Madison was standing in the entryway to the bedroom area. She was afraid to move. "There they are!" He pulled out a bunch of drapery cords, cut into pieces. "I left these here the other day, just in case I'd be back and might need them."

She could not allow him to tie her up.

"Are you afraid of a girl, Ken? You have to tie her up in order to have a conversation with her?"

He began laying the pieces of cord out on her desk, his gloved hands grasping each piece and releasing it almost tenderly and then patting it flat. "I wasn't planning to have a conversation with you. And don't try any of your tricks on me. I'm in control now." It was like he was possessed. Madison was shocked—he was a completely different person than the one she'd met and spoken to before. This person was exuding evil; the guy she'd met before was charming. Apparently he had an ability to change personalities like a chameleon, or like Dr. Jekyll and Mr. Hyde.

"I didn't say you weren't in control. Clearly you're in control." That was important to guys like this. She stood without moving at the entrance to the bedroom. She hoped that if she didn't seem like she was trying to get away, she could keep him from feeling like he had to tie her up. She couldn't make it past him to the front door anyway; her apartment was so small that if she made any sudden movement, he could grab her and overpower her in seconds. Better to give him a sense of security.

"Hey, so how did you figure out where I lived?" *Keep him talking.* If he was talking, he wasn't killing her.

"That part was easy. You gave me a scare: the private investigator tweeting about the bouncers at Hank's. You were working a little too hard to find me and getting a little too close. I had to find out more about you. So I just took your name from your Twitter account and had a cop friend get me your address. Tom isn't the only cop I know. Easy. And then I saw you." He whistled through his teeth. "And you look like that. And smart too. And your downstairs neighbor, the brain surgeon, all it took was a hundred dollars a week for him to sell you out. Those notes, weren't those great?" It had been a game to him. Taunting her with the notes. Seeing what she would do.

Having finished straightening each cord on the desk, he picked up the uppermost cord and started to make a knot in each end.

The Smith & Wesson was in her purse, sitting on her desk, right next to him. The one she'd gotten a license to carry. The one with the hollow-point pink-tipped bullets that would stop a bear. And it was out of her reach. She couldn't do anything that would cause a physical altercation between them; she just wouldn't win a fight against a guy. She had to be smart.

Keep him talking. "Did you know Tom before you found out about me?"

He finished with one cord and picked up another. He seemed eerily calm. It was like he'd come over to hang out with her. The longer she kept him talking, the longer she stayed alive.

"Yeah, how about that?" he said. "Not too much of a coincidence, not really. I know all the cops. But I did feel quite lucky the time I saw him outside your apartment, watching you. That was good info to have."

"Why did you ask me to help you with the Rescue Mission thing? The woman, Sylvia, who needed help picking up her kids from school?"

He snickered. "I can't believe you fell for that." He chuckled again. "I made all of that up because people like you think if someone is willing to help, then they're a good person."

Madison did think that. But he wasn't willing to help; it was all a facade. But it had worked. She had trusted him.

"How did you get Samantha into your car?"

He seemed proud of this accomplishment. "She was so drunk. I met up with her on the sidewalk, and she recognized me from the bar. I told her that I would give her a ride home. She got right into my car. Like taking candy from a baby. The ones I did in Sacramento were much harder. I was going to stop when I moved down here, but, well, I didn't."

So there were other deaths. Other women who'd been killed. He was a serial killer. Madison wished there was a way to leave this information for Tom in case she didn't make it. Her head was muddled, trying to think of a way out, trying to think of a weapon she could use on him. But she was afraid to move from her spot. Any move she made had to be calculated toward her survival.

Madison realized he was tying special knots at the ends of the long cords; they were like the knots in the cords that had tied up Felicity. It must be part of a ritual.

"Where's that surfer friend when you need him, right? I hated seeing those photos of him coming down your stairs after he'd been with you."

Madison got the feeling there was something about her that was different from his other victims.

"Jealous much?" she said.

Her attempt to act confident and unafraid backfired. Ken's face burst red, and spit flew out of his mouth as he spoke. "Shut the fuck up! You know, I wasn't going to kill you. Not at first. I was going to talk to you. Maybe ask you out. But then I saw how you really are. You think you're so much better than us regular guys, right? Even Tom. You walk around laughing at the rest of us mortals, right?"

This last was said with such violence that Madison flinched.

"Oh, you're scared now, right? Well, just wait." He finished tying the last cord.

Despite her fear, Madison couldn't help but recognize the refrain coming out of his mouth: she was a girl, and so she *owed* him something. She was *required* to be sweet and loving and cater to a man's needs and whims. And when she didn't, she was a stuck-up bitch.

"Why didn't you just kill me when I followed you to your yard in Spring Valley?"

"Oh, I would have, believe me. I was not happy that you found out where I lived. But too many witnesses." He started walking toward Madison. "Now this can be easy, or it can be hard. It will hurt more if you fight back."

Madison started to back up. If she kept going, she would hit her bed and fall on it, which would make things easier for him.

There was no escape this way, just her bed and her tiny bathroom and a window she couldn't fit through even if she didn't mind the broken back when she hit the driveway. And yet something was happening. A plan. A way out.

When Madison's father died, she'd thought she'd never hear his voice again—his deep, booming voice that anyone could recognize anywhere. The voice she'd heard down the hall at two years old, when she'd been left overnight in the hospital with a blood clot in her lung, left perhaps forever, as far as she knew, the voice that told her he was there and everything would be okay. She'd thought she'd never hear it again, but she'd been wrong: she heard it in her dreams. And she was hearing it right then.

Don't you dare give up, Madison Kelly.

She stepped slowly, backward, backward, backward.

Her foot hit her bed, and she fell back onto it and everything went into slow motion. She saw her antique dressing table, made of oak with an oval mirror that was heavier than sin. She had it across from her bed so that she always fell asleep thinking about the women who had sat at it: putting on makeup or reading a book, their hopes and dreams and inherent losses of life all seeped into the oak, and the strength they'd garnered as a result reflected back in the mirror. Madison needed that strength now because she was truly afraid.

Madison saw now what bravery really was: not giving up. It wasn't not being afraid. Everyone was afraid. Bravery was keeping on despite all odds. It was risking lying back on the bed, showing her belly, in the most primal of passive stances, in order to ultimately save herself. For in her love of old things was an impulse purchase she'd made and nearly forgotten about: a Czech .25 automatic pistol built in 1947 that was only the size of her palm. It was a relic, really: famously used by spies in the Cold War era, the kind of gun the guy had hidden in his sock after he'd been searched for weapons. She'd never thought of carrying it because it had no safety and she didn't want to reach into her purse and shoot herself. It required just the slightest pressure to start the eight automatic bullets flying. It hadn't fit in her safe, and on a whim she'd stuck it on a magnet underneath the bedside table.

She stared at Ken as he approached her. His eyes lit up at the sight of her on her bed, just like a girlfriend, the pieces of knotted cord in his hand perhaps unnecessary after all; he paused to consider his options. In one smooth motion Madison rolled to her right, reached under the table, grabbed the gun off the magnet and brought it up and aimed at his central mass. She emptied the clip into his chest. His arms flew up like they were choreographed: he was the dancing man outside a car dealership, arms flailing and wild, legs akimbo, silently disco-ing to a distant beat. The arms went up one last time before the air was let out of him . . . *whoooosh*. He fell quietly, almost gracefully, his body melting into a pool of malevolence onto the floor.

Madison's ears were ringing from the gunshots. She'd never fired a gun outside of a range, and it was loud. She leaped up and looked down at him, ready to run for her purse in the other room if she needed more bullets from a bigger gun. But he didn't move. His eyes looked at her, surprised. He hadn't expected that. She waited. His eyes slowly closed. She stood watching as the blood poured out of the gaping hole in his chest. She'd always wondered how she would feel. She'd done it. She had actually taken a life.

"Damn," she said. "That's gonna leave a stain."

She stepped over the body to go call Tom.

Chapter Twenty-Nine

It had been a long time since Madison had been up for the sunrise; much longer since she'd been outside to watch it. She sat on her steps with one of those aluminum reflective blankets, although she thought *blanket* was too kind a word for it. She felt like she was sitting under a piece of tinfoil. Was there really any point to these things? Or did they just let passersby know something terrible had happened to that person and they might be in shock?

Tom had gotten there even before the first patrol car. She'd dropped the gun right next to the body and gone to sit on the steps. When you told the 911 operator that you'd just shot someone, it was always best to think through your next move carefully. The police could be slightly on edge when arriving to the scene of a shooting. So she was glad it was Tom—with everything they'd been through, he still knew she wouldn't shoot him.

Tom came out of her apartment. "The coroner is almost done." Madison scooted over so he could sit down next to her on the steps. They both misjudged the space, and his right hip smashed into her; he stood and chose the step above her instead. They sat for a minute without talking.

"I asked the detective that caught the case to let you sleep for a few hours before he took your statement. He wasn't inclined to allow that. He has a lot of work to do."

Madison coughed. She'd felt like something was caught in her throat since she'd shot him. Was it gunpowder? Leftover adrenaline? "I don't need a lawyer, right?"

"I mean, you're asking the wrong guy. I don't think suspects should ever get lawyers."

Tom was making a joke but Madison was too tired to find it funny. She tried to make a "ha" sound, but it came out as a cough.

"No, you don't need a lawyer. Are you kidding? You're a hero. We got a warrant for his yard in Spring Valley, and they're searching it now. Whaddya think they'll find? And with his comment about Sacramento, I'm sure there are some unsolved cases that are about to get solved. No, you don't need a lawyer. I mean, maybe you shoulda had a hunting license for vermin, but . . ."

Madison managed to give him a smile for that. He was being uncharacteristically animated, likely an attempt to keep her spirits up.

"I called and woke up a sergeant in Sacramento. Seems Larrabee was a cop there but was fired for shoplifting."

"Shoplifting? That seems sort of small potatoes for him."

"Yeah, it would be. But get a load of what he was stealing: a hammer and dog repellent."

Madison pulled her hair back and then realized she had no hair tie. She felt slimy. She let her hair fall back down. "That seems random yet sinister."

"Yeah. They were going to give him a hearing prior to firing him, just to hear his side of the story since it was so bizarre, and he refused the hearing. He said he would just take his punishment. So they fired him and he got probation for the petty theft."

That made more sense. He'd probably been stealing the materials he needed for a more serious crime, and he hadn't wanted anyone looking into his activities.

"The sergeant thought he went to law school. That's what he told everyone he was doing. Maybe he did. Maybe we're going to find missing girls connected to a campus somewhere."

Madison cleared her throat. It had to be said. "I'm sorry I thought it was you."

"Hey. Don't even worry about it. If I hadn't set the stage by stalking you—"

"It wasn't really stalking, it was just sort of . . . a general wonderment."

"Nice *Friends* reference. It was stalking, I admit it. So if I hadn't started it with that, making me seem creepy, you wouldn't have been able to jump to those conclusions. So I'm sorry."

That was nice. They were both sorry. A happy ending. Hurray and woohoo. Madison realized she was a bit in shock; she felt punchy.

"How did he manage that BOLO? Did a cop friend of his do it?"

Ryan appeared in his bay window and looked up at where Madison was sitting on the stairs. He waved slightly; Madison waved back. That was going to be awkward for a while.

"No, and thank God for that. I can't take another story about a corrupt cop. But like I said, we don't need a warrant for a BOLO. Sometimes it needs to go out fast, like in the case of a child who has just been kidnapped. So there aren't a lot of checks on it. Once it gets seen by someone, it gets sent out fast. So Larrabee hacked into the computer system. The hows and the whys, I can't tell you, because I'm not an electronics guy; but it is all on computer and he hacked into it. We'll get to the bottom of it and put in a better firewall or whatever they do."

Madison figured Arlo could tell her how the guy did it. *The guy.* She didn't think she'd say his name for a long time.

"I just want to say—" Tom began.

"Don't say something mushy."

"No, no. It's not mushy. It's just. The reason I stalked—"

"Watched."

"Okay, okay, watched. The reason I watched you is because I've never met anyone like you in my life. You walk into a room and the whole place lights up; it isn't even your beauty. It's just a presence you have. And then to top it off, you're the best investigator I've ever met."

Madison was silent.

Tom continued. "I know we're not meant to be together. I'm meant to admire you from afar. And that's okay."

Madison figured that was the most poetic Tom had ever been in his life. He was practically reciting Yeats.

Finally she spoke. "Okay. As long as it's only from 'afar.'"

Tom laughed. Madison felt like she had a friend.

"Any word on Felicity?" Madison had been afraid to ask before then. She hadn't been ready to hear it. But she had to know.

"She's gonna make it. You saved her life."

Madison coughed again to cover the sob that ejected from her like a belch. She turned it into a coughing fit.

"Let me get you some water." Tom went down to where the trucks were parked on the street in front. Windansea looked like a war zone—police cars, crime scene trucks, coroner's van, and crime scene tape surrounding the entire thing. Seeing yellow tape always used to give her a thrill: "Someone died! I wonder what happened?" Now that she was behind the yellow tape, it just made her feel sick.

Madison heard a commotion coming from the street. There were men yelling. Then she saw a blond head and surfboard. She stood up.

"Hey, it's okay. He's with me!"

They let Dave through. He was in his wetsuit, but it was dry. He must've been on his way to surf sunrise when he saw the yellow tape and imagined the worst.

"Maddie! What the fuck?"

It was good to see him. It felt like coming home.

"Yeah. Well. There was an incident. Come here and sit down. I don't need you punching a cop and going to jail today."

He walked to the bottom of the steps, and she stood up. He set his surfboard against the building and ran up the steps; he grabbed her and picked her up in a huge hug.

"What the fuck happened?" He sat next to her on the step.

"Well, remember that murderer I was looking for?"

"Yeah . . . ?"

"I found him. In my apartment. And I shot him."

Dave looked her up and down. His mind had gone to the obvious: *did this guy hurt you?* He took in what she was wearing, her face and arms to see if she had bruises or defensive wounds. It reminded her of her beloved Labrador retriever: when she would lie on the floor to do yoga, he'd think she was injured or sick and run his huge lip with all its olfactory points over her forehead and face, ever so lightly, to assess for damage; it used to tickle. Dave seemed satisfied.

"You shot him? Epic!"

Madison laughed. And then coughed. It *was* kind of epic.

"So. Dave. The stuff you said made me think."

"Forget it. I was angry; I didn't really mean all of that."

"Yes, you did." Madison wasn't sure exactly what she wanted to say. But she wanted to say it.

Tom had started walking from the crime scene truck down the path to her carrying two bottles of water, but he saw Dave and stopped. He glanced at Madison and made a signal to indicate that he would give her a minute.

Madison tried to form the thoughts to tell Dave how she felt. In those moments when she hadn't known if she was going to live or die, she saw a lot of things. She saw art day with her mother: Saturdays when she was six and her mother took her to walk in the forest; they picked pinecones to decorate with gold glitter. She saw the moments with Dave where she'd let her guard down; why hadn't there been more of those? Her life had been full of love when she'd let it in. What had she missed out on by refusing to be vulnerable? And her father's voice. The sound of her father's voice was the sound of her dreams; it was the sound of love forever and always. At the end of her life she had remembered so much love, and she'd lamented the many times she hadn't allowed it in.

"I don't 'need' you," Madison said. "That's true. It's just the way I am. But I saw my life without you, and I didn't like it."

"I like your independence. I was just . . . tired of feeling like I didn't matter."

They watched the commotion below. There was something macabre about having this kind of conversation amongst the trappings of a violent death. But maybe it was perfect: hope rising from the ashes.

"You matter," she said.

"You matter to me, too."

Madison felt a warmth that started in her heart and spread outward. "As long as you understand that I won't change. I'm always going to be the girl who doesn't need a guy."

He leaned over and kissed her.

"Love and the Murder Scene," Madison said. "A very special episode of Madison's Life, brought to you by Smith & Wesson: make sure you have us nearby when you need us."

"Did you shoot him with your S&W?"

"No, with the Czech .25. The S&W was in my purse, and he was standing next to it."

"Damn." Dave didn't trust guns. He preferred to knock a man out with one blow. But he liked justice and standing up to bullies. "Classic!"

"So anyway. I like my life with you in it. I'd like it if you stuck around."

"I'd like to stick around," he said.

"What about Gabrielle?"

"That's over anyway. Apparently she had a problem with my lack of 'earnestness' in not telling her about you."

"'Earnestness'?"

"Yeah, she wasn't using the word right. Which kind of sealed the deal."

Madison grabbed his hand. They sat in the middle of a crime scene, watching the specialists come and go, carrying equipment, making notes, having conversations.

"There's waves, babe. Gotta go." He stood up.

"Catch a tube ride for me," she said.

He leaned down to kiss her. "And just remember this: *à cœur vaillant rien d'impossible.*"

To a brave heart, nothing is impossible. Dave spoke French better than she did. Then again, she didn't have a trust fund pay for her Stanford education. He grabbed his surfboard and hobbled in bare feet around to the alley to walk to the beach. Tom saw Dave leave and came up the path.

"They found Samantha."

Madison waited for the rest.

"She was in a shallow grave in his yard in Spring Valley. He probably intended to move her at some point. Man, that place is full of crap. It's gonna take a long time to sort through it and process everything. But they found tokens: women's jewelry, a couple of driver's licenses. And then there are Polaroids. Glad I'm not the one going through those and matching them to missing women. But a lot of families are going to get closure, that is for sure."

The enormity of what she had accomplished weighed on her like an albatross. Because it automatically made her think of what would've happened if she *hadn't* discovered all of this. How many more women would've died? How many loved ones would've never had answers?

"Like I said, you're gonna be a hero."

As if on cue, two news vans showed up on the street in front. They parked, and their huge satellite dishes were raised.

"You don't have to talk to them right now. It can wait."

Madison realized that her life was going to change. She would be on the news. People would know her name and would probably call to hire her to find their missing loved ones or solve a cold case. When this whole thing began, she'd been trying to figure out if handling murder investigations was what she wanted for her life. Now she felt like it was. She was good at this. She could make a difference in the world. She could help people.

"So are you going to keep investigating murders?" Tom asked.

"Hell yes." Madison stood up. "I'm a hero."

"I'd heard that about you."

Madison walked down the steps as the first TV reporter crossed the lawn for a statement.

Acknowledgments

There have been times when for me the act of writing has been
a little act of faith, a spit in the eye of despair.

—Stephen King

My thirty-fifth birthday was fun: a martini party with swing
music. But it feels so long ago that it might as well have been my
tenth. You think of a life as peaking around the age of thirty-
five—family started, well into your chosen career, life pretty
much set up and knowing what's to come. Not me. Just like
Madison, I wasn't settled at thirty-five. I've experienced more
changes since my thirty-fifth birthday than I did in all the years
before it. Some of the changes haven't been fun at all: the death
of my father, my own sickness, those parts of life that make it
harder to keep going with a smile on your face. But there were
good things too: for example, I graduated summa cum laude
from UC San Diego with a degree in writing—thank you Professor Cristina Rivera-Garza, for guiding me through my hon-
ors thesis, which was a short-story version of Madison's
adventures. Thank you Professor John Granger, for turning me
into a real writer. And to Danny Panella, my undergraduate

adviser, who helped me transition from a French literature major to a writing major, thank you for having an open-door policy so that this overachiever, who just had to get straight As, could come and cry in your office.

The other good thing that happened after age thirty-five was my decision to become an author. While continuing to work as a private investigator, I kept my eye on the goal of becoming a published author—throughout the not-so-fun challenges that followed. When I sat down to write this book in earnest, I was in a new home, my office had boxes stacked in it, and my desk was dirty—disorganization that normally would've rendered me unable to function. But the challenges I'd been through had an upside: they made me focused and determined, almost to a fault. So I sat down in the dust and disorder and wrote like a house on fire. Madison made me laugh, she made me cry, and no matter what, I just kept writing.

It helped to know that someone was waiting for pages: Kristen Weber became more than an editor with great ideas whom I'd hired to make sure I finished the book. She became a cheerleader, my first fan, and ultimately a friend.

My editor at Crooked Lane, Terri Bischoff, was the first to offer publication, and boy was she quick. Her swift offer made me feel she deserved special consideration, and I'm so glad she did and I did, because Crooked Lane is the perfect place for me; thanks go to Matt Martz for creating that environment and bringing me into the fold. Terri encouraged me to bring more of Madison into the book—I didn't realize parts of Madison were missing until Terri pointed it out. I'm looking forward to a long relationship with Terri, where together we bring readers much more Madison.

Madeline Rathle and Melissa Rechter at Crooked Lane were tornadoes of efficiency, making sure I stayed on track and turning ideas into action. This book was put on a fast track to publication, and they were on top of it the whole way. Nicole Lecht designed a kickass cover that leaps off the shelf; she made it better than I could explain it.

My brother and his wife have helped me in many ways, especially during the not-so-smiley challenges I've faced. Without them I couldn't have written this book.

The same goes for Kathy, a fairy godmother through and through.

My agent, Abby Saul of the Lark Group, has been with me from the beginning: sticking it out through thick and thin with encouragement and words of wisdom, suggesting edits for the book, and guiding me into a wonderful relationship with Crooked Lane. What a team we make. I can't wait to see what the future holds.

Mentioned in the book are Tim Pilleri and Lance Reenstierna of Crawlspace Media and the *Missing Maura Murray* podcast. They fight the good fight every day by bringing attention to cold cases and making sure the missing are never forgotten. You can help: https://investigationsforthemissing.org/

Aside from Lance and Tim, if you recognize yourself in the pages of this book, I did a good job as an author because the characters are all fictitious. There is no Tom Clark, so there is no one to blame other than me if I got police procedure wrong

Acknowledgments

(or I might have known it was wrong and wrote it that way anyway—poetic license!). There was no Gaslamp mystery, and the bars the girls went missing from are a product of my imagination. However, the rest of the places mentioned in the book are real, and I hope you visit them someday. San Diego is one of the most beautiful places in the world.

To the authors who have influenced me, like Thomas Perry (thank you for your encouragement), Dean Koontz, Stephen King, Lee Child, Robert Crais, Sue Grafton, Janet Evanovich, Rex Stout, Agatha Christie, and Sir Arthur Conan Doyle, thank you for your artistry, to which I aspire every day.

Finally, I would like to thank the everyday unsung heroes. You don't know who you are—because you don't think of yourself as a hero. You get up, feed the kids (or the cat, or the dog), go to work; you take care of a parent, visit a friend, lend an ear to a stranger. You volunteer, cheer, and console, often without any thanks. You're kind, you're patient, and sometimes you're ashamed of your behavior and try to do better next time. You may not be the star of the show, but you're the backbone of society and we'd fall apart with you. I dedicate this book to you and the part you play in keeping life worth living for everyone else, even if you don't realize it. I do. I see you. Thank you.